The HOME COMING

Also by Preeti Shenoy

The Magic Mindset: How to Find Your Happy Place

A Place Called Home

The Rule Breakers

It's All in the Planets

The Secret Wish List

The One You Cannot Have

A Hundred Little Flames

It Happens for a Reason

The HOME COMING

PREETI SHENOY

HARPER FICTION

An Imprint of HarperCollins *Publishers*

First published in India by Harper Fiction 2024
An imprint of HarperCollins *Publishers*
4th Floor, Tower A, Building No. 10, DLF Cyber City,
DLF Phase II, Gurugram, Haryana—122002
www.harpercollins.co.in

2 4 6 8 10 9 7 5 3 1

P-ISBN: 978-93-6569-057-6
E-ISBN: 978-93-6569-834-3

Typeset in 11/14.6 Minion Pro at
HarperCollins *Publishers* India

Printed and bound at
Thomson Press (India) Ltd

FSC
www.fsc.org
MIX
Paper | Supporting responsible forestry
FSC® C010615

This book is produced from independently certified FSC® paper to ensure responsible forest management.

To all those whose love remains in the shadows, but in their hearts shines brighter than the sun.

1

A VISITOR

2006

Some demons we cannot exorcize. They live inside us, locked away in the dark recesses of our hearts, tightly bound and mostly forgotten as we go about the mundanity of our daily lives. But they are always there, waiting for the appearance of a small chink, a tiny crack through which they seek escape. Over the years, you let your guard down, you relax, thinking the demons have vanished. But that's exactly when they strike—when you least expect it. There is not a chance you stand as you are caught by surprise, washed away in the deluge that is unleashed.

Alka was certain she had made peace with her demons. She sat in the verandah of her home in Sakleshpur in the middle of the lush 400-acre coffee estate, waiting for her two girls to get back from school. The thoughts swirling around in her head didn't involve her husband's brother Krish. She'd decided with a resigned certainty that Krish would have to be relegated to the stories that can never be. She wasn't thinking about her husband Subbu either, who was busy with the harvest season. Having been a coffee grower's wife for many years now, she knew that it was the busiest time of the year. At the start of the season, Subbu had travelled to various temples with the other coffee plantation owners to seek blessings for a good harvest. Alka, too, had whispered prayers for a good harvest even though she wasn't as devout or religious as Subbu. Their entire income came from this specific period alone, whereas the expenses of running the estate were continuous and spread throughout the calendar year. They would have to budget for the whole year's expenses based on the prices the harvest fetched.

The extra workers that Subbu had hired for the harvest had already arrived. She knew he was stressed about it. This year there was a shortage of labour just when he needed to scale up the workforce. In addition to coffee, he also had to take care of the pepper and cardamom he had planted to supplement their income from coffee. Though Alka had offered to share Subbu's burden of running the coffee estate, he had persistently refused.

'Come on, Subbu, it's not that I can't handle at least some of the tasks,' Alka had said many times in the early years of their marriage.

'Alka, you have your hands full with Nisha and Tulika. We need them to have a well-rounded education, and you know how the schools in this remote place are. The coffee estate I can handle, but their education is something only you can take care of,' Subbu had reasoned.

Her mother-in-law Anandi, who had loved Alka and supported her in every way, much like her own mother, had surprisingly agreed with Subbu on this. 'You have enough to worry about. Let him take care of the estate. It's his job,' she'd constantly advised her.

As the years went by, Alka had given up asking, not because she did not care, but because over time, their respective roles had become rigid and clearly defined. Subbu took care of the business, while after Anandi's death, the task of managing the day-to-day activities in their 200-year-old heritage bungalow, as well as their two children had all fallen upon Alka. It was a burden she was more than happy to bear, and she did it with a smile on her face and gratitude in her heart.

As Alka sipped her coffee and waited for her girls, she thought about how much her life had changed since she had left Mrs Shetty's home where she had spent her entire childhood in a small ten by ten room, assisting her mother who had worked as a domestic help.

The sound of a jeep pulling up in the driveway interrupted Alka's thoughts. The school bus had dropped the girls off at the main road. Since it was too long a stretch for the girls to walk back on their own, their trusted driver Shanker fetched them home from there in the jeep every day.

Tulika raced up the steps leading to the bungalow, looking rather excited. She had a wide grin plastered on her face as she triumphantly waved her art book in the air.

'Mummy! Mummy! I won the first prize! I've been selected for the big competition.' Tulika's eyes shone with exhilaration. Nisha waited patiently for her turn as Alka looked at Tulika's drawing.

'You've drawn an elephant and our coffee estate!' she exclaimed. 'But why did you colour the elephant red?'

'Because he is an angry elephant, Mummy. He destroyed the estate's fence and many of our coffee plants!' Tulika narrowed her eyes. Alka was astounded at the amount of information the children had picked up by overhearing adult conversations. Subbu had mentioned that the movement of elephants through Sakleshpur and Alur in Hassan district had forced the villagers to change their daily routines and reschedule their travel plans. It had stopped the planters from growing bananas and jackfruit on their lands as the smell of ripening fruits attracted the jumbos. The menace had increased to such an extent that farmers no longer felt assured about returning home safely. A few weeks ago, a tusker had entered Subbu's warehouse as well after breaking open the door and had damaged the sacks of paddy stored inside. But Alka hadn't been aware that both the girls knew about this.

'Oh, I see,' Alka said as she noted other details in Tulika's artwork.

'But he is not a bad elephant, he is just angry because he didn't get any food,' Nisha added quietly.

'He is bad, he is an enemy of the farmer. He kills people, don't you know?' Tulika was quick to retort.

'The forest department has to fence that bit of land. They're not doing their job. It is not the elephant's fault. He is just looking for food,' Nisha insisted. Clearly, Nisha had paid close attention to Subbu's talks with the other plantation owners.

Alka knew that if she didn't step in, the conversation would escalate into a fight. 'When we live amidst nature, these things become a part of life,' she announced diplomatically. And before the girls could come up with anything else, she quickly added, 'But guess what, I've baked cupcakes today! Your favourite lemon ones!'

That was enough to make the girls forget about their little disagreement. They rushed inside to put away their bags, change out of their uniforms and take a quick bath—a routine that Alka had instilled in them.

Once the girls had lunch, Alka sat with them in the spacious sunroom with its large floor-to-ceiling windows, where they always did their homework. She meticulously went through all their notebooks, checking if they had any upcoming assignments or tests. Tulika's teacher had left a note in her school dairy, saying that she had been selected to participate in the annual district-level art competition that was to be held in Bangalore in six weeks. It was being organized by the Karnataka State Council for Child Welfare. If her entry got selected, Tulika would have to travel to Delhi for the national-level competition that would be conducted by the Indian Council for Child Welfare. The note also mentioned that the travel and accommodation expenses for both Tulika and an accompanying parent would be covered. Alka had not known that the competition was so prestigious. Her heart swelled with pride.

'Oh my! Baby, this is a really big competition. You've won at the district level!' she exclaimed.

'Yes, I know,' Tulika replied. She had scrunched up her face and was focused on carefully forming the cursive letters in her double-lined handwriting notebook.

'And Nisha, you didn't mention that you've been selected to represent the school in a debate competition!' Alka exclaimed as she checked Nisha's diary.

'That's because I don't want to go, but my teacher says I have to,' Nisha grimaced.

'But why don't you want to go?'

'I don't like it. The teacher says I have to speak against the topic. And I do not want to do that.'

'What's the topic?'

'"Dogs are better than cats." How can one animal be better than the other, Mummy? They are just different animals. It is silly!'

'Hmm, I agree. But if the topic were to change, would you want to go then?'

'I don't know, it depends on the topic. But my teacher said that you will have to either write her a note or speak to her if I don't want to participate.'

'Don't worry, I'll give her a call,' Alka assured her. The topic was indeed silly, and she decided to call the teacher and tell her that Nisha was unwilling to participate in the competition.

While the girls settled in and did their homework, Alka sat back and thought about how much her mother would have loved to see her daughters. After her mother passed away, Alka had felt orphaned and alone. But then the unexpected connection with Renuka Mavshi had emerged, and she cherished that relationship so much now. She made a mental note to call her soon. It had been well over seven months since they last spoke. Residing in the coffee estate meant living in near isolation, with little communication with the outside world. The only network which worked was a BSNL connection, and that too was erratic.

Alka and the girls looked out the window when they heard Subbu's jeep pulling up outside. A steel-grey Honda Civic had followed the jeep. Subbu had arrived with two other people—an elderly gentleman dressed in a white full-sleeved shirt and grey trousers, and a lady in a pale green salwar kameez, her grey hair cut short.

'Who is that?' Nisha asked.

Alka shrugged. 'Let me quickly get ready, okay? Tell Appa I am upstairs if he asks,' she told her girls as she rushed up the flight of stairs to her bedroom.

She hated it when Subbu brought guests home without informing her in advance. She hurriedly brushed her hair, applied some eyeliner and checked her outfit in the mirror. She was wearing an old T-shirt and a pair of track pants.

'Alka! Where are you?' Subbu's voice rang out.

'Coming!' she shouted back, deciding that there was no time to change into something nicer.

When she came downstairs, the guests were already seated in the formal living room.

'Hello,' she greeted them, wishing she was dressed better.

'Meet my wife, Alka. Alka, this is Dr Sethuram and his wife Nalini,' Subbu said.

'I am Mrs Senapathy's sister. I think you might have met her at Anandi's memorial meet,' Nalini said, smiling.

Alka's back stiffened when she heard that name. She had presumed she was done with whatever had happened in the past when the secret about her identity had been discovered. It was Mrs Senapathy who had alerted her mother's old employer, Mrs Shetty, of Alka's whereabouts. Did Nalini also know about Alka's background? Even as her heartbeat shot up, Alka smiled sweetly, pretending nothing was wrong.

'How lovely. Welcome to our estate,' she said, her facial expression giving nothing away. Over the years, Alka had learnt to mask every single emotion she felt. Her face was inscrutable. Keeping secrets was something she excelled at.

If Nalini knew anything about Alka's past, she showed no signs of it. Instead, she explained that they were on their way to Coorg and had stopped over as her nephew, who was Subbu's business associate, had insisted they visit Subbu.

'Of course, how can you pass Sakleshpur and not stop here?' Alka played the gracious hostess, a role she'd perfected over the years. She instructed Gowramma and Selvi to serve some snacks and coffee. Within no time, they laid out a delectable spread of Malnad snacks—crispy roasted pathrode, roasted cheenikayi kadubu, deep fried vegetable pakoras and filter coffee. Alka was proud of the tradition of hospitality that Anandi had taught her, and she kept it up.

The guests were delighted and they chattered away happily as they dug into the food. Alka excused herself to check in on the girls who had finished their homework by then.

'Can we go outside and play?' Tulika asked.

'Only after you greet our guests properly,' Alka replied.

After the girls greeted the guests and politely answered the usual questions—What class are you in? Which school do you go to?—they went outside to play.

'Such sweet girls, and what excellent manners,' Nalini remarked.

'All credit goes to Alka.' Subbu beamed proudly. Alka smiled in response and made polite conversation, playing the role of a hostess to perfection.

After they left, Alka waited until the Honda Civic disappeared around the bend before giving in to her annoyance.

'Why in the world didn't you tell me we would have guests? How many times have I told you to inform me in advance?' she asked Subbu.

'I didn't know they were coming myself.' His dismissive tone irked Alka further.

'Do you mean to say they suddenly descended on you? Didn't you know about it in the morning? Didn't they call?'

'I got the call when I was on the estate rounds. I was busy with the labour.'

'Subbu, it would've taken you all of thirty seconds to let me know.'

'What does it matter whether I let you know or not? It's not as though you had to cook everything yourself.'

'It's not about that. I would have dressed better. And I would have at least been prepared. It was a shock to hear that she is Mrs Senapathy's sister. I'm disturbed about it, Subbu.'

'You are the one who hid your past, Alka. For an entire decade. You pretended to be someone you were not. If you hadn't done that, maybe you wouldn't be so disturbed now,' Subbu's voice seethed with suppressed fury. His face darkened with indignation as he climbed down the stairs, taking two steps at a time. He rushed to his jeep and sped away before Alka could utter another word.

All she could do was stare after him in disbelief and feel hurt.

2

WITHOUT A CARE IN THE WORLD

2006

Alka slowly walked back to the house, trying to get a grip on her emotions. The sudden appearance of Mrs Senapathy's sister had left her reeling. She hadn't processed things yet and had expected Subbu to empathize with her.

A year ago, when her secret had been exposed and Alka had left home, Subbu had been forced to confront his beliefs about class and caste. Alka had explained everything to him—the way she had lived her entire life, her insecurities, her crushed dreams, and the feeling of helplessness she had endured. She had apologized and he had accepted her explanations. She recalled how he had thundered, 'To hell with Mrs Shetty and all of them,' as he had raised his glass of wine.

After that day, they had never broached the topic again, not until today. Their marriage had slipped into familiar patterns, and it was as though the fact of Alka's betrayal had been completely erased from their relationship.

Alka had often thought about Krish. When Anandi was alive, Alka would get all the news about Krish's family from her. But with Anandi gone, that bridge of communication had crumbled. After his last visit to the estate, Alka had felt tempted to message him on many occasions, but she had never actually acted on it and reached out to him.

While Alka was lost ruminating about the past, the sounds of the girls running back home and chatting excitedly brought her back to the present. She got busy serving them dinner and then reading them bedtime stories—a ritual she loved dearly. Every night before bed, the girls got to choose the book that Alka would read out aloud from. Tonight, it was Tulika's turn and she picked *What Do You Do With a Kangaroo?* It was about an irascible little miss battling to the very end with the animals that took over her bed and tried to order her about. It was a favourite with both the girls as well as Alka, and they never tired of reading it.

Subbu hadn't returned home even after the girls had been tucked into bed. Alka ate her dinner alone, after which Selvi and Gowramma cleared the table, tidied up the kitchen and finished their work for the day.

Alka pondered whether to call up Subbu or not, despite anticipating the usual outcome—a scenario she was familiar with because it had played out countless times in the past. She decided she would. She tried his number, and then sighed as she hung up. His phone was switched off. She knew he would only return the next morning. Though she had expected it, she still felt the sharp pangs of disappointment. Alka hated it. She suspected he was having an affair. But what right did she have to ask him anything or confront him when, deep down, she was still in love with Krish? Of course, she knew that she would never pursue it. She valued her family and her relationship with her girls too much for that. It had taken her over three decades to get what she wanted from life—her very own home, a heritage bungalow no less, nestled in a magnificent coffee estate, two beautiful daughters who were dearer to her than life itself, and a tranquil existence—and she would never ever jeopardize it. Questioning Subbu would yield no results; it would only strain their relationship further. So, Alka continued to fume in silent frustration.

She couldn't help but feel that Subbu was being unfair. The fact that he had hurled those accusations at her and walked away meant that things were still simmering within him. Though he had never spoken about the incident after that one day, it was now apparent that he had never really forgiven her. What did this marriage mean then? Did he just need someone to manage the house and take care of his daughters? Was that why he had compromised and accepted her back?

She knew who she had to talk to—Renuka Mavshi. Alka glanced at the wall clock in her bedroom. Renuka Mavshi would've probably finished dinner by now, which meant that she would be free to have a conversation.

Alka propped herself up in bed with a couple of pillows and, grabbing the cordless phone from her bedside table, punched in Renuka Mavshi's number.

'Alka! How have you been?' Renuka Mavshi answered the phone almost instantly, her voice filling Alka with warmth.

'Mavshi, I am sorry for not calling all these months—'

'You don't have to explain anything at all,' Renuka Mavshi interrupted her. 'You had a marriage to save. I completely understand.'

'Yes, that I did. But I've so missed talking to you,' Alka said softly.

'Oh, I missed talking to you too. I pray every single day for your happiness. When I don't hear from you, I just presume that things are busy.'

'Yes, Mavshi. It's harvest time here in the estate which means things are very busy indeed. What's the news with Manish and Kavita? How are Ritvik and baby Meera?'

'Oh, they aren't so little anymore. Baby Meera is walking around and it's a full-time task to watch over her. Manish and Kavita manage everything, and the restaurant is thriving beyond our expectations. We've bought the adjacent plot as well and we're expanding our space, Alka.'

'Mavshi, that is fantastic news! If only my mother were alive to see this day. She would've been so proud.'

'I agree. But you know what? I am sure Seema is watching us from above and smiling at our success. I think about her often,' Renuka Mavshi's voice trailed off as her eyes misted.

'How I wish she had the courage to stand up to that Mrs Shetty. She might have lived longer. I feel it is overwork that killed her, Mavshi.' Even after all these years, Alka was still angry.

'She did it to protect you, Alka. She always feared that if Mrs Shetty had thrown you both out, you would've ended up on the streets. And she was right. The way Mrs Shetty treated Seema was unforgivable. Perhaps the only good thing Mrs Shetty did was to pay for your education.' Renuka was practical and balanced in her approach. But that didn't mollify Alka.

'Well, the money didn't come out of her pockets, Mavshi. That Inner Circle club paid for it. Sometimes I wonder if I was too harsh in the way I confronted her and told her exactly how I felt.'

'You needed to do it for Seema, and for yourself too. You needed that closure to move on.'

'Yes, Mavshi, I did. Anyway, what is done is done.'

'You're right. We can't keep thinking about the past. It's over and there is nothing we can do to change it. How are Subbu and your daughters?' Renuka asked.

'My girls are doing fine, Mavshi. Tulika is showing a real talent in painting and Nisha's excelling in her studies. But Subbu, it seems like he hasn't forgiven me.'

'What happened now? The last time we spoke, you said you'd talked to him and that everything was okay because he'd understood?' Renuka's voice was full of concern.

'Yes, but that lasted only for a while.'

Alka narrated what had happened that evening, beginning with the arrival of the unexpected guests and ending with why she felt disturbed about it. Speaking to Renuka Mavshi felt cathartic. The words flowed easily, with Renuka listening without interrupting. After Alka was done, she said gently, 'Child, you need to take a break. You're doing a lot for everyone else, but what are you doing for yourself? When was the last time you took a break?'

'When I visited you all.'

'That means it's been nearly a year now, no?'

'Yes.'

'Do you remember how worried you were about the girls when you came here, and how they were actually fine in your absence? Subbu was all right too. Everyone needs a break, Alka. And from time to time, you must take one too. Only when your own cup is full can you fill others cups.'

'I think you may be right, Mavshi. Subbu keeps getting his breaks as he goes to Bangalore every week and comes back only after a day or two. But I never get a break,' Alka conceded.

'Your mavshi doesn't have grey hair for nothing. When Subbu comes back, tell him you're going away for a few days. You can come here and stay with us.'

'Hmm. I will think about it, Mavshi.'

'Just act on it. Don't keep thinking about it. It will do everyone good. I always tell my Manish that it is only when we take care of ourselves that we are able to take care of others. I send him and Kavita away for a few days every six months while I look after the children. After they get back, they manage the restaurant and everything else on their own, and I visit my ashram in Rishikesh for a few weeks. I come back feeling refreshed.'

'Yes, I hear you loud and clear, Mavshi. I promise to give this some serious thought.'

Renuka Mavshi knew exactly what to say, but even though Alka felt much lighter after hanging up, she found herself tossing and turning through the night. She kept wondering whether she truly needed a break or not. But Mavshi was right. The only time Alka had taken a break was after she'd had that tumultuous showdown with Subbu and he had asked her to leave the estate. Besides that pivotal moment, in all these years Alka had never allowed herself the luxury of taking some time out for herself. She had never had any respite from her daily duties.

By morning, she had decided to take that break after all. But she wouldn't go to Renuka Mavshi's house, simply because she would have to take a flight to Delhi. Airfares were expensive and she wanted to wait and see how the harvest turned out. She also did not want to be away from the girls for too long.

She knew of a charming homestay in Coorg, approximately ninety kilometres away from the estate. It had been established by one of Anandi's friend's nieces, Gowri, and Anandi had spoken glowingly of it. It would take Alka only two and a half hours to drive there. The thought of driving there on her own ignited a spark of excitement in her. She'd never driven such a long distance before. For any place she had wanted to travel to, the estate driver was always there to take her. But this was a journey she wanted to go on by herself. She made up her mind to seize this chance before her courage waned.

The next morning, when Subbu got back, he pretended there was nothing amiss. He appeared to be in a great mood. Alka wanted to talk about what had happened the previous day, but she decided it was not the right time. Instead, she broached the subject of her needing a break.

'Is this some kind of tit-for-tat since I left abruptly yesterday?'

'Come on, Subbu. It's not that. You get your breaks when you visit Bangalore almost every week. I, on the other hand, have not had a single one in all these years.'

'Yes, you're right. I suppose I have to be fair here. Go ahead, take your holiday. I will manage the girls and the estate,' Subbu told her.

Once the girls left for school and Subbu went for the estate rounds, Alka flipped through Anandi's phone book, looking for Gowri's phone number. She found it easily; the entry read 'Green Tree Homestay—Gowri, Subhashini's niece', followed by the phone number. Alka had met Subhashini aunty a couple of times when she had come over to the estate. Anandi had been very fond of the quiet, serious woman.

She dialled the number and it was answered by Gowri herself. When Alka introduced herself as Anandi's daughter-in-law, Gowri immediately recognized her.

'Oh hello, Alka! I've heard a lot about you from Anandi aunty. I felt so terrible when I heard about what happened to her. My deepest condolences.'

'Yes, thank you. It was a shock for us as well,' Alka said, recovering quickly from the friendliness and warmth in Gowri's tone. She hadn't anticipated that.

'I am so sorry I couldn't attend the memorial. I had to be in court that day, you know,' Gowri said, sounding like she expected Alka to know exactly what she was talking about.

'That's totally understandable,' Alka replied, although she was completely clueless. She hadn't even known that Gowri had been invited to the memorial. For whatever reasons, Gowri seemed to be treating her like they knew each other well.

'So, what can I do for you?' Gowri asked.

'I actually, er, I wanted to come and spend a couple of days at your homestay.'

'Oh, sure. We have enough rooms available. How many do you need? And how many of you are coming? Let me guess, you have guests from out of town and you want to show them Coorg?'

'Umm. No. One, just one.'

'Oh! A single room or a single person?'

'A single room for a single person.' Alka chuckled nervously. 'It's for me,' she added.

A pause.

'Ah, I see. No worries! When do you need it for?' Gowri asked.

'For today and tomorrow. Will that be possible? I can be there in about four hours from now.'

Another pause followed while Alka held her breath.

Gowri, while initially surprised, quickly recovered her professional demeanour. 'All right, we usually never have guests arriving at such short notice, but we'll make an exception for you since you are Anandi aunty's daughter-in-law. You are most welcome, Alka. Come over! I will see you soon.'

'Thank you,' Alka exhaled. She hadn't realized that she'd been holding her breath until then.

'Do you know how to get here?'

'I've passed by the area a few times, but I am not sure of the exact location.'

'Once you pass the Siddapura police station in town, take the Karadigodu road. Then travel for about ten kilometres and keep an eye out for a signboard on the right side. When you spot it, turn and take the road that curves uphill and continue for about three kilometres. That will lead you to my place.'

Before they hung up, Alka asked her to repeat the instructions and wrote them all down. Then she began to pack hastily, throwing a few casual clothes into a duffel bag. She paused and then added a towel and some toiletries too. Before she could change her mind, she scribbled a note for Subbu, telling him she would be at Gowri's Green Tree Homestay. She instructed Selvi and Gowramma on what to do in her absence.

'Akka, please go and have fun. You know my mother and I can manage the girls and look after Subbu Anna, too,' Selvi assured her. And that was all that Alka needed to hear.

She leaped into the Scorpio and expertly navigated the winding path that ran through the coffee estate and led to the main road. Her heart raced with anticipation. She was terrified but also certain that she wanted to go even though she had never done anything like this before.

As the vehicle sped towards Coorg, Alka felt exhilaration seeping into every pore of her being. This was what it meant to be free, to be without a care in the world! She drove with the windows rolled down, laughing in delight as the wind swept her hair across her face. She pulled over and used a hair-tie to sweep back her hair into a tight ponytail. She looked for her favourite song—she had an entire playlist to choose from—and then sang along with Freddie Mercury at the top of her voice, feeling happier than she had in many, many years.

3

GOWRI'S GREEN TREE HOMESTAY

2006

Having followed Gowri's precise directions, Alka found the homestay easily. The drive had been pleasant—she'd stopped a couple of times for tea at roadside stalls and stretched her legs, savouring the feeling of 'getting away'. What it was that she was escaping from, she couldn't pinpoint. But the thrill of a solo drive was heady and invigorating. She felt powerful, in control, and strangely liberated, driving on the highway with the music turned up loud.

The colonial bungalow that loomed into view as she drove up the path looked similar to her own home, although it was much smaller in size. Adjacent to the bungalow was a new two-storeyed building constructed in the same style. The whole place was filled with bougainvillea that had seemingly grown wild and were bursting with blooms of every colour possible—purple, magenta, white, pink, yellow. Marigolds and dahlias swayed gently in neatly tamed flowerbeds as though nodding to the butterflies fluttering around. Pots of similar sizes with large palms planted in them stood in a long, straight line, the foliage forming a screen of privacy around the first floor. The garden seemed to be a celebration of every kind of flower, so unlike her own garden back home with its functional vegetable beds. The vibe of the entire place was exotic and wild, yet warmly inviting as well, and Alka fell in love with it that very instant.

As she parked her vehicle, Gowri came out of the bungalow to welcome her. Running a hand through her closely cropped hair, cut short like a soldier's, Gowri smiled warmly. She had a wide smile with perfect dazzling white teeth, like the ones featured in toothpaste ads. Alka guessed her height to be about five feet two. She also noticed her unusual attire—a loose, brown checked shirt with the sleeves rolled up and a pair of equally loose khaki shorts, both of which made it hard to discern her gender at first glance. Gowri had an air of quirky, androgynous charm about her.

'Hi, Alka! I am Gowri. Welcome! Welcome to Green Tree Homestay. So good to see you,' she greeted Alka with great enthusiasm, as if she was a long-lost friend.

'Hello,' said Alka, feeling a little self-conscious, but Gowri didn't notice it. Instead, she held out her arms and enveloped Alka in a bear hug, much to her surprise.

Gowri's genuine warmth and attitude were infectious and Alka found herself relaxing, her awkwardness melting away.

'Bags?'

'Just one.'

'The staff will take it upstairs for you. I've given you the best room. It has a view of the mountains and you'll see the most gorgeous sunrises. Unless you prefer sunsets, that is. In which case, I'll give you the next best room, the west-facing one,' Gowri chattered away.

'I'm sure whatever you suggest will be fine,' Alka said.

'Come on inside, let's have a drink. You can see your room later,' said Gowri as she led Alka into the main house.

'Drink? Now?' Alka was surprised.

'Why not? It's always the right time for a drink somewhere in the world. Don't tell me you don't drink,' Gowri frowned and playfully wagged a finger at her.

'I do. But—'

'But what? It's the middle of the day? Oh please! You are on vacation. That too by yourself. Relax and enjoy!' Gowri scoffed.

'Umm, okay, I suppose you're right.'

'Red wine? It's homemade. We have a great collection. Shall I pick one for you?'

'All right, thank you,' Alka replied. She followed Gowri into the drawing room, her eyes taking in her surroundings.

Antique bookcases, all of them built in different styles, lined the room from one end to the other. In front of them was a planter's chair on which lay a thick book that was closed shut, with a bookmark sticking out. One of the walls was made entirely of stone. Another was full of different kinds of artwork. The floor tiles had pretty patterns on them. Comfortable-looking sofas with multicoloured throws scattered over them dotted the room. It was an eclectically done up drawing room with a motley of things that looked like they had been randomly thrown together, and yet there was a method to the madness—art on one side, literature on the other, a fireplace tying them up together, and sunlight streaming in through the skylights. As she absorbed everything, Alka almost missed the two cats—an orange and a white one—sleeping in a cat hut that blended with the drawing room perfectly, almost as if it were camouflaged. They looked at Alka lazily but made no attempts to get up or come towards her.

'Hope you don't mind these two. They are the laziest fellows on earth,' Gowri said as she walked to a bar in one far corner of the room and generously poured some chilled wine into two glasses. She walked back and handed one to Alka.

Alka sank into the welcoming embrace of a brown sofa while Gowri gracefully took her seat at its other end.

'Oh no, not at all,' Alka said. 'Living on an estate, you get used to all kinds of animals.'

'Yeah, but these two, I pamper them rotten. I think there's some deep unfulfilled mothering instinct in me that I need to feed. My own children have fled the coop.'

'What do your children do?' Alka asked, still surprised at how friendly Gowri was being.

'Both are full-fledged adults now. One is a wildlife enthusiast and works at an animal conservation centre in the US. So far, she has worked with zebras, hawks, tortoises, monkeys and harbour seals. The other one is in London and is an investment banker. Both are very different from each other. Seems like it was just the other day when they were both kids, and now they are living on their own. Time sure flies,' Gowri sighed. 'I know from my aunt that you have two girls. How old are they now?' she asked.

'One is nearly ten and the other is a year younger. Bright as buttons, the two of them,' Alka said as she took a sip of the slightly sweet wine and savoured its mild, fruity notes. She instantly loved the flavour. She was about to say how delicious it was but Gowri spoke up before she could.

'Ah! Then you definitely deserve a vacation. I remember how things were when mine were that age,' she said.

'I suppose I do, but then the mother's guilt always acts up,' Alka confessed.

'Hmm. We all need to do this every now and then. Particularly so when a marriage loses its spark,' Gowri remarked, her gaze fixed on Alka. There was a level of understanding in her eyes that left Alka astounded.

'Er…' Alka fumbled, unsure of what to say. Her marriage had indeed hit a roadblock, but how could she reveal that to Gowri, a woman she had just met? Gowri did make her feel comfortable and she was clearly a chatterbox, but still, how much could she trust her?

'Wondering how I know?' Gowri smiled. 'It's because I recognize the signs. I've just come out of a bad marriage myself. I've done what you are doing just now. When my own children were younger, I needed these breaks every now and then in order to stay in the marriage, else I would have gone insane. Over the years, however, the breaks became longer and longer. It was only after my children grew up that I knew for certain that I was holding on to an empty shell. There was no marriage at all. Only the illusion of one. It took me a while to find my footing because I'd been playing a role that someone else had written for me. Now I am by myself, and I cannot tell you how happy I am,' Gowri revealed as she took another sip of the wine.

'Wow, that's quite something,' Alka said, pondering over everything that Gowri had mentioned. She was a little taken aback with how honest Gowri was being and how comfortable she was sharing such personal information with a person she'd just met. 'I am honoured that you shared all this with me,' Alka added, trying to cover up her conflicting thoughts.

'Hah! I share it with anyone who cares to listen. Women need to be told such things. We've all been brainwashed and conditioned to be good wives and good mothers. Of course, we can be all those things, but we should also live for ourselves. We should love and indulge ourselves too!' Gowri kicked off her sandals and tucked her legs underneath her, settling even deeper into the sofa.

Alka followed suit, propping up her legs. She felt cozy and at ease, sitting there and listening to Gowri talking nineteen to the dozen.

'We're conditioned that way for sure. Although, truth be told, I always did want a family. I so enjoy being a mother! I enjoy cooking for my family, dressing my girls, shopping for them,' Alka said.

'Really?'

'Yes, I was an only child,' Alka said.

'Ah, that explains why you enjoy it so much! And oh, sorry! I forgot to ask. Are you hungry? Lunch is already made, if you want to have it now. Or will you have another glass of wine?'

'Some more wine please,' replied Alka. 'This is delicious.'

'That's the spirit!' Gowri exclaimed, chuckling and pouring a large amount of the wine for Alka and herself.

They continued to converse easily, moving from topic to topic. Alka learnt that Gowri had met Anandi a few times many years ago but then they had lost touch.

'I hope you don't mind my saying this, but I think Anandi aunty wanted Subbu to marry my younger sister. They'd even met each other once. But of course, this was a lifetime ago and things never materialized.'

'Oh, I see,' Alka replied slowly, taking in all the information. She had no idea about any of it, and now her curiosity was piqued. 'Why didn't things materialize?'

'Umm … you know why.'

'No, I don't.'

Gowri suddenly went quiet. 'Oh, it doesn't matter! I just mentioned it casually since I found it amusing. That's all.'

'Come on, Gowri. I can sense there's something you aren't telling me.'

'Er, maybe it's better if you hear this from Subbu himself,' Gowri suggested, trying to dodge the situation and not give Alka any more details. But Alka was persistent.

'Listen, you said it yourself. It was all a lifetime ago. How does it even matter now?'

'I suppose it doesn't,' Gowri said, still feeling a little abashed at having revealed more than she'd intended to. It was one thing to spill her own story since she didn't mind doing so, but she had never intended to gossip about Subbu's past.

The wine had loosened Alka's inhibitions and she pressed Gowri hard for details.

'Go on. Tell me. I'm a big girl. I can take it. You can't lead me to the story and then not reveal the climax!'

After some resistance, Gowri relented.

'Yeah, you're right. It's not a secret anyway. Everyone in the coffee circles knows about it. Subbu was in love with a girl named Chanda. They were the talk of the town. All of us were certain they would get married,' Gowri said, her voice low.

'I see,' Alka said. She had never heard Chanda's name mentioned before.

'Why didn't they get married then?' she asked, hoping she sounded nonchalant.

'I don't know why. That is a mystery because all of a sudden Chanda got married to someone in the US.'

'Oh!'

'Anyway, Anandi aunty tried hard to set Subbu up with someone else by sending him on dates, and my sister was one of the women he met. He told her that he was meeting her only because his mother had insisted he do so, and that he didn't want to get married. My sister told me later that she felt he wasn't over Chanda yet.'

Alka was quiet.

'Hey, listen, I really hope I haven't upset you. I didn't want to tell you all this, but then you insisted.'

'No, it's just making me think a lot about my past,' Alka said.

The earlier light-heartedness of their conversation was now replaced with an air of awkwardness.

'Let's eat,' said Gowri, and getting up quickly, she led Alka to the dining table where her staff had laid out a sumptuous feast of butter chicken, biryani, parathas, rotis, paneer and many other North Indian delicacies.

'I thought you might be tired of the Malnad cuisine. So, I instructed the staff to make all this,' Gowri said.

'You're right. This is such a wonderful change,' Alka replied as she filled her plate and began to eat. But she grew quieter as she ate. The food reminded her of Delhi. It reminded her of another time in her life. Of all the wrong choices she had made and how she had walked away from the biggest love of her life.

After they finished lunch, Alka said she wanted to rest for a bit and Gowri guided her upstairs to her room. It was spacious, elegant and tastefully done up with antique furniture, mirroring the decor of her own home in Sakleshpur. However, the bed linen and the drapes were quite distinct, and adorned with charmingly delicate and tiny floral prints. Jute rugs were placed strategically in the room and fresh flowers graced various corners, adding a warm rustic touch to the space. Alka loved it.

'Once you finish resting and feel up to it, come downstairs for tea. If you are in the mood for a drive, I'll take you to the sunset point. It is beautiful,' Gowri said as she gently shut the door and left.

Alka sank into the soft mattress and pulled the duvet up to her chin. Her bag had already been placed in the room. The wine had made her feel relaxed, and while all her marital problems seemed far away, her mind was a whirlwind of questions about the choices she had made in her life. Soon though, the thoughts all blurred into one another as she closed her eyes and fell into a deep, restful sleep.

4
UNSOLICITED ADVICE

2006

When Alka woke up, she felt more rejuvenated than she ever had in the past decade. She had never taken time off just for herself, never engaged in extensive conversation with a person she'd just met, and she'd never thought that she would experience this kind of luxury, where she could just sit back and have plenty of time to think about things.

She explored the room and discovered a hot water kettle, two teacups and everything else she needed for making a hot cup of tea, all of it cleverly concealed inside a wooden cabinet on a counter that faced the window. Alka gazed at the imposing misty mountains outside. They were visible from her home too, but here, the view seemed sharper and more in focus, as though a painter had gone over the scenery and added an extra coat of paint. The air had a sweet citric tang to it, and Alka drew in a slow long breath, inhaling the mountain air as she made herself a strong cup of Nilgiri tea.

She reclined on the easy chair that faced the window and stared at the gorgeous view beyond. Putting her legs up on the ottoman in front of the chair, she slowly took a sip of the tea. Gowri had said that Subbu and Chanda were the talk of the town. Although Alka and Anandi had grown extremely close over the years, she'd never heard a word about Chanda from her. Curiosity welled up in Alka now. Who was this mysterious Chanda? Another thought crossed her mind. Why was it okay for Subbu to keep a secret about his past if it was unacceptable when she kept one?

A few years back, when she'd felt extremely unhappy with the sparse communication between them, she'd suggested seeing a marriage counsellor, but Subbu had ridiculed the idea.

'What is wrong with our marriage?' he'd asked, derision lacing his words.

'We hardly communicate, Subbu. I am not happy at all.'

'But what is there to be unhappy about? This is who I am.'

'Doesn't it matter to you that I am not happy?'

'All marriages are like this. But tell me, what can I do to make you happy? What do you want from me?'

'Just a connection, Subbu. I just want to be understood.'

'I do understand you. But I don't get why you're so unhappy. I do my best. I work hard. I provide well for you and the girls. I keep everything running and I don't burden you with anything.'

'That is exactly the problem! You don't share anything with me!'

But Subbu never understood what she was complaining about. After many such conversations, Alka had given up. Subbu simply didn't get her, and she had reconciled herself to that fact. But these days, the situation between them had worsened even further, making her feel isolated.

After finishing her tea, when Alka went down to the main house, she found Gowri waiting for her. As soon as she saw

Alka, Gowri rushed to apologize, 'I am sorry about earlier. It was not my place to say any of that. I get many tourists here, but there are hardly any visitors from the plantations around. So I was excited to have you visit, and I guess I got carried away.' Gowri looked sheepish.

'Don't worry about it, Gowri. It's fine, honestly. It's water under the bridge,' Alka replied.

'What would you like to have? Tea or coffee? Paneer and vegetable pakodas have already been made,' Gowri said.

'Nothing, thanks. I just had tea.' Alka smiled at Gowri's amiable hospitality.

'You can't turn down snacks! Babik, my cook and helper, will be insulted. He has made samosas too.'

'Oh my! Gowri, do you treat all your guests like this?' Alka asked.

'Only the special ones!' Gowri smiled. 'Besides, like I said, I enjoy having the company of our own kind.'

The food was delicious and Alka couldn't help taking second helpings. By the time they were done snacking, she felt stuffed.

'Shall we go for a drive? Up for it?' Gowri asked.

'Let's please walk instead of driving. I overate,' Alka requested.

'Tell you what, let's drive to a suitable trekking point, and then we can walk up the hill from there.'

Gowri drove Alka in her jeep to the foot of a waterfall from where they trekked up a narrow path that led to an ancient temple. The climb was steep and both women made their way up in silence, focusing on the path ahead. Gowri was slightly out of breath but Alka, having regularly walked on a lot of uphill paths in her own estate, found that she could climb without getting too tired. Time to time, though, she waited for Gowri to catch up.

'Look at you, a regular mountain goat,' Gowri teased.

'I do this daily at my place. I love it,' Alka replied.

When they finally reached the temple, Alka couldn't help but stare in awe at the imposing figure of the goddess inside. The idol had been decorated with a hundred red hibiscus flowers. The priest of the temple was finishing up for the day, but he waited for both Alka and Gowri to finish praying before he locked up the temple. Once done, he asked Gowri how she was doing and whether the cow at her estate had given birth yet. He also enquired about a labourer whose mother was ill. Gowri answered all his questions, and then he was on his way, telling her that he was happy she'd come to the temple.

'You seem to know everything that's going on around here,' Alka commented.

'They are all my people, including the animals. I watch out for all of them. We're a small close-knit community here.'

Both Alka and Gowri sat on the concrete platform that had been built around the majestic peepul tree in front of the temple. Far beneath them, the entire town of Coorg stretched out like a vast carpet. The cold wind tousled Alka's hair and she tied it up in a knot. Big fluffy clouds hung low in the sky, creating a picturesque tableau, a scene worthy of being caught in a pretty postcard.

Alka wondered how Gowri managed the estate all on her own.

'Don't you find it difficult to manage everything? How do you do it?' she asked.

'I had to learn how to do everything. I was forced to, actually. After my father passed away, there was no one to step into his shoes. I'd lost my mother a few months earlier. My sister and my brother both live abroad and they didn't want anything to do with the estate. My own marriage was over. So I came here and took over the reins of the estate. You should've seen this place when I came back. It was literally in shambles. Nothing was organized. Half the labour force had left. Production was on the verge of closing down.'

'That must've been such a difficult situation,' Alka mused. 'How in the world did you know where and how to begin?'

'Well, when you want to do something, the universe always shows you a way. It sounds clichéd, but I can tell you it's true,' Gowri said, gazing at the sky.

Alka waited for her to go on.

'There's a group of people who have formed an informal association,' Gowri continued. 'I took their help. I was heartbroken after my marriage ended and also very afraid. Sometimes, we get too used to things and are terrified to make changes, but these changes are needed for us to start the next phase in our lives. This is mine.' Gowri shrugged.

'Why did your marriage end, if I may ask?' Alka didn't usually pry, but she was curious about Gowri.

'He ended it. He said he'd met someone else. She's from his workplace and is ten years younger than me. A single mother with a son. Apparently, she "gets" him, whatever that means! And my biggest complaint in all the years I was married to him was that we never communicated enough. He was travelling more and more, finding every excuse possible to stay away from me. When I confronted him, he seemed relieved. Can you believe it? We think we know everything about someone, but we know only as much as they're willing to reveal.'

Alka drew in a sharp breath. Not only did she feel the same way about her own marriage, but wasn't this exactly what she'd done to Subbu? Revealed only what she wanted him to know? And he, in turn, seemed to have hidden some things too.

Alka's mind went back to a party she'd attended a few years ago, where the group of women she had been chatting with suddenly changed the topic after one of them blurted out that Subbu wasn't as innocent as she thought. Alka was almost certain now that Subbu was having an affair. Her intuition was strong. She had brushed it aside as an unfounded suspicion all this while, but the circumstances of Gowri's story seemed to bear an uncanny resemblance to her own. She would have to dig deeper into the matter when she got home.

Gowri noticed the faraway look in Alka's eyes. 'What are you thinking about? I hope I haven't bored you with all these details about my life,' she said and smiled apologetically.

'Something just struck me about my own marriage as you were speaking about yours. It seems like the same thing is going on in mine too,' Alka confessed with a sigh.

'All I can say is, don't be blindsided like I was. Be aware. Notice the signs. I was oblivious for a long time and when he told me he had met someone else, I was shell-shocked. For a while, I just refused to believe him.' Gowri grimaced.

Later that evening, after dinner, Gowri's staff got a bonfire going in the garden. Alka loved watching the dancing flames crackle and hiss. It was a mesmerizing sight. Gowri poured out some hibiscus wine for them. She said it had been bottled at their own vineyards, and since Alka liked it so much, she would pack a few bottles for her to take back home. Both the women prattled on happily, losing track of time. It was only when the fire died down that they went into the house and sat in the living room.

Gowri said she wanted to share something with Alka. She fetched a photo album, took out a photograph and showed it to Alka. 'Look at this picture,' she said.

It was Gowri with a tall, handsome man who had his hands wrapped around her shoulder. Gowri had long hair in the photograph. Both she and the man looked joyful and in love with each other as they gazed directly into the camera, laughing.

'That's my ex-husband,' said Gowri. 'It was two days after this photograph was taken that he told me he was ending our marriage. Can you believe it?'

'What? From the photograph, it doesn't seem that way at all. And you had long hair!' Alka exclaimed.

'Yes. As hard as it is to believe, that's what happened. That was the last time we gathered as a family. My son took the photo. He insisted that we both smile and refused to click the picture until we did. I have looked at this picture so many times, wondering how I missed all the signs. Anyway, many therapy sessions later, I've forgiven my ex-husband. I reinvented myself, and now I do things that make me happy. The reason I am showing you this photo, Alka, is because we lie to ourselves. We do not want to see the truth even when it is staring us in the face. Think long and hard about what you want from your marriage. And if you want your marriage to last long, fight for it. Tell him you want a hundred per cent.

Don't be satisfied with a twenty-five or a fifty. Above all, don't ever lie to yourself. Have the courage to face the truth, whatever it is.' Gowri drained her glass. 'I'm sorry again, I got carried away. All of this is unsolicited advice.'

'No, Gowri. I can't tell you how much all of this is helping. I can't thank you enough for sharing your story.' Alka blinked back the tears that had risen to her eyes.

'I'm glad then. I recognized a kindred soul in you. A minute into your phone call, when you said you were coming alone, I kind of knew why you needed to get away for a few days. I'd been in that same position before.'

'Tell me, Gowri, you live on your own and manage all of this by yourself. Doesn't it ever get lonely?'

'You know what, Alka? I was far lonelier in my marriage. Though we were both physically with each other, we were never there. Loneliness has nothing to do with the physical presence of another person in your life.'

Gowri was so right. Even though she and Subbu shared a bed, Alka did feel lonely in her marriage. Sitting in the drawing room and chatting with Gowri, she had a sudden insight into the way forward. Gowri was absolutely right in all that she had said. She needed to be in a marriage where both partners gave it their all. She had to demand that level of commitment from Subbu. All these years, she and Subbu had done the bare minimum required for them to get along. No more, she decided. It was time to face the truth and set things right, however hard it might be.

5

FLOWERS AND DIAMONDS

2006

Throughout the drive back home, Alka's mind was preoccupied with Gowri's words and her story. Gowri had packed six bottles of the hibiscus wine for her. In the back seat of the car, the bottles, securely cradled in a crate, produced a rhythmic symphony as they rubbed against each other with every winding turn of the road.

On the second day of her stay, Gowri had taken Alka to the vineyards and shown her the wine-making process. She talked about how she had supplemented her income from the plantation by setting up the vineyards and opening the homestay.

'Your estate has a lot of beautiful cottages too. Why haven't you opened them up as homestays?' Gowri asked, referring to the old cottages that were spread out all over the estate. Ever since Alka remembered, they'd been kept locked up and she was quite sure that they were all in a dilapidated state. The areas these cottages were located in all had quaint names; they'd been named by the British planters from whom Subbu's great-grandfather had bought the estate. When Subbu's father inherited the plantation, he renamed it Anandi Estate, but he had retained the British names within the property. Alka knew that four out of the five locations—Gurgling Waters, Laughing Meadows, Silver Brooks, Poet's Paradise and Misty Blue—had a cottage each. But she hadn't been inside any of them for many years now.

'I haven't actually bothered to ask Subbu. He handles all estate matters himself.'

'Maybe you should talk to him about it. There's good money in it, and it'll balance things out, especially during years when the crops don't yield well.'

Alka could only smile sadly in response. Subbu held the coffee estate like a guarded vault; it was his territory, his call alone. She had brought up the idea a few times, but Subbu disliked the prospect of letting out the cottages. Anandi had also not wanted to do anything about it. Alka had then let it be, but she didn't want to explain all that to Gowri.

When Alka got back home a few hours later, Selvi greeted her. Even though she had gone away for just a brief time, it felt as though it had been many days since she'd left. After she placed her bag in her bedroom, Alka walked into every room of her home, inspecting them for any signs of dust or dirt. She couldn't find any. Gowramma and Selvi had clearly done a splendid job of managing the house.

As Alka wandered around the house, Gowri's little slip-up about Chanda and Subbu played in her mind. She found herself walking into one of the unused bedrooms where Anandi used to store old photo albums. She opened an antique oak cabinet and took them out. There were five albums in all, each measuring roughly half a foot in length. They all had unique covers made of rich, textured silken fabric bound with satin chords. But the fabrics were beginning to lose their once vibrant colours. While Alka had briefly glanced through these albums in the early days of her marriage, she hadn't really paid close attention to the pictures. Now she found herself wanting to study them in detail. She wanted to examine every family gathering and celebration, every moment of daily life captured in the pictures. Perhaps she would be able to spot Chanda in one of them. She didn't know how she would recognize the woman. But she felt a compelling urge to find out at least a little bit more about the man she had married, and maybe, these sepia-toned photos would offer her a clue. Calling out to Selvi for a cup of tea, Alka settled back into the armchair and began flipping through the albums one by one.

The older photos were all in black and white. Alka drew in a sharp breath when she came across a picture of Krish dressed in his boarding school uniform, standing in front of a jeep, with his trunk packed and kept near his feet. There was a look of such profound sadness in his eyes that Alka wanted to scoop up that little boy in her arms and hug him. There were plenty of photographs of Krish from his school days—Krish as the school captain, Krish with his friends, Krish leading the debate team, Krish laughing, Krish surrounded by different girls. His entire childhood was playing out before Alka's eyes as she flipped through the pictures, and she found herself filled with a tender, indescribable longing for Krish. There were only a few photos of Subbu, and they mostly showed him working around the estate with the workers and the estate manager. By the time she finished with the albums, Alka was overcome with sadness as she realized just how much Subbu had missed out on by dropping out of school.

'Mummy! You're back! What are you looking at?' Nisha's voice interrupted her thoughts as the two girls rushed towards her. Alka looked up with a start, blinking away the tears that had unwittingly filled her eyes. She hadn't kept track of time as she sat engrossed in the albums and had forgotten that the girls were to return from school.

'I was looking at some old photos of your Appa and Chikkappa, baby,' Alka replied as she hugged them.

'Show us too,' demanded Tulika.

The girls giggled as they peered into the album which lay open in Alka's hands.

'Chikkappa looks smart,' Nisha commented.

'Appa is always dressed like a worker,' Tulika mused.

'That's because he works in the estate, silly. He doesn't go to an office like Chikkappa does,' Nisha replied.

Alka was amused at how observant her daughters had become. They were growing up fast. She put away the albums and asked the girls to go wash up.

'When is Chikkappa coming here? He promised he would come soon,' Tulika said as they walked out of the bedroom.

'Umm, I don't know. Why don't you girls wash up and come down to have a snack? Selvi Akka has prepared banana halwa today.'

'Yay! It's my favourite!' Nisha exclaimed as she and Tulika went to put away their bags.

Later that night, Alka waited for Subbu who got back much later that his usual time.

'What happened? Why are you this late? All well?' Alka asked as he washed up and joined her at the dinner table.

'Labour trouble. They're demanding a lot of freebies, like ten kilos of rice and free electricity. That will really cut into our profits. But don't worry. I am taking care of it. Muthu and I are negotiating with the leaders,' Subbu said as he helped himself to the akki rotis.

'Hmm,' said Alka. She knew he didn't want to discuss things further.

'How was your trip? Did you enjoy yourself?' Subbu asked.

'I did. I think these short breaks really help. You would know—you always get one when you go to Bangalore every week. But I rarely get a break.'

'Alka, I've never said that you can't take a break. You were the one who chose to stay here,' Subbu replied, helping himself to some chicken curry.

'But you never encouraged it either. You have never once offered to look after the girls and asked me to go on a vacation,' Alka shot back.

'How is this on me, Alka? You're the one who's wanted to stay with the girls all the time.' Subbu continued eating.

Alka paused to take a sip of water.

'I guess I should've done these things earlier. Anyway, Subbu, I had an insight while I was there. I feel there's something missing in our marriage. We both must put in a lot more effort into our relationship, and currently, we aren't doing that,' she said.

'What more do you want me to do, Alka? I work hard. I provide for this family. I am not a guy who will gift you flowers and diamonds, if that's what you want.' Subbu stopped eating and looked up at Alka.

'No, Subbu, I don't expect you to woo me with flowers and diamonds. But I would appreciate it if we could discuss things instead of you storming off every time we have a fight,' Alka said, looking squarely into his eyes.

'I like that. You kept your whole identity a secret, Alka, for *ten* full years. And now you talk about being open,' Subbu sounded annoyed as he put another akki roti on his plate.

'I know. I've apologized for that. I think it's best to let the past stay in the past, where it belongs. Also, it's not like you've never kept any secrets from me!' Alka couldn't stop herself from saying.

'What do you mean?' Subbu asked sharply.

'I heard about you and Chanda.'

Subbu stopped eating. His face had turned to stone and he couldn't speak for a few seconds.

'What? Who told you?' he finally managed to ask. His shocked expression took Alka by surprise.

'Gowri,' Alka replied.

She knew then that it was a mistake to have brought Chanda up. This was not the time or the place, but it was too late. The words hung in the air between them like a dark, ominous cloud.

'Oh, that woman! I should've known. She's always talked too much,' Subbu mumbled, avoiding looking at Alka as he shifted slightly in his chair.

'How is it that neither you nor your mother or Krish have ever mentioned anything about her?' Alka couldn't stop herself from asking the question even though a small voice inside her head begged her to stop. But she couldn't let it go.

'I don't want to talk about it,' Subbu said.

'Oh, I see. So, it's okay for you to keep a secret, but when I do the same it's a crime?'

'Alka, enough. I said I don't want to talk about it.' Subbu stood up abruptly and pushed away his dinner plate with the half-eaten food still on it. He stalked off to the verandah.

Alka followed him out.

'What the hell, Subbu! I don't want to fight. I just want us to go back to how things were.'

'And you do that by bringing up something that I said I don't want to talk about?'

'How is it okay for you to bring up my past, but when I ask you about something, that's not okay? Be fair.'

'This isn't a quid pro quo. What I had, well, it is different. I didn't pretend to be someone else.'

'Oh but you did. You pretended to be interested in marrying me when the truth was that you were never in it completely. You did it for your mother, didn't you?' Alka didn't know what had got into her but she simply couldn't stop. It was like picking away at a scab. It was all very clear to her now—Subbu had never loved her. Just how blind had she been? His expression told her all that she needed to know. But still, she was not willing to give up.

'Subbu, look, I want a little more from this marriage. We've spent a decade together and yet we haven't really been close to each other. Let's wipe the slate clean. You kept a secret from me, I kept one from you. We're even now. Let's start over. Let's give this marriage a proper chance. What do you say?' Alka asked.

'Let's have this conversation another day. I need some time to think.' Subbu averted his eyes and turned away from her.

Alka didn't say a word. She watched as Subbu paced up and down the verandah. It seemed as though he wanted to say something but couldn't find the words to do so.

Alka thought about all the years they had spent together. While they didn't have a whirlwind romance, they did have deep affection for each other. At least that's what Alka felt for him. They had stuck together for a decade. Subbu might not be exciting to talk to, but he was dependable. He gave her a feeling of security, which was something she'd never experienced before. He'd given her a family, a home, a sense of purpose and belonging which she valued so much. Yet, she longed for more.

'You can't keep pushing me away, Subbu. I come to you with a solution, and you're turning me away. Shutting me out. Like it or not, we're both stuck in this marriage and we better make the best of it,' she persisted.

'Please, Alka, I am not turning you away. I just need some time, okay?' Subbu's voice was hoarse, the words barely leaving his mouth. His lower lip was quivering. Alka had never seen him so emotional before.

With that, Subbu left and marched into his room downstairs. Many a time, when he had to wake up really early, he slept in one of the bedrooms downstairs. But tonight, Alka knew he was shutting her out. Again. She stood staring after him for a long while.

As she eventually made her way to their bedroom upstairs, Alka grew certain that there was more to the matter than what little Subbu had revealed. Everyone had past relationships, but no one got affected like this. She remembered Rohan, whom she hadn't thought about in a decade. She didn't have the slightest iota of feelings left for him—he was an ex, and that was what he would remain. But there was something unusual about Subbu's reaction. His behaviour was uncharacteristic and disproportionate to what anyone would feel if their past relationship was discovered. Why, then, did he care so much?

For many days afterwards, Alka thought about Subbu's reaction. He had clammed up completely. He went on his estate rounds as usual, leaving early in the morning. At lunchtime, he assiduously pretended that everything was normal. Every day, Alka waited for him to bring it up, and every day he avoided it. She was giving him time like he'd asked for. But as each day passed, he retreated even further into his shell.

After six weeks, Subbu had still not said anything. Alka felt she was neither 'inside' nor 'outside' with Subbu. He didn't want to talk at all. He was simply pushing the whole thing aside and not letting her in. She didn't want the walls between them to remain standing anymore. But if he was going to hide behind these walls that he'd built, then she was determined to break them down. She had to make him understand that no matter what mistakes they had made in the past, it was all okay as long as they forgave themselves and forgave each other. If they wanted true intimacy in their marriage, they had to be honest enough with each other. She was tired of waiting, and she wanted to know the truth. Her own truth had been revealed to Subbu already. Then why was he hiding his? What was he so ashamed of?

She decided that if Subbu wouldn't tell her, she would find out for herself. She would call up Krish and ask him what had happened between Subbu and Chanda and why Subbu had reacted the way he had. She simply *had* to know. Settling into the sofa, she dialled Krish's mobile number. She had never thought she would use it, but today, she needed to speak to him. He picked up on the very first ring.

6

SETTING UP A HOME

2006

'Hello, Krish?'

'Alka! How are you?' Krish asked, his voice gentle. To Alka, it felt like a balm on her bruised soul.

'I'm okay, Krish. How are you?' she replied.

They spoke with an easy familiarity. Though they hadn't spoken to each other since his last visit to the estate, it didn't feel that way. It was as if they'd never been out of touch.

'Umm, not so bad. I have some big news. But before that, tell me what took you so long to call me?' he asked.

Alka drew in a sharp breath as she heard the warmth and tenderness in Krish's question. How she'd missed him! But she would never reveal that to him. It was best if some things were left unsaid.

'Big news? What is it? Tell me!' she insisted, smiling.

'No, you'll have to first tell me what took you so long to call me.'

'You know why I didn't call you, Krish,' Alka said softly and sighed. 'Now, are you going to tell me what your big news is or not?'

'No! Tell me why you called me today.'

'Not unless you go first. It's unfair to mention that you have some big news to share and then not say anything. I absolutely refuse to continue this conversation unless you tell me,' Alka declared firmly.

'My goodness! When did you become so demanding?' Krish asked.

'Ever since I became a mother. Mothers just have to get things done and they refuse to take no for an answer.'

'All right, all right,' Krish relented. 'Since you insist, I shall tell you my news first. There's a massive opportunity for my company that is coming up in Bangalore. They're setting up an offshore division there and they have an opening that's perfect for me. I interviewed for it a while ago and I got it. I'm moving to Bangalore, Alka.'

'Oh, Krish! Congratulations! That's big news indeed.'

'Thank you. It's a great opportunity, career-wise. But personally also, I think I needed this, Alka. It's going to be a fresh start,' Krish replied.

'What do you mean by fresh start?'

'You know, starting life over. Manasi and I, we've filed for a divorce. And that should come through soon.'

'What? When did this happen?' Alka was shocked.

'It's been brewing for a few years now. I had decided to ask for a divorce when I was in Sakleshpur. Things became very clear to me while I was there. That's why I left so abruptly.'

'Oh, Krish!'

'This was coming anyway, Alka. I had been burying myself in my work and refusing to confront reality. But when I was there at the estate, I had the time and distance to think about it. Both Manasi and I have known for a very long time now that we were in a dead marriage. We both agreed there was no point in holding on.'

'I know what you mean.' Alka understood the feeling perfectly.

'But it didn't come without its share of bitterness. Manasi said she was tired of me acting like I was doing everyone a favour by earning money.'

Alka didn't know what to say. She knew nothing about how Krish's marriage had been. She had no words of advice for him. But Krish wasn't looking for comfort. It seemed like he only wanted to tell his side of the story to Alka. So Alka did just that as Krish continued to speak: she listened.

'She said a lot of hurtful, nasty things, Alka—that I am an absentee father, that I hate Sanal, and I don't care about their well-being. She said that she was happier when I wasn't around. And so was Sanal. Apparently, Sanal behaves better when he doesn't see me. When I suggested we get a divorce, she said she was glad I'd brought it up as she'd been thinking of ending the marriage herself. She said I could move out whenever I wanted.'

'It must have been so hard, Krish.'

'It was, initially. I am renting a studio apartment close to work now. It felt like a massive weight had been taken off my chest when I walked out of that house. But it also felt strange. Her accusation about me not loving Sanal really hurt me, it cut deep. I've made every effort I can, Alka. But I've not been able to bond with Sanal. He's on the most severe end of the autism spectrum. And I don't know if this makes me a selfish person, but I wanted to tell you that I tried. I really did.'

'I know you did, Krish. Whenever your mother visited you all, she used to come back and tell us how hard things were. But remember Krish, Manasi wanted this too. It wasn't your decision alone.'

'The worst part is, she isn't letting me see Sanal. She says I am a trigger and his behaviour changes when I am around. She says he is making progress without me. And I don't think she is saying it to be mean. She wants what is best for Sanal.'

Alka found herself at a loss for words. She understood fully well how difficult a situation it was. She recalled the time when Sanal was about six and had to be hospitalized after he had toppled the television over, which had then landed on his feet. She remembered Anandi telling her how stressed Manasi and Krish were as they dealt with his severe meltdowns, sometimes cleaning up urine, watching out for self-injurious behaviour and being on tenterhooks all the time, not knowing what the next trigger could be.

'Things have a way of taking their own course, Krish. It's not in our hands. We only have the delusion of control,' Alka said, hoping her words would comfort Krish. She could easily fathom his pain and frustration.

'I agree. It is what it is, and I have to accept that,' Krish replied.

'What's next though? When are you moving to Bangalore? Have you told Subbu the big news?'

'It just came through yesterday, Alka. I was going to call Anna over the weekend and tell him. And you would've heard it from him. I wasn't going to break any protocol by calling you up and telling you first, but after I heard your voice, I couldn't help telling you.'

'Wow, I am honoured, sir,' Alka replied, not sure of what to say. She tried to make light of it, but her heart was humming with excitement. Krish was moving to Bangalore! He would be so close.

'And listen, don't tell Anna yet. I'll call him and let him know myself.'

'No, I won't tell him. This conversation never happened,' Alka said. 'We'll be so much closer. Geographically, I mean,' she hastened to add.

'Yes, I know what you meant,' Krish replied, smiling. It was the first time in days that he had smiled. He felt lighter after talking to Alka, and surer, too, of his decision to leave Mumbai. It was time to start a new chapter in his life.

'By when will you be in Bangalore?' Alka asked. She hoped she didn't sound too eager.

But Krish didn't notice. 'In about a month's time, but let's leave that aside. You didn't tell me why you called today.'

'Oh, that's okay, Krish. It can wait. It's not important,' Alka said. She couldn't possibly ask him about an incident from her husband's buried past, especially not now when he was dealing with so many things in both his personal and professional life.

But Krish knew she was fobbing him off. 'It can't be *not important*, else you would've never called,' he said.

'Umm, it kind of is. But now is not the time. It can wait,' Alka admitted.

'I am so curious to know what it is. You can't leave me hanging like this, Alka.'

'All in good time, Krish, all in good time. Now take care of yourself. I have to go,' Alka said.

After she hung up, she couldn't stop thinking about all the possibilities that would open up with Krish being so close by. It would be nice to have him around on the weekends, if he could spare the time, that is. The girls loved him, and when he was around, there was an air of lightness and joy in the house. Almost immediately though, Alka admonished herself for having these feelings. On one hand, she wanted more closeness with Subbu. She had told him she wanted a hundred per cent out of their marriage. And yet here was her foolish heart, humming a happy song at the thought of seeing Krish more often. She wondered if she was a hypocrite. Pushing these troubling questions aside, she buried herself in her daily tasks. She did not want to think about it.

Subbu got to know over the weekend that Krish was moving to Bangalore. He mentioned it to Alka when they were all having lunch and both Nisha and Tulika squealed with joy.

'I bagsy Krish Chikkappa for a game of Monopoly,' Nisha announced.

'No, he doesn't like Monopoly. We'll play Pictionary,' Tulika piped up.

'Girls, he's moving to Bangalore, not Sakleshpur,' Alka reminded them.

'So what? We'll visit him, won't we?' Tulika asked.

'Or he can visit us!' Nisha exclaimed.

'He sounded very down though,' Subbu told Alka later. 'I hope he's okay.'

'I hope so too,' Alka replied.

'Anyway, it will be good to have him close by,' Subbu said. But Alka didn't say a word. How could she? For while she was excited about him being close, she was also terrified about what that closeness could lead to. Krish still held a special place in her heart, and she knew from the sound of his voice that the feeling was mutual. Nothing had changed.

By the time Krish moved to Bangalore, the busy harvest period at the estate had ended. Subbu was still preoccupied with multiple tasks at the estate, but not as much as he'd been in the previous weeks. As soon as Krish landed in Bangalore, he called up Subbu and said he would visit them once he'd settled down and taken charge of things at the workplace.

'Do you need any help in setting up your home?' Subbu asked.

'No Anna, the company takes care of everything,' Krish said. He had to push away the memory of how Alka had helped him set up his very first home in Bangalore all those years ago, and the time they had spent there. It was one of the happiest periods of his life, even though all he could afford back then was a tiny apartment. Compared to that, his current house was a palace.

'All of you should visit me here. My new place is a penthouse in a fancy high-rise apartment, Anna, and I even have a private pool. The girls will love it,' Krish told Subbu.

'Private pool? Inside your apartment? That sounds like you're living in a foreign country.'

'It's on the terrace of my penthouse. Bangalore has developed a lot, with all the high-end buildings that have come up. Each builder is trying to outdo the other in terms of the luxuries and amenities provided. Compared to Mumbai, housing is extremely affordable too. For my daily living expenses, I am spending just half of what I used to spend there. The kind of accommodation I can get here for the amount I spent there, it's mind-boggling. Truly.'

'I'm happy you've achieved all this, Krish,' Subbu said with pride in his voice.

'Thanks to you, Anna. You're the one who sent me to school, sacrificing your own dreams,' Krish said.

The separation from Manasi was clearly making him a lot more sensitive than he'd anticipated. His emotions were in an overdrive.

'What dreams? My life is here on the estate,' Subbu replied, as practical as ever. His response helped Krish regain his composure.

'How is it going at the estate?'

'It's a little worrying this year. It is raining, which is unusual for this time of the year. The weather forecast says it will continue like this for another ten days. The Indian Meteorological Department has issued a yellow alert for Hassan and Shimoga districts. If it continues like this, all our hard work will be lost.'

'Let's hope it stops,' Krish said. He knew how hard Subbu worked and how helpless the entire farming community was when it came to Mother Nature. There was nothing that they could do to protect themselves from her fury.

7

LOST

2006

Tulika's art competition in Bangalore was approaching. Her art teacher, Miss Shanta, was giving her extra attention. She had even sent a note in Tulika's diary, asking Alka to meet her. When Alka visited the school the next day, Miss Shanta met her in the visitor's lounge, a small room located next to the principal's office. Slender and petite, with her untamed curly hair bound in a high ponytail, Miss Shanta smiled at Alka as she all but bounced into the lounge. She wore an earthy green sari with the pallu neatly pinned up. Alka liked her instantly.

'Hello, Mrs Shekhar. How are you? she greeted Alka and took a seat.

'I'm good, thank you. Tulika talks a lot about you. She loves your class,' Alka said.

'You really have a very talented daughter, Mrs Shekhar. It's a pleasure teaching her. She works very hard too.'

'That's heartening to hear,' Alka beamed.

'Thank you for coming in today. The reason I wanted to meet you was to ask whether you'll be able to take Tulika to Bangalore or not. We have only one school bus, and as you know, Tulika is the only student selected from this school. We can't reserve the school bus for a single student. That's why we're unable to arrange transport for Tulika. If it's a problem for you to take her, then I'll travel with her by public transport to Bangalore. We'll have to stay overnight though as it'll be close to 5 p.m. by the time the competition is over, and I wouldn't want to travel back with a child so late in the evening. I'll need you to sign the consent forms as well,' Miss Shanta explained.

Alka was not comfortable sending Tulika with the art teacher and letting her stay overnight in Bangalore.

'Oh, that will not be an issue. I should be able to manage taking her myself,' Alka said.

That evening, Alka told Subbu about her conversation with Miss Shanta.

'Of course, you should take her to Bangalore. There's no question of letting some teacher take her. Maybe you can stay with Krish and come back the next day. Shanker can drive you both there,' Subbu said.

Alka's heart skipped a beat at the thought of staying overnight at Krish's place. However, while she was excited, she also knew that it was dangerous territory, something she did not want to tackle.

'Umm, let's see. I'd prefer coming back home after the competition,' Alka said as she looked away. She couldn't meet Subbu's eyes.

'Why do you want to risk driving through these Ghat roads at night, that too with a child? Just stay with Krish and come back the next day,' Subbu said firmly.

Alka didn't reply.

A few days later, Tulika came back from school in tears. She had lost three of her textbooks. She had never lost anything before, and she was inconsolable now.

'Someone … someone stole them, Mummy … I had … I had kept the books in my bag. But when I came back … from the PT period … they were all gone … my maths textbook, English textbook and my social studies textbook,' she said in between sobs, snot running down her nose.

'It's okay,' Alka consoled her and wiped away the snot.

'It's not okay, Mummy! They had all of Nisha's notes!' Tulika wailed even louder.

Tulika had never needed new textbooks. At the start of each academic year, she would always get Nisha's textbooks.

'It's not fair that I always get old textbooks,' she had complained initially. But then Nisha had pointed out that all the English poems and lessons were already neatly annotated for her. 'Even if the teacher doesn't explain something, you will understand everything as I've made all the notes in the margins of the textbooks,' she had said. Ever since then, Tulika had seen the advantages that the arrangement offered and she treasured Nisha's textbooks. Whenever her teachers asked a question about anything they'd taught in class, Tulika already knew the answers, all thanks to Nisha's notes. She revelled in the teachers' praise, and therefore, losing the three textbooks was a disaster for her.

'Didn't the teacher try to find out what happened?' Alka asked.

'Mummy, the teacher made every student open their bags. She checked thoroughly, but the textbooks were not in anyone's bag. Someone has done this deliberately. The teacher called me to their class because Tulika was crying so much,' Nisha explained.

'How … how … will I get new books now? The school store … doesn't have … any in stock!' Tulika was crying even harder now, taking in large gulps of air and barely managing to get the words out.

Alka held her until she calmed down.

'Hush. We'll get you new books from Bangalore when we go for your art competition, okay? I'll call up Gangaram Bookstore and ask them to source the books if they don't have them in stock. Don't worry, baby,' Alka comforted her.

'And I still have my last year's notebooks. So, we can make notes in the new textbooks again. I'll help you,' Nisha assured her.

That comforted Tulika somewhat.

'Promise?' she asked.

'God promise,' Nisha said.

Later, Alka called up the bookstore and enquired about the availability of the textbooks. Thankfully, they did have them, and Alka heaved a sigh of relief. Now all she had to do was travel to Bangalore and get them for Tulika.

Alka did not call up Krish to tell him about her upcoming visit to Bangalore. She was busy fighting her feelings of guilt and excitement, and she knew that he would hear about the trip from Subbu anyway.

Two days before the trip, Subbu told her he had spoken to Krish and informed him that she and Tulika would stay over at his place after the competition.

'Apparently, his apartment complex also has rooms for drivers and staff. So, Shanker can stay there too,' Subbu said as he sipped his wine and leaned back into the easy chair in the living room.

Alka didn't know what to say. She stood up abruptly and walked to the fridge, pretending to get a refill for herself.

'Why didn't you check with me about this plan?' she asked, trying to calm her racing heart as she poured a tiny amount of wine into her glass even though it wasn't empty yet.

'I thought we'd decided this already?' Subbu looked surprised.

'I told you I prefer coming back the same night,' Alka said. She regained a bit of her composure and sank into the sofa opposite Subbu. She gazed at the floor as she took a sip of the wine.

'Alka, I already told you that it's best not to risk driving at night. There have been some landslides on NH 75 near Donigal because of the rains. And after what happened with Amma, no way am I allowing you to come back at night. Just stay there and come back the next morning. What's your issue with this plan?' Subbu asked.

Alka couldn't argue with him after that. Anandi's road accident had been gruesome. She recalled how it had taken eleven hours to rescue the wreckage of her car from the ravines of the Western Ghats, and then extract the mangled bodies. The accident had badly affected all of them, especially Subbu. He was right. She couldn't risk travelling back at night with Tulika.

'Yes, I agree, you do have a point there. It's definitely safer to stay overnight,' Alka conceded. She thought about what excuses she could possibly give to check into a hotel instead of staying with Krish, but she failed to conjure up any. If she still insisted, it would only seem odd. All she could do was play it cool.

Tulika was more excited at the prospect of meeting her uncle and getting new textbooks from the bookstore than she was about taking part in the art competition.

'It's not fair that she gets to meet Chikkappa and see his beautiful house while I can't,' Nisha pouted as the girls did their homework.

'How do you know his house is beautiful?' Alka asked.

'It has a swimming pool which no one else can use and it has gardens and it is on the top floor. Appa told us,' Nisha said.

'You don't have an art competition to participate in, then how can Mummy take you?' Tulika asked.

'You have to take me on a Saturday-Sunday then, okay?' Nisha asked Alka.

'Yes, maybe we can all go again,' Alka replied only to placate Nisha.

Tulika had practised what she was going to draw at the competition. They could choose from three topics: 'Save the Earth', 'City Life' or 'Imaginary World'. Tulika had chosen 'Save the Earth'. Her piece would show a beautiful gleaming sun in the centre of the page, its rays made of solar panels outstretched like arms. The earth, positioned underneath the sun and coloured in rich hues of ocean blue and green, would be thriving with life. Tulika's brush strokes and the colours she'd chosen symbolized harmony and sustainable, eco-friendly practices. They exuded a message of hope. Tulika had understood the importance of it, and if asked to explain her painting, she could speak like a pro. Her science teacher had coached her and Miss Shanta had helped her refine her work. Her teachers were certain that she stood a fair chance of winning a place at the national level competition.

On the day of the competition, after Subbu had left for the estate rounds, Alka finally decided to call Krish. It would look odd if she just showed up at his place without calling him even once. She couldn't avoid him forever. She would have to fight her feelings and pretend everything was okay.

The moment she heard his voice, a sense of comfort enveloped her.

'Hey!' She smiled.

'Hey yourself. I'm quite excited that you'll be staying here,' he said.

'Listen, Krish, about that, I don't think it's a good idea.'

'Why not? It'll be nice to see you, Alka, and of course, Tulika too.'

'I know. I badly want to see you too, but—'

'But what, Alka?' Krish interrupted her. 'Do you not trust me?'

'Oh, Krish! I do trust you,' Alka said. It was her own self that she didn't trust. But she couldn't bring herself to say that to him.

'Come on, we're both adults here. Not the young impetuous people we were in our youth.'

'I agree,' Alka sighed. 'Anyway, I have a mobile phone now. I'll message you. It'll be easier to coordinate with you once the competition ends. I also have to pick up some textbooks from Gangaram for Tulika.'

'I'm taking an off from work. We can go there together.'

'Krish, you don't have to.'

'I know I don't have to. But I want to, Alka,' he said. His words made her heart melt.

They agreed to meet after Alka dropped off Tulika at the competition venue.

Alka spent a lot of time debating what to wear. Finally, she chose to wear an old pair of jeans so that it wouldn't look like she'd made an effort to dress up. But she teamed it up with a designer top and heels. Alka decided she would bring up the topic of Chanda when she saw Krish and would insist that he tell her the truth. She needed to unearth Subbu's past to understand him better because she wanted to give her all to their marriage. She would also make it clear to Krish that no matter what they felt about each other, they could do nothing about it. She would simply have to bottle up everything she felt for Krish and not allow it to consume her.

Yet, despite all these resolves, her heart overflowed with joy as she sat in the car with Tulika. Her mind kept wandering back to Krish. How would they be able to contain their feelings when he was specifically taking a leave from work just to meet her and spend the day with her? She had no answer to that question. All she knew was that she was happier than she'd ever felt in a long, long time.

8

WITHOUT A CARE IN THE WORLD

2006

The journey to Bangalore had been peaceful, with Tulika sleeping through most of it, including the hairpin bends that Shanker had navigated expertly. By the time she woke up, they had already pulled into the campus of the Karnataka Chitrakala Parishath, where the art competition was being held. Alka had never been there even though she knew it was a cultural landmark in Bangalore. It was a massive complex, housing within its precincts a network of museums, galleries and archives. It also had a college of fine arts that offered undergraduate and post-graduate research programs for visual arts. The sheer size of the campus took Alka by surprise.

Signboards guided them to a large hall, and at its entrance, volunteers checked the names of the children, verified their identities, and then led them to their allotted desks.

'Are you sure you don't want Mummy to hang around here while you paint?' Alka asked Tulika before she went inside.

'Mummy! I'm a big girl now. Only for kindergarten students do the parents need to wait. You can go and buy my textbooks,' Tulika said dismissively. Alka nodded, secretly proud of how fiercely independent her little girl was becoming.

'All right, I shall go to the bookstore now and get back here quickly. When you finish, I'll be outside the hall, okay? All the very best!' Alka hugged Tulika and watched her walk into the hall.

As she made her way back to the car, Alka wished Tulika had asked her to wait at the venue. While she was eager to meet Krish, part of her was also terrified. She wasn't sure if she would be able to hold back her feelings for him when she saw him.

She messaged him as she got into the car, letting him know that she had dropped Tulika off and was heading to the bookstore.

'I'll meet you there.' His reply was almost instantaneous. Looking at the message on her phone screen, Alka's heart began to beat faster. She was finally meeting him. Alone. Why was she feeling guilty even though she wasn't doing anything wrong? Was it because deep down she knew that she was still not over him? She wondered if he struggled with the guilt as well. Perhaps she could bring it up at some point during their conversation, she thought as the car sped towards the bookstore.

'Shall I park here and wait?' Shanker asked as he pulled up outside Gangaram Bookstore.

'No, please go and have lunch first. Then you can park inside Shringar shopping complex. I'll probably take a couple of hours. I'll find the car once I'm done,' Alka said. Shanker, like most people at the estate, did not own a mobile phone.

Alka always felt happy when she came to Bangalore. Even though the cacophony of honking horns and bustling engines was jarring when compared to the melody of the birdsongs she was used to hearing at the estate, she soaked it all in. She loved the city's energetic pulse, the lively conversations of the pedestrians, and the allure of the shops on the sidewalk selling everything from tiny trinkets for tourists to elaborate handmade dreamcatchers. It was a welcome change from the serene greenery which she was always surrounded by back home.

She took the stairs instead of the lift to the store's second floor where the textbooks were stocked. She found the books that Tulika needed and bought them quickly. Then she glanced at her watch and messaged Krish, telling him that she would be in the stationery section in the store. It was her favourite section. Once there, she began browsing through all the pretty notebooks which she had no intention of buying. She held one in her hand for a moment and then placed it back after running her hand over its fabric cover. Then she picked another one and began examining it as well. The simple act of looking at these notebooks gave her such joy.

When she'd first moved to Bangalore, Alka had discovered this stationery section and been so enamoured by it that she had bought four beautiful journals. Manasi, who'd been with her, had been so amused that she'd narrated the incident in great detail to Krish the next day. Alka sighed at the memory. Such different turns their lives had taken now.

'Hello there,' a familiar voice interrupted her thoughts and for a second Alka wondered if she'd imagined it because she'd been so completely lost in her memories. Then she turned around and saw that it wasn't her imagination at all. Krish was standing a few feet away, smiling at her. Her heart leapt with joy. He was impeccably dressed in formal wear—a charcoal grey shirt, black trousers, a red tie and a black blazer that matched his polished shoes.

'Hi, Krish,' Alka smiled, hoping that her excitement wasn't showing on her face.

'Hey! You still love notebooks, don't you?' A smile lit up his face.

'I guess I do,' Alka shrugged, putting back the one she was holding. It had a pretty bicycle with a flower basket on its cover.

'You know, I was going to buy one for you. But now that you are already here and browsing, you can choose one yourself,' he said as he picked up the notebook Alka had just put back.

'Krish, that's so sweet of you, but there's no need for that.'

'And I say there is. So, are you going to pick something you like? This one, perhaps? Or shall I pick one for you?' he asked, glancing at all the notebooks displayed on the shelves.

'Hmm, you're stubborn as ever. Fine, you pick one,' she conceded.

'You want to make this difficult for me, don't you?' Krish raised an eyebrow.

'You're the one who gave me a choice! And now you're blaming me?' Alka exclaimed, pretending to be indignant. But a second later, she and Krish were giggling away like a pair of teenagers.

'How about this one then? Like it?' Krish asked as he rummaged through the notebooks and handed one to her.

Alka fell in love with it instantly. He'd chosen a charming hardbound notebook made of recycled paper. The deep maroon fabric cover had a rough, woven texture. When she opened the notebook, she saw a label at the back which said it was made from recycled hand-spun silk sari yarn from Nepal. The strangest thing was that the notebook Krish had picked up was the same one she'd placed back on the shelf just before he arrived. It was uncanny how well he knew her taste.

'This is perfect. Would you believe it if I said that I would have picked the same one?' she asked softly.

'See, I know you so well, Alka.'

'That you do. Thank you,' she said.

Krish insisted on paying for Tulika's textbooks too, refusing to listen to Alka when she tried protesting.

Alka was trying hard to not look at him too much. He had a striking presence and she could see the respect he commanded amongst the bookstore staff. They were almost standing in attention, fawning over him as he took out his wallet to pay. She had to remind herself that this was not a date.

'How long do you think Tulika will take?' Krish asked.

'Well, the competition is for three hours. I told her I'd be there when she gets done,' Alka replied.

'Pretty cool that she got selected. Anna was so proud when he told me about it on the phone,' Krish said as they walked out of the store. He was holding the plastic bag containing all their purchases.

'Aayi would've been so proud. She once told me that she used to paint in school,' Alka said. She rarely spoke about her mother and the sacrifices she'd made working as a house help to take care of Alka. But with Krish, she had a level of comfort she had never felt with anyone else.

'Amma used to paint too, before she had Anna and me. In fact, her paintings should be lying somewhere in the attic at home, I mean my home in the estate, not my home here,' Krish clarified.

Alka felt touched by how Krish still referred to the house in the estate as his home, and rightfully so. But it was a little strange as well, for it was her home too. They were so close to each other, and yet so far away, separated by the social norms and diktats because she'd walked away from him and married his brother instead.

'Where shall we go?' Krish asked as they walked down M.G. Road. When a group of men going in the opposite direction passed them by, Krish put an arm around her protectively. Alka drew in a sharp breath.

'India Coffee House?' she suggested.

'Of course! I should've known. You've always loved that place,' Krish said as they began walking towards it.

'Why are you dressed in formals? I thought you were taking an off today?' Alka asked. They had reached India Coffee House and Krish was guiding her to a table beside a window.

'I had a meeting before you came. I only took a few hours off actually. I have to go for another meeting in the evening,' Krish said as they sat opposite each other.

Alka looked at him and he looked right back at her. All that existed in those few moments was the two of them. It felt exactly like it always had when they used to go out together, before they both got married to other people.

'This place hasn't changed a bit,' Alka said hurriedly. They were still communicating with their eyes, just as they always had. She looked away now, feeling slightly disconcerted. On the wall behind Krish, she saw the same portrait of Mahatma Gandhi that'd been hanging there since their college days.

An elderly turbaned waiter in a pristine white uniform came to take their orders.

'Masala dosa, cutlet and filter coffee. Two of each. Bring us the coffee after we finish the food,' Krish told him without bothering to ask Alka what she'd have. This was what they'd ordered every time they'd come to India Coffee House in the past.

'Astounding memory. And why did you presume I'd want the same things?' she remarked.

'I haven't forgotten a thing, Alka. And you haven't changed at all,' he said.

'Different times, Krish. It seems like a lifetime ago.'

'And yet, isn't it strange how some sights and sounds can transport you back in time?'

'The illusion of time,' she said, not willing to admit the effect this meeting was having on her. Things were veering into dangerous territory now.

'I have to be content with illusions now,' Krish said, looking into her eyes again. But this time, Alka couldn't gaze back at him. Instead, she looked steadily at the portrait of Mahatma Gandhi on the wall.

They sat in silence, both lost in a world of nostalgia. The silence wasn't awkward. In fact, it was a comforting one, the kind that only two people close to each other could share. The waiter brought their order soon, but Alka left the food untouched. She was trying not to feel too excited and happy about being with Krish. *It's not right to have these feelings*, she chided herself mentally. But her heart, heedless of her rational restraint, thumped with joy.

'Not eating?' Krish asked as he broke a piece of the cutlet with his fork and tasted it.

'Yes, I will,' she said, following suit.

Then she remembered that she had to ask him about Subbu and Chanda.

'Listen, Krish, there's something that's been really bothering me.'

'What is it?' he asked, putting away the fork and using his hand to break a piece of the masala dosa.

'Who is Chanda?' Alka asked straightaway.

Krish stopped eating and fell silent, as if she had just dropped a bombshell.

When he looked up at her, he had an inscrutable look on his face.

'How did you hear about her?' he asked.

'Doesn't matter how I heard.'

'It does matter. People gossip. I don't know what you heard. But whatever version you heard, I doubt it's the right one,' he said as he recovered from her question and resumed eating.

'Then tell me everything,' Alka demanded. But Krish said nothing.

They ate their dosas in silence. When they finished, Krish said he'd go wash his hands, and when he returned, Alka did the same. She glanced at herself in the mirror above the washbasin. Her eyes were glowing and her face was flushed with happiness, such was the effect Krish had on her.

When she returned to their table, she saw that the waiter had served their filter coffees.

'Why don't you want to tell me about Chanda and Subbu?' Alka asked Krish again.

'Didn't you ask Anna about this? He should be the one explaining, not me. Let's have the coffee while it's hot,' he said and avoided looking at her.

Alka took a sip of the coffee. It still tasted the same—heavenly.

'So good, isn't it?' Krish remarked. Alka nodded.

They drank their coffees quietly, both of them relishing it.

'I did ask Subbu,' Alka said when she'd finished her coffee.

'And?'

'He clammed up. The man is like a bank vault. I couldn't get a word out of him. It's been haunting me for a while now, ever since I went on a solo trip, to be exact. It was the first time I did something like that. I went to Gowri's place in Coorg. And it was she who inadvertently told me about Chanda. But when she saw that I knew nothing about it, she clammed up too. When I got back and asked Subbu about it, his reaction was so extreme that I was astounded. I've never seen him like that. He almost cried. Since then, though, he has simply refused to talk about it.'

'Let sleeping dogs lie, Alka. It's for the best,' Krish's tone was firm. But it only ignited Alka's curiosity more.

'Krish, you have to tell me. If it's all in the past, then why does it matter so much?'

'It's not my place to tell you.'

This angered Alka. How could he not tell her after everything they had shared?

'Your brother won't tell me anything himself. You know it and yet you won't answer my questions. What kind of a friend are you? And how is it fair when you both know everything about my past but are keeping family secrets from me? Are you trying to protect your brother?'

'Alka, people are looking at us. Keep it down,' Krish said.

'I don't care about people, Krish. I want to know what happened and why no one is telling me anything.'

'Come on, Alka, I care about what people will think! My office is just down the road. People who know me are likely to be around. Please! Not here,' he pleaded and then signalled to the waiter to bring the bill. Once he'd paid and left a tip for the waiter, he led her outside.

It gave Alka a few minutes to cool off. She didn't know what had come over her in the cafe. Perhaps it was the thrill of being so close to Krish yet having to keep her emotions and feelings in check that had made her erupt.

Now they walked side by side on M.G. Road in silence. The sky had turned a dark grey, as if to match their sombre mood. The clouds hung low, but Alka didn't notice them.

'Please don't insist on me telling you something that Anna should tell you,' Krish begged her.

But Alka was determined to get to the bottom of the matter.

'If I mean anything at all to you, if our friendship means something to you, then tell me. Because Subbu simply won't. And Amma is no longer around. What am I to do?' Alka felt frustrated, angry and helpless.

Krish sighed. 'All right, I will. But not here. You're staying over tonight, so I'll tell you later.'

'All right,' Alka sighed.

The skies opened up just then and rain came pelting down in a sudden shower. The cold droplets struck them angrily, catching them both by surprise. People hurried to take shelter as deep puddles began to form on the road. Alka and Krish were in front of the Deccan Herald office and they, like many others, took refuge under its wide porch.

'See, even the gods above don't like you getting angry. They've sent this shower to cool you down,' Krish teased her. Alka playfully punched him in the arm, just like she used to do all those years ago, and they both chuckled.

'We still have an hour left to pick up Tulika. Do you want to go to my place? It's five minutes from here,' Krish asked.

'Shanker is waiting in the car. He's parked inside Shringar shopping complex. He doesn't have a phone though.'

'Well, that's where I parked too. Let's make a dash for it?' Krish asked.

Alka hesitated only for a second before agreeing.

'I love, love, love the rain,' she said as she stepped out of the shelter, the cool drops of rain hitting her face. She smiled widely even as water began running down her hair and face.

'You're crazy! But yes, I love the rain too. Follow me,' Krish said. He tucked the packet of books he was carrying under his suit jacket and ran towards Shringar shopping complex. Alka laughed as she followed him.

By the time they both got to his car, they were completely drenched. Krish removed his jacket and tossed it on the rear seat. The packet of books went next. His shirt was wet too.

Alka felt carefree and young. She couldn't remember the last time she had had so much fun, running like a lunatic on the roads, in the rain.

'Your car seats will be ruined. Thank God the textbooks are in a plastic bag though, else they would've been done for,' she said, giggling as she climbed into the car.

'I haven't got drenched like this in years now. You're completely crazy, Alka!'

'You suggested it! And you know you loved it!'

Krish reversed his car expertly and they spotted Shanker just as they were exiting the complex. Alka rolled down the window and asked him to follow them, ignoring the look of utter surprise on his face.

A few minutes later, as they pulled into the basement of Krish's apartment building on Vittal Mallya Road, Alka's teeth began chattering.

'God, it's c-c-cold. But it was worth it! I ... l-l-l-loved it,' she said, finding it hard to speak.

'Good thing we've reached,' Krish said as he parked the car and got out. Shanker had pulled in behind them. Krish pointed out the visitor's parking spot and then showed him the driver's room where he could wait. Then he led a shivering Alka towards the elevator to his home.

9

A CHANGE OF PLANS

2006

The building had looked rather nondescript from the outside, but Alka knew it was one of the most expensive residential addresses in Bangalore.

'I wish you had some towels in the car,' she said, still shivering as they stepped into the elevator.

When Krish opened the door to his apartment, a thousand memories came flooding back to both their minds. This was the reason Alka had not wanted to come to his place on her own. She was afraid the memories would overwhelm her, and that was exactly what was happening as she entered his home. His living room was done up in a mature and refined palette. The luxurious sofa in a rich, textured royal blue, the elegant powder blue patterned armchair next to which stood a majestic Areca palm in a stone planter, the white hand-tufted rug—all of it exuded an understated and sophisticated vibe.

'Wow!' Alka couldn't help exclaiming in sheer delight.

'This is why I wanted you to see it. Remember that first apartment I had in Bangalore? You had helped me do it up.'

'How could I forget, Krish?' she asked softly.

He led her to a room on the left. 'This is the guest bedroom. You'll find towels and bathrobes in there,' Krish said as he gestured to the wardrobe. 'I'll get out of these clothes too. My bedroom is upstairs,' he added as he left the room.

The guest bathroom too was styled with elegance. Alka got out of her wet clothes and wrapped a bathrobe around herself, feeling vulnerable and excited at the same time. Her hair was dripping wet and she was using the hairdryer to dry it when she heard Krish call out.

'You okay? I got you some clothes if you'd rather not be in a bathrobe. Leaving them on the bed. Also, we can put your wet clothes in the dryer once you are out,' Krish's voice rose above the din of the hairdryer.

'Thank you,' Alka shouted back.

Krish had read her mind once again.

When she came out, she saw that he had laid out a T-shirt and a pair of men's pyjamas. She quickly got into the clothes. They were oversized and she laughed as she looked at herself in the mirror. She resembled a scarecrow.

'I must say those clothes look better on you than they do on me,' Krish said when she emerged from the guest bedroom. He took her wet clothes from her and put them in the dryer.

'I'll win the fashion award for the best dressed scarecrow! I do have my own clothes in my car, you know,' Alka added as she sank into the plush sofa, tucking her legs beneath her.

Krish smiled. 'That's okay. You can wear these while your clothes dry.'

He handed her a steaming hot cup.

'What's this?'

'Hot chocolate. I used to have this back in my boarding school. You must try this one. It's deliciously rich and the texture is simply divine. I got it from France,' Krish said.

As Alka took the cup from him, his fingers touched hers. It felt like a bolt of electricity had passed between them. The air became charged with anticipation.

'Aren't you the regular Mr Butler?' she said simply to dispel some of the thrill and make the atmosphere a little less tense. They both laughed a little too loudly, even though it wasn't really funny. All Alka could think of was how much she wanted to hug him, hold him and kiss that sexy mouth of his.

Krish was thinking along the same lines—how attractive Alka looked and how much he wanted her in his bed. But neither of them were giddy teenagers anymore. Krish had decided he would do nothing about it, and Alka was too aware of the lines she would end up crossing if she initiated anything.

So they sat across from each other, demurely sipping their hot chocolate and trying to calm their racing hearts. Then Alka remembered why she was there in the first place.

'Okay, now tell me all about Chanda,' she said.

'I don't know where to begin, honestly. And I feel like I would be betraying Anna by telling you this stuff.'

'What about me? Aren't you betraying me? Don't I have a right to know? Everyone seems to know about Chanda except me. You said you'd tell me.'

'Yes, I did, and I won't go back on my word,' Krish said, inhaling deeply. 'You have to promise me that you'll never reveal that you know about Chanda. You cannot drag me into this.'

'I take full responsibility of that. You have my word.'

'Brace yourself then. Anna was madly in love with Chanda. Sometimes, I feel he's still in love with her. They were the couple that everyone in our circle wanted to be like. But Chanda's father was terribly strict, so she kept the affair a secret from her family. When her father found out about it, he was livid. He simply couldn't stand Anna. He hinted that Chanda, having done her masters, couldn't possibly marry an uneducated, uncouth villager. It hurt Anna deeply, injured his pride. Her father said he would consider Chanda getting married to Anna only if he managed to graduate. Anna took this demand very seriously and enrolled in a college, entrusting the estate to the manager. But within a month, without any warning, Chanda's father got her married to a guy from the US. Anna was heartbroken.'

Alka sat in silence, thinking about what Krish had said. Krish got up and walked towards the balcony. He didn't go out, but stood looking at the greenery outside.

'I see. So, it was a very intense past relationship. What's so bad about that? It's in the past, right?' Alka asked as she got up and walked towards him.

But Krish said nothing. Silence hung over them like a shroud and Alka intuitively knew the answer to her question.

'Don't tell me it's not in the past?' she asked quietly, looking into his eyes.

'You … you have to ask him, Alka. I-I can't do this. It's not my business and I can't get involved,' Krish pleaded.

'I was right then. It's not in the past.' Alka shook her head.

'Listen, Alka, I said that I'd tell you about Chanda, and I did. Now you'll have to ask Anna whatever else you want to know. This is between you and him. You cannot arm-twist me like this,' Krish said.

Alka opened her mouth to speak, but then thought the better of it and said nothing.

'And all this while, he was mad at me for having a secret,' she muttered.

'I don't know, Alka. I really don't, and I don't want to be dragged into this. You have to sort it out with him,' Krish repeated. He had decided that the topic was closed. Alka was angry about Krish not revealing anything else. But she also knew that there would be no use asking him for more information. Once he'd made up his mind, he wouldn't relent.

Krish's phone rang just then. When he looked at the number flashing on the screen, he frowned.

He showed the number to Alka. It was from the estate. Alka's mind immediately went into panic mode. Why was Selvi calling Krish? Was Nisha okay? Was there an emergency? And if there was one, why wasn't Selvi calling on her phone? Or was it Subbu who was calling?

'Hello,' Krish said, answering the phone.

This was followed by a stunned silence as Krish listened carefully. The expression on his face changed slowly, his eyebrows furrowing with worry. Alka knew at once that something had gone terribly wrong.

'Oh no! When? How did you know? Oh God ... okay .... No, she's here with me. We'll start from here immediately.'

Alka bit her nails anxiously, waiting for Krish to hang up, her heart sinking with each word he uttered. What had happened? Why did he say they would start off immediately?

When Krish finally hung up and looked at Alka, his face was pale.

'Krish, what happened? Is Nisha okay?'

'It was Muthu who'd called. Selvi found my mobile number in the phone book you keep next to the phone. They couldn't reach your mobile, so they called me. They didn't know what else to do.'

'What happened, Krish? Where is Subbu? You're scaring me.'

'Anna is in the hospital, Alka. It's an elephant attack. A lone tusker came out of nowhere and charged at Anna. He is hurt and has been rushed to the Sakleshpur government hospital.'

Relief washed over Alka for a brief moment when she realized that Nisha was safe. She had feared the worst. But the next moment, she was filled with worry. How bad were Subbu's injuries?

Every year, twelve to fifteen people lost their lives due to elephant attacks in various coffee estates in the area. She knew just how dangerous the lone tuskers were, but she'd never thought something like this would happen in *their* estate, that too to Subbu. She had always thought that the damage caused by the elephants would be limited to the warehouses.

'We have to leave now, Alka,' Krish said.

'But Tulika?' Alka asked.

'Let's head over to the competition venue and pick her up. What time does she finish?'

Alka glanced down at her watch. 'In another forty minutes. I should've left already to pick her up. I … I really lost track of time.'

'It'll take us less than thirty minutes to get there. We can pick her up and leave quickly for the estate.'

Alka nodded.

'Let me get your clothes from the dryer. Change, and then let's head over to the competition venue.'

'Okay.'

'How bad is it?' Alka asked a little later as they took the elevator down to the garage.

'He's unconscious.'

'Oh good Lord. Is he … is there something you aren't telling me to shield me? Tell me the truth, Krish. Please.'

'No, Alka, he's alive,' Krish said.

But Alka wasn't sure if Krish was merely saying that to comfort her. He looked stoic as they walked to Alka's car.

'Shanker, hurry and drive fast to pick up Tulika. Subbu sir is injured and he's in the hospital,' Alka said as she and Krish got into the car.

'Oh, what happened, madam? Is he okay?' Shanker asked, looking worried.

'An elephant attack. I'm sure he'll be okay,' Krish replied with a conviction he wasn't feeling.

Shanker drove like a man possessed. Alka and Krish said nothing as they sat in the back seat. Alka clasped her hands, trying to calm herself down. Once they reached Karnataka Chitrakala Parishath, Alka led the way to the competition hall with Krish closely following her. They spotted Tulika waiting outside the hall. When she saw Krish, she rushed towards him, exclaiming, 'Chikkappa! You came to pick me!' Krish hugged her.

'Mummy, you're late. You said you would be waiting outside. But since you brought Chikkappa, I won't be angry with you, okay?' Tulika told Alka.

'Okay, baby. How was the competition? Did you do well?' Alka asked, swallowing the lump in her throat. She didn't know how to tell Tulika about Subbu.

'I finished early, Mummy. I'd practised the drawing so many times that I drew it really fast. Everyone was looking at my painting. The aunty who collected it said it was very good. Does that mean I will win?' Tulika asked as they walked back to the car.

'If it has to happen, it will. But what matters is that you did your best and I am proud of you,' Alka said.

'Tulika baby, I'm coming with you to Sakleshpur. Your appa is in the hospital, but don't be worried, okay? He'll be all right,' Krish said as he settled her in the rear seat of the car next to Alka and shut the door. He then got into the front seat, and Shanker immediately started the car.

'Hospital? Does he have fever or typhoid?' Tulika asked. Her friend had recently been admitted to the hospital and she had learnt about typhoid then.

'No, baby. An elephant attacked him,' Alka said.

'Oh, the horrible elephant! Is Appa going to die?' Tulika asked, her voice quivering.

'Of course not. He's going to be fine.' Alka said.

'Yes, of course, he'll be fine,' Krish said as he turned around and smiled at her. But he didn't really know if his brother was going to be okay at all.

Alka's insides twisted and she held Tulika close to her, hoping and praying for Subbu to be okay.

10

HOPES AND PRAYERS

2006

Once they were on the way, Alka called Selvi for updates. Selvi was whispering as she spoke. She said that Nisha had come back from school and that she hadn't told her about Subbu yet.

'Good, don't tell her anything. I'll come back and tell her,' Alka said.

Krish called Muthu to check what was happening at the hospital. But Muthu had no new update other than the fact that Subbu was in the ICU and the doctors were asking for his family members.

'Tell them we're on our way and we'll be there soon,' Krish said.

Since Tulika was hungry, they stopped en route at a bakery and bought veg puffs and a fruit drink, all of which she gobbled up. It was a rare treat for her since there were no bakeries near the coffee estate.

The gentle motion of the car and the day's excitement hit Tulika soon and she curled up on the back seat, with her head in Alka's lap, and fell asleep. Alka covered her with a blanket she'd left in the car. They hit the highway in no time and were making good progress till the car came to a halt behind a long row of stalled vehicles.

The rain had caused a landslide on the highway. A large bulldozer was clearing the mud that had slid down onto the road, blocking the highway and dividing it into two parts. Vehicles stood in serpentine queues on both sides of the landslide, waiting for the mud and the debris to be cleared. Alka reached for the pillow she'd brought and gently shifted Tulika's head from her lap onto the pillow. Then she got out of the car and joined Krish as he stood surveying the situation. Most people had gotten out of their vehicles and were stretching their legs, waiting for the road to open up so they could resume their journeys. The sun was setting and the sky was a deep crimson.

'Oh, Krish, I wish I hadn't come to Bangalore today. I wish I was at the estate!' Alka cried.

'That was not up to you, Alka. Tulika had the competition today.'

'I know, but I feel helpless. I just want to be in the hospital. Like right now.'

'Me too. Trust me, if there was a helicopter to get us there, I'd have taken it. I am very worried, honestly. This tusker coming out of nowhere is a shocker.'

'Do you think he is …' Alka trailed off, not wanting to complete the sentence.

'No. I'm certain he is alive. Muthu would've told me immediately if something like that was the case.'

Much to Alka and Krish's relief, the landslide was cleared up soon and they began letting vehicles on the opposite side of the road go first. When the line finally cleared, cars on their side of the road started moving slowly too.

Alka called Selvi once again. When she hung up, she turned to Krish and said, 'Selvi says Nisha had dinner and is getting ready for bed.'

'Then let's drive straight to the hospital. Do you think Tulika will still be asleep when we get there?'

'Yes, she woke up really early and I think she's exhausted after all the travel and the competition.'

By the time they reached the Sakleshpur government hospital, it was close to midnight. Alka and Krish left a sleeping Tulika in the car, with Shanker keeping an eye on her, and rushed inside the hospital. The nurse fetched the doctor on duty—a tall, thin, bespectacled young man who looked a little annoyed.

'Are you the family?' he asked.

Alka and Krish both nodded.

'Why did you take so long to come? We have been waiting for the consent forms to be signed. We cannot act without your signatures. He has to be shifted to the speciality hospital in Hassan. It's urgent.'

'Sorry, doctor. We were driving here from Bangalore. Can we see him now?' Alka asked.

'He's in the ICU; he's not conscious. You can see him for a few minutes. But just to prepare you—he has four broken ribs. There seems to an intracranial haematoma as well, that's a brain clot, to put it simply. But we can be sure only after a scan. One of you can have a look at the patient. The other one, please sign the consent forms so that we can shift him immediately.'

'Alka, I'll take care of the paperwork. You go see Anna,' Krish said, taking charge of the situation.

Alka stood at the entrance of the ICU and peered in. A nurse asked her who she was there for. When Alka explained the situation, she said she could see Subbu for a few minutes.

Subbu's bed was behind a screen that afforded little privacy. Alka followed the nurse, her heart sinking as she took in the eerie silence in the room, punctuated only by the beeps of the various machines the patients were attached to. It being night-time, the lighting was low and that only added to the feeling of dread hanging in the air. When she finally saw Subbu, Alka stood very still, shock and pain mingling together, attacking her senses and choking her till she felt she couldn't breathe. There were all kinds of tubes going in and out of him—one from the nose, one at his arm, and she noticed a catheter as well. His eyes were shut and swollen, his head was swathed in bandages and his left hand was in a plaster. Alka was filled with conflicting emotions as she stood there, not knowing what to say or do. She couldn't believe that only a few hours ago, she'd been angry with him for keeping a secret from her, and now she couldn't bear to see him this way. How fragile life was.

The doctor on duty came in just then, accompanied by two attendants, and they asked Alka to wait outside.

When Alka stepped out, Krish was waiting for her. He said, 'We're shifting him to Bangalore instead of Hassan. I hope that's fine.'

'Why? Isn't Hassan closer?'

'Alka, too much time has elapsed. The doctors feel he has a better chance of survival in Bangalore. I'll go along with him in the ambulance.'

'I'm coming with you then.'

'Listen to me, Alka. Go home now. There's nothing you can do. Tulika and Nisha need you. You can't leave the girls like this. Nisha doesn't even know anything. I'll look after him. We'll have a clear picture and a proper course of action by tomorrow. You can come then.'

'How can I just leave him like this, Krish?'

'Trust me on this, Alka. There's no point if we both go. We can't do much anyway. He's not conscious either. I promise I will keep you updated.'

The attendants carried Subbu out on a stretcher, with one of them holding up the IV bag. Alka watched helplessly as they took him to the ambulance and gently eased the stretcher inside.

'Only one person is allowed in the ambulance. Who's coming with the patient?' one of the attendants asked.

'I am,' Krish said. 'Listen Alka, go home. I'll keep calling you. Take care of Nisha and Tulika. They need you.'

'All right,' Alka said. As the ambulance left, she wearily made her way towards the waiting car and went home. Once they reached home, Shanker carried Tulika inside in his arms and lay her on her bed.

'Madam, please keep me posted about sir. I will offer prayers at the Anjaneya temple. Everything will be okay,' Shanker said. Alka could only nod gratefully.

By the time she went to bed, it was past 3 a.m. Alka closed her eyes and was out like a light, the exhaustion taking over her mind and her body as she sank into a deep slumber.

When she awoke, the events of the previous day came rushing back and she sat up with a jolt. It was past 10 a.m.! She hadn't intended to sleep this long. She rushed to the kitchen and found Selvi making the afternoon meal.

'Why didn't you wake me up?' Alka demanded.

'Akka, you were fast asleep and I didn't want to disturb you. I sent Nisha and Tulika to school. I packed their lunch,' she said, handing Alka a cup of steaming filter coffee.

'Thank you. Did you tell Nisha?'

'Tulika told her. I told them he'll be coming back soon.'

'That's good. He was shifted to Bangalore last night.'

'Oh, Akka! Is he going to be okay?'

'I hope so,' Alka replied. She rushed to the phone and called Krish. He answered almost immediately.

'Why didn't you call me?' she asked.

'The news isn't too good, Alka. Anna has had a massive haemorrhage and has gone into a coma. He probably needs a surgery. Right now though, nothing is certain. They are waiting for the senior neurologist.'

'Oh good Lord,' Alka whispered as the news slowly sank in. 'I'll start for Bangalore right now.'

'Yes, you do that. When you reach, come to the ICU section. I'll be outside.'

'Thanks, Krish.'

'No need to thank me, Alka. He's my brother. I'd give my life for him.'

❧

The journey to Bangalore felt like it would last forever. Alka was thankful for Shanker, who drove carefully. He asked her about Subbu's condition and assured her that he would recover. They had the best doctors in Bangalore, after all. Then they fell into a worried silence. There was nothing more to say. When they reached Bangalore, Alka heaved a sigh of relief to have finally arrived. Throughout the drive, she'd kept thinking that had she not been in Bangalore, the consent forms the government hospital had needed could've been signed sooner. Maybe, the situation wouldn't have deteriorated so much then. But as Krish had pointed out, there was nothing she could've done. She had to take Tulika for the competition.

Alka told Shanker that she didn't know how long she would take inside the hospital or what her plans were. She slipped him a hundred rupee note and asked him to grab a meal and refresh himself.

'Thank you, madam. And do not worry. Everything will be okay. I'll be waiting in the car,' he said.

Alka met Krish outside the ICU. His eyes were red from the lack of sleep, and he was clearly exhausted.

'Hey, Krish, I'm here now. Go and sleep for a while and come back after you've rested.'

'No, Alka, I am fine.'

'Please, listen to me, you haven't slept at all. Did you eat?'

'No. Actually, it never crossed my mind. The doctor in charge, Dr Mohan, will come for his rounds in about two hours. I want to speak to him.'

'Let's speak to him together. Meanwhile, you have two whole hours. You can go home, rest a little, change your clothes and come back by then. There's no point in both of us waiting here. You said the same thing to me yesterday. Why doesn't that apply to you now?'

Krish realized that Alka was right. 'All right, I'll hurry back. You don't worry too much, okay? Anna's in the best hands.'

Krish was trying to reassure himself more than reassuring Alka. He couldn't bear the thought of anything happening to Subbu.

A little later, when he got back, Alka was waiting for him.

'Dr Mohan wants to speak to both of us. They asked us to meet them in their consultation room. Let's go,' she said.

When Krish and Alka entered the room, they saw that there was another doctor along with Dr Mohan. He introduced himself as Dr Murthy, the senior neurologist.

They asked Krish and Alka to have a seat and then they both explained the nature of Subbu's injury in detail. Dr Murthy grabbed a writing pad and a black marker from the desk, and drew a human brain on the paper. Around this, he drew another circle to represent the skull.

Then he explained, 'Subbu has had a traumatic injury. Head injuries can cause the brain to swell or bleed. When that happens, the fluid pushes up against the skull.' He drew arrows to indicate this.

'This causes the brain to push down on the brain stem, damaging the Reticular Activating System, or the RAS, the part of the brain responsible for awareness. That's what has happened in Subbu's case. We'll have to go in for a surgery to remove the clot,' he continued.

By the time he finished his detailed explanation, the paper was a mess, full of arrows and squiggles going in several directions.

'Will he recover fully and come back to normal after the surgery?' Alka asked.

Dr Mohan said, 'It's a long process and we won't be able to predict that. Right now, he's unaware of his surroundings and is incapable of voluntary movement. He's in a vegetative state. He may progress to wakefulness, but it is difficult to say whether he'll regain higher brain functions or not. His circulatory system and lungs will work. He will have sleep-wake cycles. But beyond that, we'll have to wait and see how much he recovers. Let's just hope there is no irreversible brain damage. The longer he's in a coma, the worse the prognosis.'

Krish and Alka both sat in stunned silence as the full weight of what the doctors were saying sank in. The air in the room seemed heavier. Alka felt numb and Krish felt as though an invisible force had tightened its grip around his chest. Both the doctors were looking at him, waiting for him to speak.

'Is … is there no way to know?' Krish asked. He couldn't believe what the doctors were saying.

Dr Murthy said, 'Well, the thing is, not all head injuries are the same. Patients recover at different rates and to varying degrees. It's difficult to determine at what point a patient will start understanding and interacting with their caregivers or their family in a meaningful way. It's important to have patience. Recovery from a brain injury can take weeks, months, or even years. So, we have to give it time. He needs care.'

'What happens if we don't go in for the surgery? I mean, is that an option?' Alka asked.

'Yes, that option is, of course, there. But it poses a risk to his life. His organs could fail. That's why the surgery is highly recommended. But the final call is yours.'

'There's no choice then. We'll go for the surgery,' Alka said.

'When can the surgery take place?' Krish asked.

'We'll schedule it for the earliest. But we had to explain the implications and the risks to you first and check if you still wanted to opt for it. Dr Ghanshyam will be the chief surgeon; he's one of the best in the country. Now, you'll need to sign the required consent forms before the surgery.'

'Yes of course, if that's what is needed then we don't have a choice,' Krish said.

'Then please complete the formalities and take care of the other requirements at the administrative desk.'

'Thank you, doctors,' Alka said politely as they left the room.

What she actually wanted to do was shake the doctors and tell them to assure her that things would be fine. That's what they were supposed to do, weren't they? Instead, they'd said it wasn't in their hands at all.

When Krish and Alka went to the administrative desk to complete the formalities, they were asked about Subbu's medical insurance. Alka said that Subbu did have a medical insurance policy, but she wasn't sure of the details. The administrative staff said that since the surgery was scheduled as an emergency, the details of the insurance policy and other things could be completed later. They could just sign the consent forms for now. Alka signed the necessary forms and handed them over to the staff. She did not know how she was functioning so calmly. Her heart felt heavy and her head was spinning with all the information that the doctors had given them. She was in a daze and it felt like they were caught in a nightmare. She and Krish walked towards the ICU and looked at Subbu. He was unrecognizable beneath his swollen facial features, the tubes, the bandages and all the machines that were hooked to almost every part of his body.

Alka sighed as she sat on the cold metal chair outside the ICU. Both she and Krish had thought that Subbu would recover immediately after the surgery. But now, after speaking to the doctors, they weren't sure at all. Krish sat down beside her. He reached for her hand and gave it a tight squeeze.

It was then that Alka started sobbing.

11

A FIGHTER

2006

Krish put his arm around Alka and held her as she wept. Around them, life in the hospital continued as usual—there were patients being moved on stretchers, nurses rushing around with reports and medical files, relatives waiting anxiously outside the ICU, a group of doctors heading towards the canteen. Nothing had changed around them and yet, everything had changed for them.

Alka did not know what lay ahead or what she was going to do with Subbu being in the hospital, but the worst thing was not knowing if he would ever recover.

Krish couldn't imagine his beloved Anna, the person who had raised him and looked after him, being reduced to a vegetative state in a hospital. He didn't know how to console the love of his life, who was sobbing in his arms. All he could do was blink back his own tears. He had to take charge of the situation. He had to be strong.

Alka stopped crying. It was almost as though the thoughts in Krish's head had somehow been transferred to hers. She felt the same way as Krish. She knew how much Subbu meant to Krish and how close the two brothers were. She sensed that

Krish was in as much pain as her, perhaps more. She had to be strong for both Subbu and Krish's sake, and also for her daughters. *Enough crying. Do what needs to be done.* She sat up straight, wiped her tears and rummaged in her bag for a tissue to wipe her running nose.

'Alka, there's no point in you hanging around here. I'll stay here. Why don't you go back to the estate? Things have to be managed there, no?' Krish suggested gently.

'No, Krish. I just *have* to be here. Subbu is going in for a surgery. How can I leave? I *want* to be here. Selvi can take care of the girls, and I am sure Muthu can handle the estate for a day or two.'

'All right then. Shall we go get something to eat? Have you had anything at all?'

It was only then that Alka realized her stomach was rumbling. She had set out from Sakleshpur without eating anything. It was strange how the human body was capable of adjusting to hunger, thirst and everything else when under extreme stress.

'I haven't, and now that you mention it, I am ravenous. Let's go to the hospital canteen,' Alka said.

The hospital canteen resembled a large, modern commercial restaurant, impeccably designed and well-appointed. The interiors were sleek, with muted colours and pretty artwork adorning the walls. The polished floor, the ambient lighting, the open kitchen, and the soft background music—all of it exuded an air of sophistication, which was a sharp departure from the sterile and depressing atmosphere of the rest of the hospital.

'Oh my! I didn't expect anything like this from a hospital canteen,' Alka said.

'Yes, rather surprising. Everything smells so delicious as well. What will you have?' Krish asked.

'Some vangi bath perhaps?' Alka said, quickly scanning the menu.

'Good choice. I'll have the same. Go sit, I'll get the food and join you,' Krish said, pointing to an empty table.

Alka went and sat down. She looked around—the restaurant, rather the canteen was buzzing with activity. A group of doctors was chatting and cracking jokes. Another table had two healthcare workers eating quietly. While for the hospital staff it was a normal day at work, Alka couldn't help but notice the other people in the canteen who looked like they were caregivers and family members of patients admitted there. They were of all age groups. Some of them sat alone, and a few sat together as they ate their meals. But there was one thing that was common among them—they all looked sombre and grave. She thought about how one could have everything in the world, but if one's health was affected, then nothing else mattered.

Krish came back with two plates of steaming hot vangi bath and they ate their meal in silence. Alka kept thinking about how much things had changed since the time they had eaten together the previous day at India Coffee House. She'd been fighting her feelings and demanding that Krish tell her about Subbu's past. All of that seemed irrelevant now, as if it had happened eons ago.

She felt slightly better as she ate. Her thoughts took her back in time to when her mother used to make her rice and comfort her when things had gone wrong. She would tell her that no matter how terrible things seemed, everything would feel better with some food in the stomach. Her mother was right after all.

Krish's phone rang just then. He excused himself and answered it. Alka could sense the impatience in his voice as he explained to the caller that he had no new updates yet and that he would keep him posted.

'All of Anna's plantation friends have called, asking about him and wanting to visit,' he informed her as soon as he hung up. 'I told them he isn't allowed visitors yet. I'm guessing they don't have your mobile number?'

'No, they don't. I got my mobile phone only recently as you know, and I hardly use it. It's nice that they are calling up though.'

'Yes, but it's also a bit annoying. There's one other thing, Alka—'

Before Krish could complete his sentence, his phone rang again. This time, the caller was one of the nurses from the ICU, who wanted Krish and Alka to come back. They finished their meal hurriedly.

When they reached the ICU, a nurse came out with a packet in her hand and enquired whether they were Subramaniya Shekhar's relatives. When Krish and Alka both nodded, she asked, 'What is your relationship with the patient?'

Alka and Krish spoke at the same time.

'He's my husband,' Alka said.

'I'm his brother,' Krish said.

'Okay, one of you can take this then,' the nurse replied, handing over a large brown paper packet and a smaller envelope.

'What's this?' Alka asked.

'His personal belongings. Please check the documentation and then sign here, also write your name and relationship with the patient,' the nurse instructed.

Alka opened the envelope first and saw that it contained Subbu's gold ring and the gold chain he usually wore. Her eyes filled with tears. The larger packet contained his clothes, all stained heavily with blood.

'Krish, please, could you sign … I can't …' Alka said, moving away as she broke down despite her resolve to stay strong.

She was transported back to the day she lost her mother. She remembered how she had taken a flight for the first time in her life, and how her mother's body had been kept in the small room reserved for the domestic help, the same room they had occupied all their lives. She could still recall how cold her mother's body had been when she'd touched it, and how it had been so hard for her to accept its lifelessness. She hadn't shed a single tear when her mother's body was taken to the crematorium, but once she was alone in that room, she had howled in pain, not recognizing the sounds that were coming from her. Then she remembered Anandi's death. Anandi had also been snatched too soon. They hadn't been able to even see the body, so gruesome had been the car accident, and they'd had to cremate her mangled remains. Alka missed Anandi terribly. And yet, a part of her was also relieved that Anandi was spared the agony of seeing her firstborn in this state. It would've been too much for her to bear.

Alka was only too aware of the searing pain of grief that comes when someone close to you is taken away suddenly. Subbu was too young, there was so much left for him to do. Their girls hadn't grown up yet. This simply couldn't be happening. And yet it was. She dreaded each minute that passed, not knowing how things would turn out. The blood she'd seen on Subbu's clothes had shaken her badly. She didn't feel hopeful at all, not anymore. But she said nothing. She stood staring out of the hospital window. On the road below, life went on as usual—cars honking, a loudspeaker blaring out music somewhere, autos weaving in and out through the traffic, and two wheelers trying to get on the pavement, too impatient for the traffic signals to change. Alka took a deep breath and blinked back her tears.

A few minutes later, Krish joined her and gently patted her on the back.

'He's going to be fine. He's a fighter,' he tried to reassure Alka. But it only made her cry. Just when she thought she'd stopped crying, she began again.

'Sorry, I can't seem to help but cry ... I don't want to,' she said, wiping her tears.

'It's okay, Alka. It's better to cry than bottle it up inside.' Krish was crying too. When he managed to regain his composure, he added, 'The surgery is going to take place soon.'

A little later, they saw a flurry of activity inside the ICU. Subbu, with all the tubes still attached to his body, was wheeled out by the nurses and an attendant and taken to the operation theatre. Krish and Alka followed them, and then stood side by side, staring at the forbidding doors of the operation theatre that were now closed.

This particular operation theatre was located in what seemed to be an isolated corner of the hospital. There was no one else outside besides the two of them. Krish walked to the end of the long corridor and saw a few more operation theatres on the left. There was an anxious crowd of family members waiting outside, just like the both of them. Krish wondered what their loved ones were undergoing. He walked back to Alka, who was on the phone talking to Selvi, asking her if the girls had eaten and whether they were in bed. Krish marvelled at how even at a time like this, Alka's thoughts were still with her daughters. He wondered how women did it—balancing being a wife and a mother while also handling so many other things. For a brief second, he contemplated calling Manasi to tell her about Subbu, but then he decided against it. There was nothing concrete they knew just yet and telling her about Subbu at this point would serve no purpose. A few of their relatives and cousins had called as soon as they got the news, and Krish had patiently repeated the story. He walked to the end of the corridor now, not knowing what else to do. Pacing up and down seemed to help calm his runaway thoughts.

Time crawled at an agonizing pace. The corridor seemed longer than ever, and eerily silent too. Outside, a million stars twinkled in the midnight sky. Alka sat very still on a steel chair, her head resting in her hands, and prayed hard. She prayed to all of Subbu's favourite gods, begging them for a miracle, begging them to make him perfectly okay after the surgery. Krish prayed too. It was all that they could do.

12

STEPPING INTO BIGGER SHOES

2006

Two days had passed since Subbu's surgery, but he hadn't regained consciousness. The doctors, however, had said the surgery was successful. Now all that was left to do was wait and see how much and how soon Subbu would recover. He was still being kept in the ICU and wasn't allowed visitors.

The wait was excruciating for both Alka and Krish. When they had to change or shower, they took turns going to Krish's home. They hardly slept, waiting anxiously outside the ICU. They became familiar with things outside the ICU—the four black metallic chairs, the window that overlooked the trees and the city's skyline, the small faded stain on the wall opposite the chairs. At one point, Alka told Krish that she could see the outline of the US in that stain. Krish stared long and hard at it, and then said that it looked like a fish to him.

'Come on, you can clearly see that it's the US. Look at the shape,' Alka insisted.

'How are you able to see a map in there? It's a large whale,' Krish held firm.

They were talking about mundane and seemingly meaningless things to try and take the edge off the dark cloud hovering over them.

'Growing up in Mrs Shetty's house, I had studied the US map in great detail. Mrs Shetty's daughter, Tanvi, would often visit her father in the US, and she would come back with things we hadn't even seen or heard of. One time, she brought back a Walkman, and I so badly wanted one as well. She would let me listen to songs on it sometimes. And then her mother would yell at me to finish up some task or the other.'

Alka had a small smile on her face as she spoke. But there was so much sadness hidden behind that smile that Krish noticed immediately. He wanted to hug her right there and tell her that she now had him. And that as long as he was around, he would always take care of her. But sitting in a hospital corridor, with his brother fighting for his life, it didn't feel like the right time or place to say such things. So Krish came up with his own story from his boarding school days, when he often longed to just escape and go back home.

It was Subbu who'd insisted Krish go to a boarding school and complete his education, something that he himself had been denied. Krish told Alka about the pranks the boys would play, the teachers they liked and disliked and how they would sneak out to meet girls.

Sometimes, though, Krish and Alka would fall silent, painfully aware of the hours ticking by and of their utter helplessness in the situation. All they could do was hope that Subbu would open his eyes soon.

On the third day, Krish urged Alka to go back home. 'You know how important this time of the year is at the estate.

Someone needs to take charge of things. How long will Muthu hold fort?'

Alka knew that Krish was right. There were multiple processes that had to be completed right before the migrant labourers left. The washing of the beans, the sorting, drying, roasting, bagging, storing, all of it had to be supervised. The trees that provided shade had to be trimmed too. While Muthu could handle these essential activities, Alka knew it was not a one-man job. Subbu was always around at this time. If these tasks weren't done before the monsoon set in, the ventilation and sunlight necessary for the coffee plants would be affected, harming the next harvest. She also couldn't let Selvi take care of Nisha and Tulika indefinitely.

'Krish, while you are right, I have zero idea about how to even handle the estate's labour. Subbu always kept me out of it. I'll get easily overwhelmed by all this,' Alka confessed.

'I know, but you have to take charge now. You can't afford to *not* oversee the work. Your presence makes a difference there. Also, you need to find the insurance papers for the hospital. We'll need the details to claim the bills. I will manage things here, trust me. And Anna is not conscious, Alka. There's nothing you can do here anyway.'

Alka reluctantly returned to the estate. She had never felt so alone and so weighed down by guilt. She kept thinking about how life could change in a split second. If only Subbu would wake up soon.

She thought hard about how she could take charge of the estate, and decided to begin by going through the estate's financial records meticulously. That had always been her strength and forte back at management school. The language of numbers was one that she understood well. She would also need to know every single detail about the estate. She could always seek Muthu's help in areas she wasn't familiar with. She could also ask him to explain things to her. Alka had been a coffee grower's wife for nearly a decade and she did have an idea of the overall picture. What she needed to focus on were the smaller, finer details.

In a way, it was the enormity of this impending task that saved her from thinking too much about Subbu fighting for his life in the hospital. While on one hand, Alka was still reeling under the uncertainty about what would happen to Subbu, on the other, she knew that she had to be practical about the whole situation. This was not the time to let emotions take charge. She had to put them aside and do whatever it took to keep their lives running. Being amidst the greenery of the coffee estate, with its chirping birds and fresh, unadulterated air, Alka felt like she could finally breathe once more. She could push back the worries and fears about Subbu's recovery for at least a little while—something she'd been unable to do in the hospital in Bangalore.

When the girls got back from school, Alka told them the news as gently as she could.

'Is he going to die slowly then?' Tulika asked when she had finished.

'No silly, he'll just be sleeping forever,' Nisha said.

'That's the same thing as dying.'

'No, it's not. Dead people don't breathe. Appa will be able to breathe but with tubes, and another tube will give him food. Am I right, Mummy?'

Alka drew in a sharp breath. Only children could be capable of such brutal honesty.

'Yes, baby, you're absolutely right.'

'See, I told you!' Nisha exclaimed with a triumphant note in her voice.

'But it's not that he'll be sleeping forever. He could wake up too. We have to pray really hard for Appa. But the doctors also said that even after he wakes up, he may not remember some things. He might need help for a few months with things like walking or even eating. Or he may recover quickly too. We'll have to wait and watch. Different people respond differently to these things, okay?' Alka explained calmly.

'Is there a chance that he won't know us? My science teacher told me about memory loss. Will he lose all his memory?' Nisha's curiosity knew no end and she said whatever came to her mind.

'The doctors don't know that yet. Let's just pray for him, okay?' Alka was as honest as she possibly could be.

'Okay, Mummy, we'll pray hard for Appa,' Tulika announced and Nisha nodded in agreement.

After she had put the girls to bed, Alka went to Subbu's room. A sharp pain shot through her heart as she saw all his clothes hanging neatly in his wardrobe. Turning away, she went to his file cabinet and opened it. While she knew that Subbu kept all his files in there, she had never gone through them before. She hadn't expected the cabinet to be so organized and neat. It was strange how even though she'd lived with him for ten years, she was still learning about him in his absence, simply by going through his belongings.

Alka rifled methodically through all the files in the cabinet. There was a large box file marked 'Medical' and Alka opened it. Subbu had filed away every prescription, every medical treatment that Anandi, Alka, both the girls and he himself had undergone. Subbu had rarely fallen sick—there was just that one time when he had come down with a viral fever. There were Alka's pregnancy records as well, all filed neatly—every scan, every prescription and all the vaccination details. Going through the papers was like going back in time. It was towards the end of the file that Alka found the medical insurance policies. She made a note of all the details and then called up Krish to pass them on to him.

'This is a big help, Alka. How are things over there?' Krish asked.

'I somehow managed to tell the girls; they seem very practical about it. Tonight, I'll go through all the papers and financial records of the estate so I know where we stand. I am guessing it'll take me a few days to get the full picture. I will also begin going on the estate rounds with Muthu and supervise the labour.'

'I am glad you are doing this, Alka.'

'I have to, like you said, we have no choice. But the guilt over leaving you alone there to manage everything, its eating me up.'

'Don't think that way. You have to do what needs to be done. I now feel a bit like Krishna giving Arjuna advice while he lay down his weapons on the battlefield.'

For the first time since Subbu's accident, Alka smiled.

'What about your work, Krish? How long can you be on leave? How are you managing it all?'

'I've told my bosses about what is happening. They said I could take as much time as I needed to take care of my brother. By the way, I forgot to mention this, but the hospital needed the blood from the blood bank to be replaced and eight people from my office showed up. They're a really supportive bunch.'

'That's such a relief to hear, Krish.'

'Yes. A few of our relatives turned up here last evening. But there's really nothing much they or anyone else can do at this point as visitors are not allowed. I'll manage things here. You should just focus on the estate and get that going.'

❧

Long after her conversation with Krish, Alka sat up late into the night and looked through the papers. She wished Subbu had involved her a bit more in estate matters when she'd requested him to, then none of this would've been new to her. Since she had no idea where to begin, Alka decided she would go through *all* the paperwork that Subbu had maintained.

The papers dated back many years, and the more Alka studied them, the more she understood how the estate was run. She pulled out bank statements, vendor invoices, sale invoices, statistics on annual yields, labour costs, transportation costs, processing costs, overheads and every other financial transaction she could lay her hands on. She was, at long last, putting her MBA degree to good use. Alka drew up a spreadsheet classifying all the estate expenses into fixed and variable costs. She looked at the costs over a longer period to study the representative averages. She studied the pending loans. She made notes. When one pen stopped working, she picked up another. She cracked her knuckles, made herself a cup of coffee and kept going.

After a while though, the lines began to blur and the numbers stopped making sense anymore. That was when she glanced at the clock.

It was past 2 a.m. Her body was protesting and she needed sleep. Alka turned out the lights and reluctantly went to bed. She was asleep even before her head sank into the pillow.

Outside, the stillness of the night was broken by the sound of crickets. Moonlight enveloped the towering trees outside, casting long shadows while Alka and the girls slept on.

13

THINGS THAT COULD HAVE BEEN

2006

Alka could barely get out of bed the next day when her alarm clock rang. Her limbs felt heavy. Her body ached and her head throbbed. It felt as though there wasn't enough air in her lungs as she inhaled deeply. She reached out from under the blanket and turned the alarm off.

The next time she opened her eyes and reached for the clock, it was past noon. She sat up with a start, her heart beating fast. She was supposed to have gone on the estate rounds with Muthu. How could she have overslept like this? Her body still hurt, but her headache had vanished.

'Selvi?' she called out.

'Akka, you're up? Let me make coffee for you. I've sent the girls to school,' Selvi said.

'Why, why didn't you wake me up?'

'Akka, I think you have a fever. You need to rest. I've kept the thermometer on the bedside table. Please check your temperature,' Selvi said, sounding like an efficient nurse.

Without a word of protest, Alka popped the thermometer under her tongue and waited. By the time she was done, Selvi appeared with a steaming cup of coffee and some biscuits.

'What is the temperature reading?' Selvi asked.

'It's only slightly above normal,' Alka answered.

'Please take a Crocin after you have the coffee,' Selvi urged.

'Selvi, you should've been a nurse!' Alka smiled as she took the coffee mug gratefully.

Selvi's face fell. 'Yes, Akka, I wanted to. But I couldn't because the nursing college fees was too high.'

Alka's eyes softened when she heard this. Memories of her mother slaving away in Mrs Shetty's house came rushing back.

'I understand, Selvi, but anytime you want to write your exams, please let me know. I will do everything I can to help you.'

'No, Akka, that was more than six years ago. Now I've made peace with it. Some things are just meant to be dreams.'

'Selvi, there's nothing like that. No one puts an expiry date on dreams. You can always fulfil them. How is it that in all the years you've been here, you've never talked about this? You said you didn't want to continue studying, didn't you?'

'That was because I failed the class twelve exams,' Selvi admitted, feeling a little embarrassed and self-conscious now. She felt foolish about having told Alka that her family couldn't afford the fees when the truth was that she had failed to clear the qualifying exams.

'Ah, but you know that you can always clear that too, right? I am here if you need any help.'

'Yes, Akka, thank you. How are you feeling?' Selvi asked, clearly in a hurry to change the topic now.

'Like I've been run over by a tractor,' Alka replied.

'You should rest today. It's the strain of the last few days with all the running around in the hospital. I will bring you some idlis,' Selvi said as she drew open the curtains and left.

Alka felt blessed to have a person like Selvi handling her home. She reached for her phone and called Krish. There was still no progress with Subbu. Krish said that according to the doctors he was recovering well, but since he hadn't regained consciousness yet, all they could do was hope.

As soon as Alka finished her food, she went back to the study to pore over the numbers from last night. Selvi peered in from time to time, fetching her refreshments. After a while, however, Alka found herself going over the same line repeatedly, and her head began hurting too, forcing her to rest.

When her daughters returned from school, Alka got up from the bed and asked Selvi for some coffee. She supervised her daughters' homework and then felt her fever returning. She decided to take another Crocin.

'Akka, do you want me to call Dr Mahalingam?' Selvi asked. The coffee estate had an arrangement with a doctor from Sakleshpur city who came to the estate thrice a week for an hour, during which time the estate workers could consult him free of charge. He had a small dispensary set up in the sorting shed. He also made house calls on request, and he was always called for treating any minor ailment that Nisha and Tulika experienced. Over the years, he'd become a family friend.

'No, I'm sure I'll be fine with a little rest,' Alka said. She knew that word of Subbu's accident would've probably reached the doctor. But she wasn't ready yet to discuss the situation with anyone.

'Mummy, you should go and rest. We're old enough to do our own homework now,' Nisha declared. Tulika nodded in agreement.

'All right, you girls. Mummy is only lying down and not sleeping. If there's anything you need, you can ask me, okay?' Alka said as she went to her bedroom to lie down. This fever was draining her of all her energy. Her brain felt foggy, perhaps due to the extensive probing of numbers she had done earlier. She couldn't think clearly. *It is strange how a little bit of fever can almost incapacitate someone*, she thought.

Alka found herself being abruptly awakened by the ringing of her mobile phone a little later. She got up with a jerk, thinking it was Krish, but the number flashing on the screen was an unknown one.

'Hello?' Alka answered feebly, her heart still pounding. Was it the hospital calling with some terrible news about Subbu?

'Alka?' a familiar voice asked.

It took Alka a few seconds to recognize the voice, and when she did, warmth flooded her insides, all her troubles temporarily suspended.

'Manasi!' she exclaimed. 'How *are* you, my friend?'

With some people, no matter how many years have passed, when they get back in touch, it feels as though no time has elapsed at all. Manasi was one of them. Her voice had transported Alka right back to their college days when they'd been thick as thieves.

'I'm doing okay, really. I cannot believe it's taken us so many years to speak on the phone. But you know how it has been,' Manasi said.

Alka had always regretted losing touch with Manasi after the birth of their children, even though they were sisters-in-law. Sanal's severe autism and other problems had taken a toll on Manasi, as well as Krish. Alka too had been busy with both her girls. And after Anandi's death, they had lost touch completely.

'I know. Amma always used to talk about how hard it was to raise Sanal and what a splendid job you're doing.'

'Ah, I try. Sanal is much better now. But it was really hard when he was younger. I suppose you know about the divorce?'

'Yes, I got to know,' Alka said awkwardly, not knowing what were 'permissible' and 'not-permissible' topics to discuss when a couple was getting divorced. She decided she would let Manasi take the lead and talk about whatever she wanted.

'It was for the best, really. I know Krish tried to be a good father, but there simply wasn't a connection between them, you know? And unfortunately, he ended up being a trigger for Sanal. I had to tell him not to see Sanal anymore. Anyway, I didn't call to chat about me. I wanted to check how you're doing. I heard about Subbu,' Manasi said.

'I'm just hanging in there. The surgery was successful, but we're waiting for him to come out of the coma. By the way, how did you hear about Subbu's accident?'

'I heard from Manish's sister. Remember Manish from our batch? He works with Krish.'

'Ah, I remember him vaguely. Our MBA days seem to belong to a different era, don't you think?'

'Yes, so much has changed of course. But that's life.'

'True. But I'm curious to know how you got this phone number. Very few people have it. I only got a cell phone recently, and you know how the connectivity at the estate is.'

'How do you think I got it? I called up Krish and demanded that he give it to me!'

'Ah, he never mentioned it.'

'He couldn't possibly have. The moment I got the number, I called you. Do you need any help, Alka? Anything at all that I can do? I feel terrible about the whole situation.'

'There's nothing any of us can do, Manasi. Just keep us in your prayers.'

'I will, I will. Now, tell me about your daughters. What are they up to? I want to hear about everything.'

Alka and Manasi chatted for a long time. Alka learnt that Manasi had met someone named Rajat at the development centre Sanal went to, and that they'd slowly fallen in love.

'I never meant for that to happen. But he's so gentle with Sanal, and he knows so much about Sanal's condition. He was easy to talk to, and we grew close over time. I did feel this was unfair to Krish, and if Krish hadn't asked for a divorce, I would've done it myself. Life is very short, Alka. There's no point staying in a marriage that doesn't bring you joy.'

'I am glad you found each other, Manasi. You deserve every bit of happiness in this world,' Alka said. She would never forget everything Manasi had done for her, and how she had called up every single person in their batch and made them attend Alka's wedding because she knew Alka would be alone otherwise.

Alka wanted to tell Manasi about everything that had happened after Anandi's death. But they had been talking incessantly for nearly an hour now. It would have to be a conversation for another time.

Manasi hung up after reiterating that Alka could call her any time of the day if she wanted to just talk to someone, and that she could ask her for help if needed. She also told Alka to keep her posted about Subbu. Alka said she would.

After that, Alka sat quietly for a long time.

She thought about the decision she had made to walk away from Krish, all because of Manasi. Who knew at that time that their marriage would eventually break up? Who knew what lay ahead?

Alka wondered if she would've made the same choices if she had possessed all the knowledge that she had now. The answer filled her with a deep ache and longing for Krish.

Perhaps they would've been happy together. Perhaps Manasi would've found Rajat and been happier. Perhaps Alka wouldn't have struggled to find peace and happiness in her marriage with Subbu.

Alka felt a pressing need to call Krish. And when she did, he answered on the very first ring.

'Hey, I had to give your number to Manasi. You know how she is, she wouldn't take no for an answer,' Krish said.

'It's okay, Krish. I'm glad you did. It was so overwhelming to reconnect, but we spoke for over an hour. She sounds exactly like her old self. If I didn't know about all the issues with Sanal, I wouldn't have imagined that she's been through so much,' Alka admitted.

'I know. She definitely sounds happier. I'm glad she has found happiness with that guy,' Krish agreed.

'I feel … I feel like … never mind,' Alka said, unable to go on. She wanted to say that she felt foolish about her decision to marry Subbu. But when she made that choice, she had only been twenty-three. She'd been hurt and shocked to learn that Manasi was carrying Krish's child. It was at that point that Anandi had called her up with the marriage proposal for her and Subbu, and she had accepted after thinking about it.

And now here she was, so many years later, stuck in the impossible situation of being married to Krish's brother.

Krish understood what Alka was unable to put into words. He could sense her pangs of regret. It was something that had always haunted him too. The fact that he and Alka could've been together had Alka not walked away on that fateful day. He would have found a solution. But Alka had denied him that chance.

'Leave it, Alka. All these things are destined. It was meant to be this way.' Krish didn't know what else to say to her. Too many things had happened and there was nothing they could do about the situation. Expressing what he felt deep down would only make things worse.

'How is Subbu?' Alka asked.

'It's not looking good, Alka. The recovery process seems to be very slow. What about things at your end?'

'I am making some headway, but it's slow here too.'

'The insurance claims have gone through. I'd gone to the insurance office yesterday. They were very helpful and I was surprised at how easy it was. I had to fill a few forms and it was done. You'll have to sign some papers when you're here next. So there's good news on that front. Also, Anna's policy will cover everything.'

'That's really good news, Krish. I didn't know it was that easy to claim health insurance,' Alka said.

'They were probably extra nice because the person who heads the division is my senior from our institute. He was very helpful,' Krish added.

'Ah, I see,' Alka said, happy to hear that.

That night, after she put the girls to bed, Alka returned to the study and began going through the files once again, making detailed, meticulous notes till her head began to ache. She did not like what the numbers were telling her. With each bill and invoice that she analysed, Alka was becoming more and more certain that there was something which wasn't adding up.

She was determined to get to the bottom of things, but it would have to wait for the next day.

14

NEW RULES

2006

Alka had fallen into a new routine now. As soon as she sent Nisha and Tulika off to school, she would call Krish. He always had updates for her—about relatives who wanted to visit, friends who had called expressing support and sympathy, and his conversation with the doctors.

'The doctors explained the GCS score to me today. It's the Glasgow Coma Scale. Apparently, they measure the eye opening, and the motor and verbal responses of the patients. If they are in a deep coma, they score very low. In the deepest coma, where they are not at all aware of anything, the score is three. A score of fifteen means the patient is fully conscious,' Krish told Alka.

'And what is Subbu's score currently?'

'They said that while the injury is severe, he's recovering well and is responding to treatment. But they wouldn't tell me the exact score.'

'Does that mean it's bad news, Krish?'

'No, Alka. You know how doctors are. They prefer to err on the side of caution. They mentioned the score only to explain how the rate of recovery is very varied between people.'

'It's all the uncertainty which makes it hard to bear this,' Alka sighed.

'I know. But we have to hang in there and be strong. He is alive and there's hope still. That's all we have to focus on.'

'Yes, you're right.' Alka took a deep breath.

'What's the news there?' Krish asked.

'I am going through the financials and something isn't adding up, Krish. I am yet to finish going through all the paperwork, but I am doggedly at it and I'll keep you posted.'

'All right, you do that, and try not to worry too much,' Krish said before hanging up.

It was quite late into the night when Alka finally finished going through all the files. She made some calculations based on the year-wise figures she'd gathered from the files. She couldn't believe what the numbers were telling her. Twice she went over every single figure she had written down, just to make sure that there were no errors. Had she missed a zero? Was this data right? There's no way she had made a mistake. She was absolutely certain of her numbers. The coffee estate had been steadily making losses over the past six years. The yield per acre was abysmally low. Alka was shocked to see that they were deep in debt. Subbu had been borrowing from two different banks to keep the estate afloat. But the estate was, in reality, a sinking ship.

Alka made herself a cup of coffee and sat thinking. Subbu had shared nothing with her, and now this mess was hers to handle. But she had no idea what to do. When she finally went to bed, she tossed and turned restlessly. Sleep eluded her and she lay awake in the darkness, contemplating things.

She couldn't wait till the morning. Her plan was to confront Muthu and confirm whether what the numbers were telling her was the truth or not. He would surely know, having been the estate manager for over two decades now. She hoped there was something she had missed—a valuable piece of information, perhaps—and that Muthu would tell her it wasn't as bad a situation as she thought.

At 5 a.m., Alka jumped out of bed, impatience coursing through her veins. Outside, the world was still calm and sleepy. But Alka moved with an urgency she'd never experienced before. She went through the motions of her morning routine with her brows furrowed in determination. She washed her face and brushed her hair, the dishevelled strands falling obediently into place. After a hurried cup of coffee, she threw on a jacket and headed out with the keys to the jeep in one hand and the estate files in the other. The tyres of the jeep scrunched the gravel as Alka drove out into the darkness, the headlights illuminating the familiar path. She was oblivious to the fact that her driving to Muthu's house at the crack of dawn was very unusual behaviour, such was her determination to find out what state the coffee estate was in.

When she reached Muthu's house, she parked the jeep and got down. A light was on inside, which was a good sign. It meant he was already awake. She walked up to his door and rang the bell.

Muthu opened the door, dressed in a vest and a lungi, with a toothbrush in his mouth. He blinked for a few seconds before slow recognition dawned on his face.

'Madam? Is Subbu sir okay?'

He had clearly imagined the worst on seeing Alka there so early.

'Yes, I mean, hopefully he will be. I … I am sorry I've come at this ungodly hour,' Alka said as it finally struck her that it was too early to be ringing Muthu's doorbell.

'Come in, madam,' Muthu said, clearly flustered. 'Please give me a second to wear a shirt.' He looked around the room and reached out for a shirt that lay draped across the back of a chair.

'No, no. I shall wait in the jeep. I had some things to discuss with you. But I am sorry to turn up like this at your place. I did not think about the time,' Alka said sheepishly.

'No, madam, it's fine. Another half an hour and I would've been ready to go on the estate rounds. I've never once been late in the past twenty years. Subbu sir knows,' Muthu said.

'Yes, I know how dedicated you are, Muthu. This is entirely on me. Please, take your time.'

'Madam, some coffee?'

'No, thank you, Muthu. I had my coffee before coming. Let me not stop you from having yours though. I shall wait for you in the jeep. Take your time, please,' Alka said as she walked to the jeep.

'Okay, madam. I will hurry up. Please give me ten minutes, I'll be ready.'

Alka waited in the jeep till Muthu came out, his hair combed, his face freshly scrubbed. He had changed into a checked shirt and khaki pants.

'Yes, madam?' he said as he got into the jeep.

'Subbu sir might be out of action for some time. It's going to take him a while to recover. Meanwhile, I am taking over. I'll be in charge from now on,' Alka said.

'Okay, madam,' Muthu nodded, and then hesitatingly added, 'Usually, we start the estate rounds by 6.30 a.m.'

'I know, Muthu. We'll continue that from tomorrow. But today is an exception. Let's go to the yard office first. I want to discuss something.'

'As you say, madam,' Muthu said. Alka wasn't sure if it was a tone of mild exasperation that she detected in his voice, but she did not care. She had an estate to save and she needed answers. She needed them soon.

Muthu was silent throughout the journey to the yard office, as was Alka. She'd decided to show him the files and ask him to explain things to her.

As they made their way to the office, the first rays of the sun appeared, painting the sky in hues of orange and pink. The birds had started chirping too, announcing the arrival of yet another day. As Alka approached the building, her eyes were drawn to what looked like a cluster of gunny sacks filled with coffee beans in the yard. She was about to ask Muthu why they'd been left in the open when she realized that it was actually a group of people, wrapped up in blankets and fast asleep. The ground beneath them served as both their bed and their shelter. Men, women and even children lay huddled together for warmth. Alka was shocked.

'Who are these people? Migrant labourers?' she asked Muthu.

'Yes, madam.'

'Why are they sleeping here? Out in the open?'

'That's how it has always been. They prefer this.'

'How can they prefer this? And prefer this to what? Have you offered them any alternative?'

'Madam, they're here only for a few weeks. They will finish their work and go. They are okay with this arrangement. Even Subbu sir was okay with this.'

'That might've been so. But they have a right to basic facilities like everyone else does. You cannot treat them this way.'

'Madam, there's no other place for them.'

Alka took a few seconds to think. She remembered the line houses in the labour colony. Those had to be empty and available. Then why were the migrant labourers not using them, she wondered.

They entered the yard office. It consisted of a small room with a metal desk behind which was an executive chair that Subbu always used. There were two metal chairs for visitors. Alka took Subbu's chair and gestured for Muthu to sit when he continued standing.

'Sit down, Muthu. This will take a while.'

'Er, okay, madam.' He hesitated slightly, and then sat down at the very edge of one chair, his eyes darting towards the door as though he wanted to run out and end this ordeal.

'What about the line houses, Muthu? We have about twelve to fifteen of them on the estate, don't we?'

'Yes, madam.'

Alka had seen those houses many years ago when she'd been out on one of her usual treks through the estate. She had wandered into one of them and explored it with awe. It had seemed well ventilated and spacious. She had come back and asked Anandi about them.

'You know, Subbu's grandfather was a very progressive man,' Anandi had said, explaining how the houses had come about. 'The usual line houses in other coffee estates are dark and cramped. The coffee business itself was started by the British planters who treated the workers as slaves. That culture continued even after the British left India and the Indians took over. They exploited the workers, threatened them with horrifying consequences if they dared to quit their jobs. The workers who belonged to the Adivasi and Dalit communities would take loans from their employers who charged exorbitant interest rates, thus ensuring that the labourers were bonded to them until the debt was paid. They were mistreated. They were hunted down, tied to trees, flogged and even had dogs set on them.' Anandi had shuddered while narrating all of this.

'But Subbu's grandfather changed all that in this estate. He was a pioneer. He recognized the fact that treating the labourers well would ensure that they wanted to work. "How can they live in cramped houses when they are the ones who have grown the coffee beans for years? When they are the ones with all the knowledge? We have to respect them and take care of their needs," he used to say. He got these houses constructed for them. Later, when the estate expanded, an entire colony of houses was built for the labourers, and these line houses have lain vacant since then.'

'Why don't you allot the line houses to the migrant labourers?' Alka now asked Muthu. 'At least two or three families can live in each house. They are large enough, from what I know.'

'Madam, they are not empty. The relatives of our permanent labourers have occupied them.'

'What do you mean the relatives have occupied them? Aren't they meant for our own labour?'

'Yes, madam, but they live in the labour colony. Their relatives live here in the line houses. It has been that way for a few years now.'

'Do these relatives work for us?'

'No, madam.'

'Then they have no place in the estate.'

Alka had no experience in running the estate, but years of working at Mrs Shetty's house had ingrained the fact that there were no free lunches. Why then, should the relatives of the workers stay in the line houses, free of cost, while the migrant labourers slept out in the open?

'But, madam, it's been the tradition.'

'Hmm. Let me see what we can do about it. They cannot occupy the houses meant for our labour. They will have to vacate those houses.'

If she was taking charge, she would have to make some hard decisions and be ruthlessly efficient. She would have to change these traditions which Subbu had adhered to.

'Madam, they aren't going to be happy about it. As it is, they are demanding a lot of things and Subbu sir was having issues with them.'

'I appreciate the warning, Muthu, but it's time we made some new rules and got everyone to follow them,' Alka said firmly.

Muthu had gone very quiet and only nodded in response.

15

CENT PER CENT COOPERATION

2006

'Coffee?' Alka asked, wanting to ease the tension in the air a bit. She didn't want Muthu feeling cornered and resentful. She wanted him on her side.

'Yes, madam. I'll make it,' Muthu said, hastily pushing back his chair.

'No, let me make it for you,' Alka insisted. She stood up and walked to the small kitchenette adjoining the office. It had a single-burner stove, a few vessels, cups, tea, coffee and some other supplies. There was also a mini-fridge in which milk was stored.

'Madam, no. I always make it for Subbu sir,' Muthu said, rushing to the kitchenette.

'Ha, me too!' Alka smiled and that got a smile out of Muthu too.

'Madam, it is my duty to serve you. Please allow me to make the coffee,' Muthu said. He felt uncomfortable about Alka making coffee for him.

'Try my coffee, Muthu. I promise I'm not a bad coffee maker,' Alka said, smiling.

'As you wish, madam.' Muthu fidgeted and looked away, but he did not move.

'Go and sit down, I'll get the coffee,' Alka said, chivvying him out of the kitchenette.

When Alka emerged from the kitchenette with two cups of hot coffee, she found Muthu going through a file labelled 'Daily Roster—Labour'. He was engrossed in calculating the payments that were due.

'Here you go,' Alka said as she placed the tray with the coffee cups on the table and sat down on the chair opposite Muthu.

'Thank you, madam,' Muthu said and took a sip of the coffee. 'This is very good. It's better than what I make,' he admitted.

Alka smiled as she sipped her own coffee.

'Muthu, over the past few days, I have been painstakingly going through all the estate accounts. I want to know if the estate has been making losses for a few years now or have I missed something?'

Muthu took a few seconds to answer her. 'It has been running at a loss, madam,' he replied finally, his eyes downcast.

'Would you be able to explain to me why we've been making steady losses? This has come as a shock to me. Subbu said he was handling everything. I was hoping you would tell me that my calculations were off.'

'No, madam. Your calculations are correct,' Muthu said, continuing to look at the floor.

'What is the reason for these losses, Muthu? You need to tell me what the problems are so we can begin to fix them.'

Muthu was torn between loyalty and responsibility. He had been Subbu's guide and right-hand man ever since Subbu's father had passed away. He had helped Subbu run the estate successfully for many years. He couldn't imagine anyone else taking charge of it. He knew he had to be transparent with Alka. But he felt he would be betraying Subbu if he disclosed exactly what had been going on. Weighed down by this burden, he continued gazing at the floor in silence.

Alka knew she had to win him over if she wanted to truly make a difference in the running of the estate.

'Muthu, look, from what I could understand, the estate's finances are completely in the red. Subbu had been borrowing regularly from two different banks. Do you want the estate to continue functioning?'

'Of course, madam.'

'Then you'll have to help me understand the issues. If you don't, you'll be out of a job because I'll be forced to sell the entire estate to repay the loans. We are deep in debt.'

That made him look up.

'No, no, madam. What are you saying? We cannot sell the estate. It is Subbu sir's heart and soul!' he exclaimed, a shocked look on his face.

'Yes, and it is mine too. You have no idea how much I've grown to love this place over the past few years. Look, Muthu, our goal is the same. To turn this estate around from a loss-making unit into a profitable one. If we fail, we will have no estate to run. I know your loyalty lies with Subbu, but he has clearly gone wrong somewhere. Now, unless you give me your frank opinion, I won't know whether I am on the right track or not. It will take me months to figure out the operations.

And time is a luxury we do not have. By the time I get down to taking any steps, it might be too late. Do you get what I am saying?' Alka asked, twisting the ring on her finger.

Muthu nodded slowly. He knew Alka was right.

Alka sighed. She saw that she was getting through to him at last. She needed his cooperation more than anything,

'I am not your enemy, Muthu. I need help, and I am asking you for it. Are you willing to help me or not? I need a clear answer. If you aren't willing, then I'll have to look for someone who is,' she said. Though her voice was soft, the threat was clear.

Muthu blinked as what Alka was implying sank in. Then he looked up at her and said, 'Yes, madam. You are right. I will help you. You can expect cent per cent cooperation from me.'

'That's good. Thank you, Muthu. Could you please begin by telling me about the decisions that Subbu made that led us to this sorry state of affairs?' Alka asked.

'Madam, there are multiple reasons,' Muthu began. 'I kept telling Subbu sir that we have to keep our minds open towards non-traditional cultivation techniques. But he believed in sticking to the same old methods.'

'What would you say are the main problems? If we had to change one thing immediately, what would it be?'

'Disease-ridden crops, madam. Subbu sir knows it. He has been trying different things, but nothing's been working. From forty acres, we are hardly getting two tonnes of pepper. We can get ten times that yield if we regulate it. I had suggested this to Subbu sir, but he wanted to focus more on the coffee, not the pepper.'

Muthu had spent all his life on the coffee estate and was extremely knowledgeable. His father had worked for Subbu's father. He was pleasantly surprised to see Alka listening to him carefully. When she reached out for the pen and paper kept on the desk and began making detailed notes of all he was saying, his jaw dropped. With Subbu, Muthu was accustomed to listening and taking orders. Any suggestions he offered were met with stiff resistance. Muthu was used to carrying out Subbu's orders, even when he didn't agree with his decisions. And here Alka was giving him such a place of importance that he was secretly flattered. Many years ago, while still in school, there was a teacher who Muthu had admired, and for a while, a young Muthu had nurtured dreams of becoming a professor in a college. Sadly though, those dreams had never materialized. In Alka, he now found a willing student, and Muthu was soon grabbing the other pen and drawing diagrams to help her understand things better. Alka kept nodding keenly and asked many questions, which pleased Muthu.

They spent two hours talking about coffee production in detail. The more Muthu opened up, the more Alka learnt. Subbu had been a traditional planter, averse to innovation.

By the end of those two hours, Alka's head was spinning. She couldn't believe the mistakes Subbu had made.

'When times change, we have to evolve. Subbu sir wanted to stick to the same things that his father had done. He thought he was honouring his father's memory by doing things the same way. But Subbu sir's father would've never been okay with the losses we've been making. He always said that there is enough for everyone if we do things the right way.

Part of it is luck, and part of it is bad decision-making. We got a raw deal in both,' Muthu said.

'All right, Muthu. Thank you so much for sharing all of this. Let me think about what can be done. I will head home now and send the kids to schools. After that, we'll go on the estate rounds,' Alka said.

'Yes, madam. I can pick you up if you wish,' Muthu offered.

'That would be splendid. Thank you, Muthu. Pick me up in about two hours,' Alka said.

❧

When Alka got home, she saw that Selvi had already gotten the girls ready and packed their lunches as well. They were about to leave for school.

'Did you pack your bags as per your timetable?'

'Yes, Mummy!' they chimed.

'Did you forget any assignment? Tulika, your math assignment is due. Did you take the book?'

'Of course, Mummy. I am not a silly girl,' Tulika replied.

'Have a lovely day, my darlings,' Alka said as she kissed the girls on their foreheads.

'You too, Mummy!' they called out as they ran to the car waiting outside.

After they left, Alka sat on the verandah for a long time, thinking about what could be done to resolve the massive problem she had on her hands. She picked the phone and called Renuka Mavshi. Today, she needed to hear her calm voice.

'Hello, Mavshi, how are you?' Alka asked when she picked up.

'Top of the world! What's the news with you? Did you take my advice and go on a break or not?'

'Oh, I did.'

'Good girl! Did it help you?'

'Yes, it did, Mavshi. But a lot has happened since then.'

Renuka Mavshi listened as Alka recounted everything in detail.

'Oh my! That sounds terrible. How are you holding up?' Renuka Mavshi asked.

'I'm okay, I guess. It's not like I have a choice,' Alka answered.

'I wish I knew at least a little bit about coffee farming and production. Then I would've had some advice for you. But you know what you should do? You should ask for help. Approach some other planters who have been through this. There's nothing wrong in asking for help when we need it, Alka. Yet very few of us do so. We are somehow afraid of people saying no to us. If there's one lesson I have learnt in my life, it's that you should always ask. If you don't ask, the answer is always going to be no.'

'You're right, Renuka Mavshi. But the problem is so big, and I don't see any solution in sight.'

'Just one step at a time, Alka. And I shall definitely pray for Subbu's good health and quick recovery. Before you know it, you'll be calling me up and complaining about him once more. Wait and watch,' Renuka Mavshi assured Alka.

'Thank you, Mavshi,' Alka said.

Speaking to Renuka Mavshi gave Alka some comfort and hope. She began thinking about whom she could ask for help.

That was when Muthu pulled up outside her home to take her on the estate rounds. The rest of the day flew by as Alka went with Muthu and supervised everything that had to be done. They had to check on the coffee plants, inspect the leaves for any signs of disease, monitor the soil's moisture level and check for weeds that were known to sprout overnight. Muthu was clearly an expert, and all Alka had to do was follow along.

'Madam, the current group of labourers that has turned up from Assam is not adept at the work. They require training. Subbu sir had said they would directly start the job, but if we train them, their efficiency will increase,' Muthu explained.

'Please organize the training programme then, Muthu. Is there any local worker who can do it?'

'Yes, madam, there are experienced workers around. They can harvest up to 80 kgs of ripened coffee beans a day. And sometimes they even go up to 100–120 kgs. But the issue is communication. The new labourers speak only Assamese and a bit of broken Hindi.'

'Is there no one who can translate? What about Subhankar?'

A few years ago, Subhankar had come from Assam to work as a seasonal migrant labourer. He had fallen in love with the daughter of one of the local workers and had stayed back in Coorg after the rest of his family returned to Assam at the end of the harvest season. When Alka had found out that he was only twenty, she had insisted that he complete his education. She had mentioned it to Anandi, who said she would arrange for it. A couple of years later, Subhankar managed to complete a course in electronics from a polytechnic in Hassan, and opened an electrical shop in the city. He was doing well for himself now. Alka recalled how he'd quickly picked up Kannada.

'Madam, Subhankar will be able to translate. But he's busy running his shop.'

'Get me his number. I'm quite sure I can convince him to help us,' Alka said.

'Yes, madam,' Muthu said. He took out a small, thin notebook from his shirt pocket and carefully made a note.

After about three hours of estate rounds, Alka was exhausted and dehydrated. Her feet hurt and so did her head. Even though she was used to going for long walks, what she wasn't used to was handling the estate's problems and sorting things out. It was mentally tiring. For the first time, she understood what Subbu's everyday life was. No wonder he was in no mood to speak to her when he got back home after his rounds. All he wanted to do was relax. Alka wanted to do the same now. Muthu sensed her tiredness and said that he could finish things up, but Alka insisted on accompanying him.

By the time they were done, it was well past lunchtime. The girls would come back soon, so Alka told Muthu to drop her home.

'I will meet you tomorrow, Muthu. Pick me up at the usual time when Subbu used to go on his rounds.'

'Madam, that's before sunrise,' Muthu said.

'Yes, I'll be ready,' Alka replied.

She wanted to do things the right way even though every cell in her body was protesting at the thought of rising so early.

When Nisha and Tulika arrived, Alka was waiting for them in the verandah. Tulika ran ahead, waving an envelope in her hand.

'Mummy! Mummy! I won the competition. We have to go to Delhi!'

'To Delhi! To Delhi, to buy a fat pig!' Nisha sang and Tulika giggled.

'To Delhi, to Delhi, to paint and win!' she chimed in.

'That's really wonderful, baby. A big, big congratulation! Let me see the letter.' Alka took the envelope eagerly from Tulika.

The letter inside stated that Tulika had been chosen to represent Karnataka at the national-level competition coming up in ten weeks. It also said that all the travel expenses for the child and an accompanying adult would be covered.

'Mummy, my teacher said we'll have to go to Delhi. Will you take me?' Tulika asked, skipping around in excitement.

Alka knew she couldn't possibly take time off to accompany Tulika to Delhi, not while Subbu was still recovering and the estate was drowning.

So, she simply said, 'We'll figure something out.'

How she was going to manage it all, she didn't know.

16

GOWRI'S VISIT

2006

The next morning onwards, Alka was up at the crack of dawn and going on the estate rounds with Muthu. The more she went around the estate, the more she learnt. Muthu was thoroughly enjoying the estate rounds with Alka. She did not order him around like Subbu, instead, she treated him like an equal. She was open to his suggestions too. He began pointing out various things about the estate to her. Alka, meanwhile, couldn't believe the number of details that had to be taken care of to run the place. Subbu had never once taken her on estate rounds or explained the functioning of the estate to her. She had, of course, been given the tourist version of the estate tour before her marriage, when she'd visited with Manasi and Krish. But once she was married, neither Anandi nor Subbu let her go on the estate rounds. Alka now realized that they'd just been trying to make things easy for her. Running a coffee estate was extremely hard work, involving bumpy jeep rides that rattled your bones and long hours of being on your feet, sometimes walking on damp ground through mulch, soil and uneven terrain. Alka had also become pregnant soon after the marriage, and there was no way a pregnant woman could've handled the physical strain of going on estate rounds. At the time, she had been resentful about not being able to accompany Subbu. But now she completely understood their perspective. They were only being protective of her.

By the time Alka came back to the house for breakfast, the girls had already left. Selvi informed her that she had received a phone call from Gowri.

'Akka, Gowri madam said she heard about what happened to Subbu Anna. She wanted to know how you are holding up.'

'Umm, and what did you tell her?'

'That this is a difficult time for us, but you are doing fine and that you'd gone on the daily estate rounds. Akka, she said she is dropping in today.'

Alka, however, was in no mood to receive visitors. She was worried to death about Subbu, and about the rising costs of running the estate. She wanted to talk to Subhankar and put the training programme in motion. There were a hundred other things on her mind. She wished she could tell Gowri that it wasn't a good time to visit, but that would definitely come off as being rude, especially so since Gowri had been extremely welcoming and hospitable to her.

'Did she mention what time she would come?'

'She should be arriving soon, Akka. She had called just after the girls left and said she would be here in two hours. So, it's almost time for her to be here.'

'Oh, I see,' Alka said.

Selvi seemed to have read her mind.

'Sorry, Akka, I didn't know how to tell her not to come.'

'Of course, I am glad you did no such thing. Keep some snacks ready and put fresh coffee in the filter.'

'Already done, Akka,' Selvi smiled.

Gowri arrived at Alka's home in a stylish red SUV. She stepped out of the vehicle with a cheerful wave and a bright grin on her face. Despite her initial apprehension about Gowri's visit, Alka felt a genuine sense of happiness upon seeing her. Gowri's personality radiated like sunshine, casting a warm glow that Alka couldn't help but bask in. Descending the steps from her bungalow, Alka embraced Gowri warmly.

'Hello and welcome!' Alka exclaimed, her greeting filled with sincerity and the joy of reconnecting with her vivacious friend.

'This is such a delightful place. The last time I visited was ages ago. You weren't in Subbu's life then, and Anandi aunty had prepared such a feast for me and my mother that we actually had to nap after we ate. We were too stuffed to drive back,' Gowri smiled at the memory as they walked into the living room.

'Ah yes, the first time I visited the estate, Amma did the same. I could barely move after the meal. She loved to feed people,' Alka recalled as they sat down opposite each other. The sunlight streaming in through the windows painted a cheery picture.

'How is Subbu doing? The minute I heard, I wanted to call you. But I thought you might not be in the right mental space to talk.'

'Yes, true. He is recovering, but we'll have to wait and see how things turn out. He isn't allowed visitors yet.' Alka did not want to delve into further details. Talking about how all the uncertainty over Subbu's recovery was killing her would only make her cry, and she did not want to do that in front of Gowri. There was nothing anyone could do, so she deftly changed the topic.

'You tell me about your life. What's happening in your part of the world?' Alka asked.

Gowri understood Alka's reluctance to talk about Subbu. So she chattered away, filling Alka in about the happenings at her estate, how business was good and how she'd recently bought a new vehicle.

'It's such a big accomplishment and I felt proud buying it entirely with my own money.'

'That must feel so good, Gowri. Hearty congratulations!' Alka was genuinely happy for her friend.

'Thank you!' Gowri replied.

Selvi wheeled in a trolley laden with refreshments—momos that she had recently learned to make, along with pathrode and crisp savouries. She had also brewed filter coffee, which she served in silver tumblers.

'The last time I came here, Selvi was a little girl. Now she is all grown up. And her mother, Gowramma, where is she? It still amuses me that we both essentially have the same name, Gowri, but they add an amma to it,' Gowri observed.

'Hello, madam. My mother has gone to visit my brother and his wife. They live in Hanumasagara village. They've just had a baby,' Selvi beamed.

'Gowramma is so enjoying being a grandmother,' Alka added.

As Selvi left the room, Gowri said, 'Ah, the joys of having grandchildren. You can spoil them and you don't have to be responsible for them!'

'Yes, true. I do feel bad that my mother never got to see her granddaughters.' Alka smiled sadly.

Gowri instantly regretted making that remark. She was trying to cheer Alka up as she could see the worry on her friend's face.

'How are Tulika and Nisha doing?' Gowri asked.

'Tulika won that painting competition I told you about. She has to go to Delhi in about ten weeks, but I don't know how I'll be able to take time off from all of this. And we don't know how Subbu will be at that point.'

'Oh, Delhi? I love going to Delhi. One of my closest friends lives there. I can easily take Tulika if she'll go with me and if you are okay with it, that is,' Gowri offered.

'Really? Do you mean that?' Alka asked.

'Of course! I would've never offered to do this if I didn't mean it. We can take a call closer to the date, depending on what the situation is then. My staff can easily manage things while I am away.'

Alka nodded gratefully.

'Also, Gowri, I really need some tips from you on running the estate. I've just discovered that things here aren't rosy. Subbu used to handle all of it. But now that I have taken charge, I am learning that there's so much to handle.'

'What do you mean by "not rosy"? Is the estate not making any money?' Gowri asked, her face reflecting real concern.

'Oh, Gowri! Where do I even begin? I think we're drowning in debt. I've gone over the figures. Come, let me show you the files. I hope you don't mind taking a look?' Alka asked.

'Certainly not. I'll be happy to help in any way I can,' Gowri replied, following Alka to the study. She sat down on the carved wooden bench as Alka handed her the files. Alka had made neat summaries of the financials, and once Gowri went through them, she let out a small whistle.

'My goodness, this is terrible. How Subbu managed to run the estate till now with these numbers is a mystery,' Gowri said.

'The way I see it, I think the priority has to be to clear these bank loans. Look at the interest that has piled up. It's eating into so much of our funds. I am considering selling about twenty-five acres of the land. That should tide us through. What do you think?' Alka asked Gowri.

Gowri didn't speak for a while. She kept looking at the numbers instead.

'Do you have a piece of paper and a pen?' she asked finally.

Alka handed her a writing pad and a pen. Gowri made some quick calculations and then spoke slowly, 'Alka, try not to sell the estate, not even a part of it. You don't have to amputate an entire leg if you're hurt. Not unless life itself is in danger and there's no other way out. Instead, you should wait for the wound to heal. What we need is proper medication and a good doctor,' Gowri declared.

A second later, she realized that it was an insensitive metaphor as Subbu was still in the hospital. 'What I mean is, I have some experience in this,' she hurried to clarify. 'When I took over my estate, it was making heavy losses. I was tempted to sell too. But I am glad I didn't.'

'I don't want to sell it either. But that was the easiest and the most obvious solution which came to my mind. However, I am not as experienced as you. So if you tell me what I could do instead, that would be helpful, Gowri.'

'When I was trying to revive my estate, I contacted a group called CoRe. CoRe stands for Coffee Rescuers. They're a group of about four to six very experienced planters who are now retired. They come from families that have been in the coffee business for at least four generations. They've made it their life's mission to save coffee estates from being sold. They know that property developers will swoop in like vultures, especially if it's a distress sale. They helped and guided me and I'm sure they will be willing to help you too.'

'Gowri, it's such a relief to hear that. I will definitely get in touch with them. Could you give me their number please?'

Gowri told Alka to contact Mr G.M. Chinappa, the man who led the team.

'You could mention my name as a reference. They know me really well. We've worked closely and I am one of their big success stories,' Gowri said.

'Thanks, Gowri. I'll contact them today itself,' Alka replied.

'Yes, you do that. Also, Alka, have you considered opening up homestays in the estate? Remember I'd broached the topic with you earlier? They can be a good source of additional revenue.'

'It looks like I will have to, Gowri. We're over our heads in debt. I still cannot believe that Subbu withheld all this information from me.'

'I am guessing he didn't want to worry you. This is quite typical of this generation of coffee planters. They think they shouldn't burden their families. Male pride and all that. He must've believed that he could turn things around and clear off the debts. My father too, believed that. He refused to open up the estate. Now, as you know, I've changed it all. In the first year of opening up the homestays, I made as much from them as I do from my coffee harvest in a year. Can you believe it? It's that lucrative! Which is why I am strongly advocating it to you too. You have an unused asset on your hands. If you don't mind a few tourists coming over, then what is the harm in opening up the estate?'

'I guess Subbu was very possessive and particular about who had access to his world. This is his whole life, you know.'

'I know and I understand. My father didn't like "outsiders", as he called them, entering the estate either. But we cannot ignore the money homestays will generate.'

'I agree. I'll look at all the cottages that can be offered as homestays. They are in various states of neglect though. But thank you, Gowri, and thanks for the contact details of CoRe too. I'll speak to them immediately.'

'Well, I must leave now. But please feel free to call me anytime. And Alka, I do mean it. If you want me to come down here and help you, I will. I can assign my manager to take care of things in my estate because I have systems in place. That's the other thing you should do, put watertight systems in place so that anyone with even minimal experience can run it,' Gowri advised as she stood up.

'I'm going to keep all that in mind,' Alka said gratefully.

The two of them walked to Gowri's new SUV. Alka felt a surge of pride seeing Gowri driving away confidently in her swanky vehicle. She hoped that someday she could achieve what Gowri had managed to.

Alka called up Subhankar and spoke to him, telling him about Subbu's accident. Surprisingly, he hadn't heard of it and was shocked to learn of the developments. She told him she needed his help as a translator and that she would pay him for his time and services.

'Please, madam, do not insult me by talking about money. Anandi madam has done so much for me that I am happy to pay back in whatever manner I can,' he replied warmly. He assured her he would coordinate with Muthu and help out with the training programme. Alka thanked him and then immediately called up Muthu to inform him that Subhankar had agreed to help.

'Ah, madam! You're a genius!' Muthu exclaimed. Now that Alka had given him a place of importance, he had become generous with his compliments.

'I'm not a genius at all, Muthu! Remember, our goal is to turn this place around, and we will do whatever it takes.'

'Of course, madam, and we'll do it.'

It is amazing how circumstances can quickly change our needs and wants, Alka thought. Just a few weeks ago, she had wanted to improve her marriage, know who Chanda was, and understand why Subbu didn't want to talk about her. Those problems seemed so minor compared to what she was facing now. All she wanted now was for Subbu to recover and for the estate to become profitable again.

17

A BIG SECRET

2006

Later in the day, Alka called up Mr G.M. Chinappa. He answered the phone after several rings, sounding breathless, like he had hurried to pick up the call. His voice was distinguished and deep, and Alka nervously fiddled with a strand of her hair as she spoke.

'Mr Chinappa? This is Alka … eh … I'm Subbu's wife. Gowri gave me your number and said I must get in touch with you.'

'Hello, Alka. Good morning. How are you doing? I heard about Subbu the day it happened. But you know how the grapevine is. I wasn't sure if the details were true. People do tend to exaggerate. Then, when I read about it in the newspapers the next day, I knew it was true.'

'Oh, I had no idea that the newspapers had covered it. I'm doing okay. Thank you for asking.'

'Yes, they did and they also mentioned that he had been shifted to Bangalore for a surgery. It's most unfortunate,' he said. Mr Chinappa sounded kind and friendly, and it put Alka at ease.

'The surgery was successful and Subbu is recovering. He'll take a while to get back to the estate, of course,' Alka informed him.

She didn't want to tell Mr Chinappa that Subbu was in a coma. Alka hated the very word and didn't want to entertain the thought that Subbu might not ever come out of it.

'Yes, these things take time. How is Gowri doing? Her estate is doing fabulously well now. It was one of our favourite projects, honestly.'

'Gowri was here just a little while ago, and she was raving about the work the CoRe team is doing. That's why I've called you. I have taken over the running of the estate, and we're drowning in losses. I wanted to sell a part of the land, but Gowri suggested I speak to you first.'

Mr Chinappa smiled when he heard that. 'Gowri is a smart girl. She's got the right spirit. We don't want to sell at the first sign of trouble. We are happy to consider your case. But you'll have to come and meet the CoRe team. It consists of myself and three other members. Our mission is to provide a philanthropic service of sorts to those estate owners who need help with making their plantations profitably sustainable. Now that you have requested for help, I'll contact the other members. Once you meet with all of us, we will explain the whole process to you. After that, if it's agreeable to both sides, we'll draw up a long-term plan and sign a contract.'

'Yes, of course, I'm happy to meet the team. Just let me know when and where, and I'll be there,' Alka said, a little taken aback. She had not expected it to be so formal and organized. She had presumed that Mr Chinappa would simply give her a few pointers and that would be the end of it.

'I will let you know soon. It may take a few weeks, though,' Mr Chinappa promised as he hung up.

That evening, Alka called up Krish and told him she would come to the hospital the next day. She wanted to see for herself how Subbu was doing. She also wanted to speak to Krish and update him about the developments at the estate. Alka felt very lonely, making all the decisions and managing everything by herself. Speaking to Krish and using him as a sounding board would give her a little more confidence, she decided.

'There's something I want to speak to you about as well. How about we meet at my place first? It'll be easier to talk at home than in our corridor outside the ICU. We can go to the hospital together after that,' Krish suggested.

It is funny how the hospital corridor has become 'our corridor', Alka mused as Shanker drove her to Bangalore. They had left by 4 a.m. as she wanted to return home the same day. She didn't want to stay away from the estate for too long, especially since she had just begun getting the hang of things.

Alka made her way up in the elevator to Krish's flat, thinking about how different things were now compared to the last time she had gone up in the same elevator, drenched and shivering from their dash in the rain. The thought of going to his place all by herself sent a frisson of excitement up her spine, but the feeling was quickly replaced by guilt for having such thoughts while Subbu was in the hospital. She wondered what Krish wanted to talk to her about.

Krish opened the door before Alka could ring the bell. He looked resplendent in an ivory shirt and slate grey trousers that complemented his demeanour. He was wearing the same perfume he'd worn the night when they had first made love all those years ago. Alka could recognize it anywhere—that woody note with just a hint of spice. The fragrance was unmistakable and the emotions it evoked in her took her by surprise. Perhaps it was all the stress and sadness she had been holding inside herself, but it seemed to bridge the past and the present, and all she wanted to do was melt into Krish's arms. She wanted him to hold her and assure her that things would be fine.

Krish, on his part, couldn't hold himself back when he saw Alka. She was wearing a white T-shirt and a pair of baggy navy blue cotton pants. She didn't have any make-up on and her hair was pulled back in a ponytail. She looked lost, sad and defeated, exactly like she had when she had lost her mother while still in college. He knew that expression so well, and he couldn't bear it.

He pulled her into a tight hug and they stood in the doorway, finding comfort in each other's arms and aware only of each other's presence. Alka took a deep breath, as though committing the smell of Krish's perfume to memory. When they finally broke away, he kissed her tenderly on the forehead. Both of them couldn't speak for a few seconds.

'Coffee?' Krish asked when he recovered. His feelings had been so intense that he was a little embarrassed now.

'Yes please,' Alka nodded, her face flushed.

Krish ushered her inside and came back a few minutes later with two mugs of coffee. They sat next to each other at the island counter in the kitchen, wanting to say so much but not finding the words. They were aware that what had just transpired was powerful—a connection so deep they could feel it within their souls.

Alka was the first to break the silence.

'What's the latest update on Subbu?' she asked, staring straight ahead as she spoke. It was as though she wanted to remind both of them that Subbu was still in the hospital and that no matter how strongly they felt connected to each other, they were bound by their respective realities—she was Subbu's wife, and Krish was her brother-in-law.

But Krish didn't need any reminding. He was painfully aware of it every second he spent with Alka.

'He's still the same. The doctors say he is improving, and I sense an underlying tone of optimism when they speak. And yet, when I see him like that, with all the tubes and machines attached, it's so hard to not lose hope.'

'I can imagine how hard it is, Krish,' Alka said, reaching out to place her hand on his. He didn't make any attempt to move it away. 'But things are going to be fine. You'll see,' she said to comfort Krish; she hated seeing him so helpless.

'Yes, before you know it, he'll be back at the estate, supervising everything.' Krish smiled. Alka nodded, hoping what he said would quickly come true.

'Speaking of the estate, there's so much I want to share with you.' Alka got off the bar stool, walked to the kitchen sink, and began washing her coffee mug. Krish's kitchen was spotlessly clean and she didn't want to leave the mug unwashed.

'Hey, my house help will do it, you know,' Krish pointed out.

'It's okay, Krish. It's just a single mug,' Alka answered.

'Then wash mine too!' Krish said and handed her his mug.

'What the hell!' Alka exclaimed, but she smiled as she took the coffee mug from him and rinsed it. In that moment, Krish wanted to hug her from behind and kiss her, just like he had done multiple times in the flat they had set up together many years ago, before they'd both got married. Alka was thinking about the same thing. She badly wanted to feel Krish's arms around her, his lips on her neck. But Krish moved away quickly.

They went to the living room and sat across each other, keeping a safe distance between them.

'What did you want to tell me about the estate?' Krish asked.

Over the next five minutes, Alka shared a continuous stream of information, telling Krish about everything—how she had found the discrepancies in the estate's books, the rounds she had gone on every morning, what she thought about the migrant labourers sleeping in the yard, and how she had convinced Subhankar to help them out. She spoke about how she had managed to get Muthu on her side and how the shared goal of turning the estate profitable was moulding her and Muthu into a team. Alka's face was animated as she spoke passionately, waving her hands occasionally. Krish couldn't help but admire how determined and gorgeous she looked sitting there; she was working so hard and trying to set things right. He was so proud of her. He must've been staring at her because she paused and asked, 'Did you get all of that? Or did I jump topics?'

'Got it, got it. I think you've got it all under control, Alka. I am so proud of you.' He smiled.

Just then, his phone rang. 'Excuse me, I have to take this,' he said as he got up and walked away to answer it, glad for the distraction this time. He was quiet as he listened carefully to the person on the other end.

Then he took a deep breath and said, 'Yes, she is here. Yes, I'll be telling her now.'

Krish hung up the phone and then walked towards Alka, not sure about how to approach the conversation.

'Alka, there's something I have to tell you, but you'll have to promise to be calm about it, okay?' he said softly.

Alka looked up at him fearfully. Her palms went cold as she clutched them together. 'What is it, Krish? Is Subbu not going to make it?'

'No! No, no. That's not it at all,' Krish was quick to reassure her.

Alka sighed. 'Krish, you scared me. What's wrong then? Why are you asking me to be calm?'

'Umm, it's about the thing we were speaking of earlier, when you were last here.'

'Speaking of earlier? When? The last time I was here? What about it?' Alka was puzzled.

'Yes, just before Anna's accident. Remember?'

Alka frowned as she tried to remember. 'What is it, Krish? Why are you speaking in this roundabout way? I don't remember what we were talking about.'

'Alka, you had asked me about Chanda.'

'Oh? That seems so irrelevant now. But what about her? Why are you bringing that up now?'

Krish sat down next to Alka.

'Listen, I don't know how to say this to you. I haven't been entirely honest with you. That phone call I just received, it was Chanda who called.'

'She called you? Why?'

'Yes, she wanted to know how Anna was doing.'

'Oh! She's heard about the accident?'

'No, I mean yes. I told her about it,' Krish replied, squirming uncomfortably.

'You told her about Subbu's accident?' Alka couldn't understand where this was going.

'She called me a few days ago,' Krish said and then fell silent for a while. He seemed to be fighting a battle within himself. He cracked his knuckles nervously. Then he took a deep breath and said, 'I don't know how to tell you this. Anna, well, his connection with Chanda is not just a thing of the past. It's very much a part of his present too. He … he and Chanda have a son.'

'What? What the hell?' Alka almost screamed. It felt like someone had punched the air out of her lungs. 'What are you saying, Krish?'

'It came as a huge shock to me too. Apparently, Anna spends one day a week with her, in her house. And the week of the accident, when he didn't turn up, she knew something was wrong. So she called me.'

'How did she get your number?'

'Anna had instructed her that if there ever came a day when she didn't hear from him, she was to get in touch with me. And so she did.'

Alka couldn't believe what she was hearing. Her head spun with this information. Her husband had a son! A son? Oh good Lord!

'Where does she live? This Chanda?' Alka asked. But she suspected that she knew the answer already. All of Subbu's weekly visits to Bangalore, his staying out the whole night whenever they had a fight, there being no emotional intimacy between them even after all these years—everything began making sense to Alka now, like the pieces of a jigsaw puzzle coming together.

She thought about how Subbu had behaved over the years and it became obvious to her that Subbu was still in love with Chanda. He was being forced to stay in this marriage because of his sense of duty. That explained *everything*—his aloofness, his lack of communication and his pent-up anger.

'In Bangalore itself,' Krish replied, confirming her suspicions.

Alka tried to compose herself even though her mind was a whirlwind and her stomach churned. She braced herself and asked, 'So what does Chanda do now?' She had to know, as torturous as it was for her.

'She said she runs a travel agency.'

'I see.' Alka sat in silence, shaking her head

Betrayal hit her like a dagger to the heart. Piercing and deep. She was angry, hurt and profoundly sad, all at the same time. Her whole marriage felt like a lie as the foundations of trust crumbled beneath her.

'And Subbu married me despite knowing about his son?'

'No, Chanda said that he found out about the child only after Nisha and Tulika were born.'

'How is that even possible? Did he cheat on me when I was pregnant?'

'No, Alka, Chanda's son is a few years older than both your girls. She wrote to Anna about three years after her own marriage.'

'Why?'

'She had a fallout with her husband while living in the US. She said he'd left her for another woman, but then he began harassing her for child custody. Chanda had always had her doubts about whether it was Anna's baby she had given birth to or her husband's. So, she got a paternity test done. And as soon as the results came back, confirming that the child was Anna's, she returned to India. Initially, she had no plans of telling Anna. Later, though, she decided that he had a right to know. So she wrote to him.'

'Oh hell,' Alka swore softly.

'I'm sorry, Alka,' Krish paused for a second and then continued, 'But Chanda is a very genuine person, and she is very worried about Anna right now.'

Alka recalled the whispers that had stopped just as she had entered the Ladies Club meeting a few months ago. Did everyone except her know about Chanda and Subbu? Was she the only fool?

'Did you know about this earlier? About this … this secret son?' she asked Krish.

She was furious now. How could Krish have withheld this big a piece of information from her? And she thought she had a connection with Krish! That he was on *her* side!

'I didn't know about his child at all. I only knew that they were deeply in love. And that for Anna, Chanda has always been special on a level that I could never comprehend. When you pressed me for details that day, I felt it wasn't my place to reveal how deep their connection was. But now that Chanda has been in touch, I felt I must tell you everything. She wants to visit Anna at the hospital.'

'Why did you hide it from me till now? Why didn't you tell me as soon as she called you?' Alka demanded, her eyes blazing.

'Alka, it was a lot for me to process too. I was flabbergasted.'

'Come on, Krish. That's a weak excuse. You were a coward, admit it,' Alka retorted, directing all her anger at Krish.

'Yes, I was. I admit it. I didn't know how to tell you.' He looked crestfallen.

'Both of you—you, your brother—are the same. It's okay for you to have a secret. But when I don't mention my past, it becomes such a big deal. And this, this is okay?' Alka demanded, her voice rising.

'Wait a minute,' Krish shot back. 'I never once condoned what my brother did. And I never faulted you for hiding your past. I supported you when you had that big fight with Anna. How can you accuse me like this and put me in the same bracket as him? I understand you are upset. But this is not on *me*, Alka.'

'You're the one who continued speaking to her, *behind* my back. How is that okay?'

'The plan was always to tell you. I might not have rushed to tell you about it the moment I found out, but I am telling you now. Please remember that I knew Chanda even before I knew you. I can't just brush her off and not receive her calls. She loves Anna, Alka. She truly does. How can you of all people not understand that?'

This enraged Alka even more. 'You know what, Krish? I need time to process this. I am leaving for the hospital, alone. Thanks for being there,' she said formally as she stood up and began to walk out.

'Come on, Alka. You can't be childish like this. Are you seriously walking out on me right now and going to the hospital by yourself?'

'Yes, I am,' Alka fumed as she marched out and slammed the door behind her.

Krish made no attempts to follow her. If she wanted to behave this way, then he wasn't going to stop her. He decided he would give her time to come to terms with what had happened. It must've been a shock for her, just as it had been for him when he had first heard about Subbu's son.

Krish had met Chanda a few times, but that had been many years ago when she and Subbu were dating. But after she suddenly got married and moved to the US, they'd had no contact whatsoever. The fact that she was the mother of Subbu's son, did endear her to Krish, but there was no way he was going to mention that to Alka, especially not when she was in such an agitated state.

Krish recalled a conversation he had with Subbu over the phone many years ago when he was working in Mumbai. He had called him just to catch up on what was happening at the estate. Subbu rarely called Krish. He was a practical man who used the telephone only to communicate 'essential news'. After they'd caught up with all the news and run out of topics to speak about, Krish idly asked about Chanda.

'Anna, what news of Chanda? Are you in touch with her?'

'Why will I be in touch with her? Don't you know she is married now?' Subbu had sounded terse.

'Well, that doesn't mean you can't be in touch—'

'That chapter is closed, Krish. I don't want to talk about it,'

Subbu cut him off, and since that day, Krish had never brought the topic up again.

Krish sat in his living room now, wondering how his brother must have felt on discovering he had a son. How did it feel to keep this big a secret? Had he told their mother about it? Did she know? How did one carry on with life like before? But then again, he and Alka had hidden their love from their families too. Granted that it had been before their respective marriages and they had never kept in touch afterwards, but it was evident that their love for each other had never died. When Krish had visited the estate last year, he and Alka had tacitly acknowledged it, but had decided they would do nothing about it.

Subbu, however, had gone straight ahead and met Chanda every week, despite being with Alka and the girls. Krish felt that it was unfair to Alka and that perhaps it was wrong on his brother's part. But love made its own rules. If Subbu had stayed away from Chanda and his son, it would have been unfair to Chanda, and the child would've never met his father. Krish's heart was filled with compassion for Subbu, Alka and Chanda. What a tangled situation they were all in.

❧

Alka reached the basement and found Shanker waiting for her. She told him to drive her to the hospital.

'Krish sir is not coming?' he asked, looking surprised.

'No, some office work came up so he'll go there later,' Alka lied.

On the way to the hospital, Alka kept thinking about what Krish had told her. She was still upset with him for not immediately sharing all the information with her. A part of her burned with anger and jealousy knowing that Krish was talking to Chanda and giving her updates. But as Krish had said, how could he not? She was furious about Subbu's betrayal, but she could also understand how worried Chanda must be. After all, she knew what it meant to love someone deeply.

Perhaps the gods were punishing her, Alka thought. She had loved Krish with all her heart and then walked away from him. This betrayal by Subbu and the pain she had to endure because of it, maybe this was her atonement.

18

SPLIT INTO TWO

2006

At the hospital, standing outside the ICU, Alka felt both abandoned and bitter. She had calmed down enough to know that it was Subbu she was angry at, but she had taken it out on Krish. Without Krish there, 'their corridor' seemed empty. She spoke to the nurses on duty who let her into the ICU briefly. Subbu was still tethered to the machines that monitored his body's vital signs. He seemed to be breathing normally, but the incessant beeping of the machines sounded ominous to Alka's ears. The intricate network of medical devices around him made any physical contact, like a hug, impossible. She gently stroked his fingers instead, mindful of the intravenous needle taped to the back of his hand. Looking at him lying there so helplessly, Alka was filled with both tenderness as well as pain. She wondered if Subbu and she had ever actually understood each other. How did Subbu feel knowing he had a son and that Chanda was raising him? Did he long to leave her and the girls and be with Chanda instead? Was it only a moral obligation that kept him bound to her? Or was it because his life was rooted in the coffee estate? Many questions rose to her mind and she rebuked Subbu silently.

'Can't you see me standing here? Can't you see that the coffee estate needs you? Why can't you open your eyes and end all this uncertainty? We need to talk, Subbu. Wake up.' But Subbu continued to lie there peacefully amidst the symphony of beeping machines in the sterile confines of the ICU.

Alka came out after a while and found the senior staff nurse, Sister Pushpa, addressing a group of interns outside the ICU. 'This is our ICU wing and the patients here need extra care. We have to treat all the patients like they are our very own. It's our restorative touch and smile that help patients recover faster. Don't look at them as cases. Look at them as someone you know—your friend, your neighbour, your classmate, your elderly relative's son or daughter. Also, never let whatever emotions you're going through show on your face. Leave them outside the hospital. This is an essential part of the job, and we'll be assessing you on this too, apart from the theoretical and practical medical knowledge,' she said. Some of the interns looked bright eyed and eager as they nodded enthusiastically. A few others looked nervous. And one of them, standing right next to Alka, rolled her eyes, which Sister Pushpa missed.

'You may go inside in pairs now. The ward sister will tell you what to do. You can go to the other ICUs too. All of you don't have to wait here for your turns,' she said.

Alka waited till the group had dispersed. Then she greeted Sister Pushpa and told her that she was leaving, but that Krish would be visiting soon.

'Yes, your brother-in-law is always here. He mentioned once that it's hard for you to be here often because of the coffee estate and your daughters. Don't worry, we're taking good care of your husband,' Sister Pushpa assured Alka warmly.

'Do you see any improvement at all in him, sister? To me, he looks exactly like he did when he was first admitted,' Alka confessed.

'There is definitely an improvement. His haematoma has been removed and the clot is no longer there. I can make out some subtle changes too. See, his eyes may be closed but his eyeballs are moving now. He is fighting back.'

'Thank you, sister. I really needed to hear that,' Alka blinked back the tears in her eyes.

'Don't lose hope. Doctors tend to not give any guarantees, and this can be disheartening for the relatives. I have seen many similar cases in my twenty-nine years of service. Sixty per cent of the people will open their eyes after four weeks and thirty per cent will usually come out of the coma within a year.'

Alka didn't want to ask about the remaining ten per cent.

On the way back to the estate, Alka felt optimistic. Sister Pushpa had said there was visible eye movement even though Subbu's eyes were closed. She wondered if Krish knew this. If he didn't, he deserved to know. She was still sore over the fact that he had not told her about Chanda sooner. But she could also understand what a shock it must've been for him too. He'd always been there for her, as he had pointed out. She would have to speak to him sooner or later, to coordinate things at the hospital. Therefore, she decided to apologize to him for her behaviour. But she didn't want Shanker to overhear her conversation with Krish. It was too private; she would call him only after reaching the estate, when she would have some privacy.

❧

When she reached the estate, she found Muthu waiting for her in his jeep at the entrance to her home.

'Hello, madam, I needed your signature urgently on all these payments that have to be cleared today,' he said.

'All right, follow me,' Alka said as she climbed the steps leading to the house.

She called out to Selvi to bring coffee for both of them, and then asked Muthu to sit down.

'Madam, it's okay,' he said and continued standing.

'Muthu, I want you to explain each of these payments and I want to go through them before I sign. Please sit down,' Alka said, gesturing to the chair opposite her. 'Also, you can't have your coffee standing.'

Muthu sat down at the edge of the seat. In all the years of having worked in the estate, he had never once sat down with Subbu like this. Mostly, they would either be out somewhere in the estate or he would be at his desk in one corner of the office he shared with Subbu. He was not used to this unconventional way of working where he was treated with respect, but he liked it and was getting used to it.

Alka went through all the pending payments carefully.

'Why are we clearing this invoice now? It says here that we have a credit period of forty-five days. Only thirty have passed.'

'Yes, madam, but the man calls up daily to ask for the payment. He's a pest,' Muthu vented.

'A pest who sells pesticides,' Alka remarked and Muthu guffawed. It was fun working with Alka. Subbu was so serious all the time.

'Tell him we'll make the payment only at the end of the credit period, and if he pesters you, ask him to talk to me,' Alka said firmly.

'All right, madam,' Muthu replied.

Selvi entered the room just then and served them coffee with murukkus and biscuits.

'Thank you, Selvi,' Alka nodded.

'Have the murukku too, Muthu. These are special dal murukkus made by Selvi.' Alka offered the plate to Muthu.

'Thank you, madam,' Muthu said. He picked one up and took a bite. 'These are so crunchy and tasty.'

Selvi beamed. Alka knew how much these little gestures of appreciation mattered. She remembered how the women of the Inner Circle club at Mrs Shetty's house wouldn't acknowledge her mother and how bad she used to feel as a child, watching her mother trying to make herself invisible as she served everyone at the same time.

Alka continued signing the papers for the payments, asking Muthu to explain things that were not clear to her. The cash outflow was a lot. She would have to find a way to cut it down.

'Madam, I also wanted to inform you that we've managed to empty the line houses. These houses have now been given to the migrant labourers, who are very happy. But the relatives of the permanent workers did protest.'

'That's okay. We need to take care of the people who work for us. They deserve better than having to sleep out in the open. So, no one is sleeping in the yard now?'

'No, madam, they are all housed in the line houses,' Muthu said. 'There's one more issue that has come up, but I don't think we should get involved.'

'What is the issue?'

'One of our labourers, Dayanna, has a sister who works in the adjoining estate. Her name is Mallama. Apparently, Mallama's sixteen-year-old daughter is missing. Mallama is accusing Dayanna's wife's nephew of having eloped with her. She even sent a search party to our estate last night to look for her daughter.'

'Wait, let me understand this—Mallama's daughter eloped with Dayanna's wife's nephew and Mallama sent a search party to our estate?'

'Yes, madam. About twenty men came to our estate last night. They found the nephew, Shiva, and questioned him. But he denied the accusations completely. So, they beat him up and left.'

'What? How can we allow that? Was he beaten up badly?'

'No, no, madam. He wasn't hurt badly. His family wanted to lodge a police complaint against the people who beat him up, but I dissuaded them.'

'Why, Muthu?'

'The police won't really do anything unless they are bribed. And this matter will only create unnecessary tension between the two estates. I do feel terrible about the girl disappearing. But such issues have come up earlier too. The girl probably eloped with someone from outside Karnataka and moved away. If we get involved, we alienate ourselves from the neighbouring estate owner, as well as from the labour who will not be happy, no matter what we do. However, if we do nothing, it will probably die down on its own. That's why I said we shouldn't interfere.'

'All right, Muthu. I'll trust your call on this; I do hope she is found quickly,' Alka said.

Once the coffee tray was cleared, she asked, 'What do you think of opening up the estate to visitors?'

'You mean setting up a homestay?'

'Yes, short term rentals for which we can get a good return.'

'Madam, there'll be people walking into our estate and Subbu sir doesn't like that.'

'I know. But I want to know what you think about it?'

'I think it's a good opportunity. I had suggested this to Subbu sir a few years ago, but he wouldn't hear of it. What I wanted to suggest to him was that if we don't want people all over the estate, there's a way around it. We can easily demarcate the areas where the visitors can roam about freely and places we don't want them to enter can be cordoned off. Walking paths and trails can be blocked by a wooden gate, like a check post, where necessary. That way, we can have our privacy while the visitors also get to roam around.'

'That's a good idea, indeed. I was thinking of having a look at the cottages at Silver Brooks, Misty Blue, Gurgling Waters and Poet's Paradise.'

'Madam, they're all in a terrible state, surrounded by thick vegetation and anthills. They haven't been opened for years,' Muthu said, shaking his head.

'That's precisely why we have to go and do a recce, Muthu. We'll have to assess what condition they are in. Will you drive me to all of them?' Alka asked.

'Now, madam?'

'Why not? You must've finished the estate rounds. We can go now.'

'All right, madam, but we'll have to drive to the office first to get the keys.'

Alka climbed into the passenger seat and Muthu drove them to the office. Along with the keys to the cottages, he also got a tiny bottle of machine oil.

'What's that for?' Alka asked.

'The locks will be rusted, madam. Unless we use this, they might not open.'

'Ah yes. And we should try to get there before sunset.'

'Yes, madam. The cottages won't have any electricity.'

'Then we'd better hurry if we want to get a good look,' Alka said as Muthu stepped on the accelerator. The jeep bumped along on the mud road, making its way to the Silver Brooks cottage which was the one closest to them.

The cottage itself was a very pretty one, built in the colonial style with local material. But it was in stark contrast to the picturesque image that its name suggested. The once-well-maintained garden had succumbed to neglect, allowing nature to claim its territory. Vines and creepers grew on the large bushes that blocked the path to the cottage. Some of the vines had bright purple flowers, and Alka could imagine how beautiful the garden must have once looked. Through the bushes, she could see that the verandah might have been a charming spot in the past, but now it was covered with fallen leaves, twigs and a thick layer of dust. The wooden railing too, showed signs of decay. The cottage looked weathered, dilapidated and beaten.

'Madam, there's no path to even get to the cottage. We'll have to get some labour and cut all these bushes down. Only then can we enter this place. Also, there's the danger of snakes lurking around. Shall we come back tomorrow?'

Alka glanced at her watch. Having come this far, she was determined to at least peep into the cottage. 'Why don't we go get the labour today itself and see how long it takes to clear a path? They don't have to clear the whole thing today. Just enough for us to enter.'

'Very well, madam, let's head back and bring a couple of men along with us,' Muthu said.

They were back at the cottage fifteen minutes later with two labourers who had brought a wheelbarrow, secateurs, machetes and spades with them. The labourers unloaded the tools from the jeep and Muthu instructed them to clear the path up to the cottage. Tying turbans on their heads, they got down to work. The men chose the most direct route to the cottage, navigating around the larger plants where necessary. Beads of sweat formed on their foreheads as they exerted themselves. The thick vegetation that had once stood tall and engulfed the cottage now lay scattered on the ground as they progressed methodically. With each swing of their machetes, the exterior of the cottage became more accessible.

'I wonder who lived here and why this place stopped being used,' Alka mused.

'I've heard my father say that Mr Davies, the old British planter, got them built for his sons, madam. He had three sons, and they were always fighting with each other. One of them was a poet and writer. He used one of the cottages as his writing place. Hence, Poet's Paradise.'

'How interesting!' Alka exclaimed. 'I've lived here for ten years and I've never really thought of who lived in the cottages or why they had those names till now.'

'Madam, there are other stories too. But it's just hearsay and it's not very pleasant,' Muthu said.

'What is it, Muthu?' Alka asked, her curiosity ignited.

'Apparently, the sons were not at all happy in the estate. They wanted to go back to England. But Mr Davies wouldn't permit that. Then the oldest son fell in love with an Indian woman, the daughter of a labourer at the estate. But this was a social taboo, and Mr Davies didn't approve of their relationship. He said he did not want a mixed-race grandchild. But the couple were deeply in love, and they eloped to England, leaving behind Gurgling Waters. The second son, who lived in this cottage in front of us, suffered from a mental problem. From what people say, I think it was probably schizophrenia, but in those days, they probably hadn't diagnosed it yet. So people just thought he was mad.'

Then Muthu's voice dropped to a theatrical whisper. 'Madam, it was in this cottage that the second son killed himself.'

'Oh! I seem to have chosen the worst one then,' Alka smiled nervously. She was a little shaken by what Muthu had just revealed. But she wasn't one to head back just because of a story.

'What about the third son?' she asked.

'The third son, the poet, was an alcoholic. He struck a deal with a local businessman to sell the cottage, which he had no authority to do. He took some money from the businessman too, but then the whole matter went into litigation. So the cottage was locked up. Later, after the businessman died, no one bothered about the case. Right from my father's time, this cottage has remained locked up, madam. These are not good places.'

'A place is never good or bad, Muthu. It is just four walls. But the people living within those walls can make that place heaven or hell,' Alka explained, thinking of the tiny room in Mrs Shetty's house where she and her mother had lived.

'That is true, madam. That is very true,' Muthu nodded in agreement.

By now, the path to the cottage had been cleared. Alka and Muthu walked up to the cottage where the labourers stood leaning against their spades, pleased with their efforts. Muthu carefully tested the wooden stairs leading up to the verandah by putting a bit of pressure on them. They did not give away but creaked from the years of abandonment.

The exterior of the cottage seemed perfectly fine, although there was a lot of moss growing in the crevices of the stones. Muthu poured some oil into the lock, and after fiddling with it for a while, he managed to open it.

'Sir, please wait. We will check it out first; there might be some creepy crawlies inside,' one of the labourers said. Muthu duly stepped back.

The labourer picked up a machete in his hand as he went inside, cautiously stepping around as if he expected to be struck by a snake any second. His movements were deliberate and measured as he went around the dimly lit interiors. It was only when he was certain that there were no snakes inside that he told Alka and Muthu to enter.

The air inside the cottage was thick, and a stale, musty odour assaulted their nostrils. Alka used the sleeve of her T-shirt to cover her nose as she went in behind Muthu. The windows were covered in grime and allowed only minimal light to filter in, casting deep shadows on the neglected furniture and the worn-out floorboards within.

The labourer went about opening all the windows to let some fresh air in. However, some of them were stuck, and when he tried to prise them open, creaks and groans echoed through the cottage. It was as though the cottage itself was grumbling at being woken up from its deep slumber.

Alka and Muthu surveyed the interior. The floor was covered entirely with dead insects and layers upon layers of dust. Animal droppings were scattered everywhere, evidence of the wildlife that had claimed the cottage as their temporary refuge. A family of pigeons, startled by the sudden human intrusion, fluttered out from a hidden corner somewhere. A couple of squirrels scampered out hurriedly, their tiny paws leaving imprints in the dust.

When all the windows were finally opened, Alka had a good look at the place. It consisted of three rooms—a hall with a fireplace, a bedroom and a kitchen. She was surprised to see that the cottage had a few pieces of furniture as well. They appeared to be well preserved, but for the layer of dust. Muthu inspected them and declared that they were termite free.

'All very good furniture, madam. Everything made of rosewood. We don't get this type of quality these days,' he told her.

'Yes, that's true. Old furniture was built to last, and these are so beautiful,' Alka agreed.

She wondered which room the second son had killed himself in. Was it in the hall? Or was it the bedroom? Perhaps the kitchen? How had he killed himself?

Muthu, somehow attuned to Alka's thoughts, gently answered her unspoken questions.

'Madam, this is where it happened,' he said, pointing towards a planter's chair next to the fireplace in the hall. 'He shot himself in that chair,' he whispered, his voice barely audible.

Puzzled, Alka asked, 'Why are you whispering, Muthu?'

His hushed tone had made the information sound eerier than it actually was, adding an unsettling layer to the already sombre atmosphere of the cottage.

'Madam, the labourers do not know about this. We don't want them to spread rumours. They may get scared and refuse to come to work. These stories can spread fast within the estate,' Muthu answered, still whispering.

'Ah, I see. And how do you know it was that chair?' Alka asked. She lowered her voice too, to match the discreet tone of the conversation.

'Everyone who has been in the estate for a long time knows this, madam. As children, we overheard the stories our parents discussed. So we used to pretend to shoot ourselves and die! As a young boy, my friends and I used to come to this cottage, peep in just to see this chair, and then run away,' Muthu said.

Alka shuddered involuntarily as she pictured a dead person in the chair, the weight of history pressing on her senses.

'I want this whole place cleaned up, Muthu,' she declared, determined to restore some semblance of order to the neglected cottage.

She hesitated for a brief moment as she contemplated asking Muthu to get rid of the chair. After a short internal debate, however, the practical side of her won and she decided against it. The chair, despite its troubling past, was a beautiful piece of furniture. She couldn't be certain about the rumours being true. Besides, the chair did add a layer of intrigue to the cottage. She told Muthu to ask the labourers to have the entire place cleaned up. She wanted the lights fixed as well.

'I want this place to look as good as new. Please see to it,' she instructed Muthu, who readily agreed.

The sun had begun setting by now, and as Muthu drove Alka back, she was filled with a sense of excitement about the three remaining cottages. She couldn't wait to see what they looked like.

It was only after she had put the girls to bed that she thought of Krish and Subbu's betrayal. Alka found it interesting to see how much her immediate physical surroundings influenced her thoughts. The outburst of that morning felt like it belonged to another life. She felt she had split into two Alkas—one who had taken charge of the estate and was excited about running it, and the other who was fuming at Subbu's secret life. It now seemed silly to have gotten angry at Krish and picked a fight with him. She would apologize to him first thing in the morning, she decided.

19

A MIRROR OF HONESTY

2006

It was well past ten by the time Alka got a chance to speak to Krish.

'Hey, Alka, how are you doing?' he asked. He did not sound angry or upset at all.

The moment she heard his voice, Alka was filled with tenderness towards him. No matter what he did, she couldn't stay annoyed with him for long.

'I am sorry, Krish. I owe you an apology.'

'For what? It's already forgotten,' he said.

'Thank you, Krish.'

'You don't ever have to thank me, Alka,' Krish said softly.

She then told him about her conversation with Sister Pushpa and how it filled her with hope.

'You know, I've heard her speak to other patients and their families too. She is always assuring them that everything will be fine. But the doctors are still saying that Anna cannot leave the ICU yet,' Krish voiced his concerns. 'And I don't mean to be a damp squib here. I am simply tired, Alka.'

'I know. I am not there all the time, and I can only imagine how hard it is on you. I will visit again tomorrow,' Alka promised. She then told him about Silver Brooks and the story that Muthu had narrated.

'I've never heard that story, but then I was away at boarding school, and they shielded me from a lot of stuff. When Anna wakes up, we'll have to ask him if it is true. I am glad you decided to keep the chair though. It would've been a shame to get rid of it. I'm also happy you are getting the entire cottage cleaned and ready.'

'I am going to see the other cottages today. If they can also be done up, I think we might have some really good rentable properties on our hands. I know Subbu was always against it, but to leave the cottages locked up seems like a colossal waste,' Alka declared.

'Yes, especially when the estate is making a loss. I think what you're doing is absolutely the right thing to do and you're doing a splendid job,' Krish said.

Alka felt happy to hear that. She'd been taking all these decisions on her own, and to hear Krish supporting her meant a great deal.

'Thank you for saying that, Krish. I'll see you soon,' she said as she hung up.

The next cottage that Alka and Muthu visited was Misty Blue. True to its name, the cottage stood adorned in a light blue hue that had faded over time into a nearly ethereal shade of white. The labourers accompanying them repeated the previous day's exercise of cutting down the foliage around the cottage to clear out a path to its entrance, and Muthu opened the lock after using some oil to remove the rust.

'This is not in a bad state at all, Muthu!' Alka exclaimed, stepping in. Despite its weathered exterior, Misty Blue appeared to be in a relatively good shape. Since all the windows had been sealed tightly shut, the interior of the cottage was free of any signs of wildlife. One of the labourers pushed against the windows, and they opened a little more easily than the ones in Silver Brooks. The layout of the cottage mirrored that of Silver Brooks, except that it was slightly smaller in size.

'Look at these exquisite floral curtains, Muthu!' Alka exclaimed with delight, her fingers gently tracing the intricate patterns on the thick curtain fabric. Unlike the previous cottage, where the windows and bed had borne no adornments, Misty Blue's interior boasted of gorgeous upholstery. The bed linen was immaculately preserved too, as if the occupants had departed only yesterday instead of decades ago. Everything inside was reminiscent of the colonial era, and there was a touch of timeless elegance within the cottage's walls.

Alka told Muthu she wanted this cottage cleaned as well.

'See if the curtains can be dry-cleaned,' she instructed. 'I don't want any tear in the fabric. These are precious. You'll have to take them to a good dry-cleaner in Sakleshpur city. And please do not hand it over to any of the labourers.'

'No, madam, I shall do this personally. They will not know the value of these items,' Muthu assured her. Alka's excitement and delight were infectious, and Muthu was swept up in them.

They visited Poet's Paradise next. It was an exact replica of Misty Blue, and because it too was sealed shut, it looked well-preserved. By now, the labourers knew what to do. They worked fast, clearing the path to the cottage and then checking inside for any danger before letting Alka and Muthu walk in. Alka was happy to see that the cottage wouldn't need too much refurbishing.

When Muthu and Alka reached Gurgling Waters, the final destination on their agenda, the soothing sounds of the stream that ran nearby greeted them.

'Oh, this one is true to its name. The water is indeed gurgling. Imagine waking up to this sound every morning. I can't believe we haven't used this cottage in so long,' Alka remarked as she walked to the entrance.

She was pleasantly surprised to find that the path to the cottage was gravelled and therefore devoid of any intrusive foliage. The gravel also added a touch of manicured elegance to the property, contrasting beautifully with the natural surroundings.

However, upon entering the cottage and looking around, Alka couldn't hide her disappointment because the furniture had been ravaged by termites.

'Oh! These are all almost destroyed. We'll have to replace them,' she groaned.

'Madam, if we are going to replace them, we will have to get the new pieces done in the same style,' Muthu mused.

'Absolutely, the charm of these cottages lies in the style of architecture and furniture used. But I think this one requires some major structural repairs too,' Alka added while walking to the kitchen sink. It had almost given away and was barely hanging off a flimsy hinge.

'Yes, madam, I am making a note of everything,' Muthu said as he scribbled away furiously in his pocket notebook.

'I want an estimate of the costs and how quickly these repairs can be done. Also, how soon we can expect these cottages to be functional? We have to revive the cash flow quickly,' Alka said.

'I will speak to various contractors and get the estimates, madam. Give me two days. I will have all the information ready for you. Subbu sir should've done this a long time back,' Muthu said.

'I know. I had suggested it too. Anyway, I am glad we're doing this now.'

'I am looking forward to it, madam.'

'What about food for the guests, Muthu? Do you think we can offer them food from our kitchen?'

'Yes, madam, that will be a good option. We can also provide them with the facility to cook as all the cottages have a small kitchen. But I think most people would want to taste our cuisine. My cousin works at a homestay in a neighbouring estate, and he was telling me about how much the guests love our local food and the campfires. Many of them come for the whole estate experience.'

'I remember how fascinated I was when I visited the estate for the first time. We will need someone to take the guests around the estate, show them the yard, the process of coffee making, explain how the beans finally turn into coffee powder. We'll have to package the whole experience well and make it eco-friendly. I do not want anything made of plastic in these cottages. We will renovate the cottages using local labour and local material. And we will employ only local women for all the maintenance work on the cottages.'

'Madam, excellent idea!'

By the time Alka got back from inspecting the cottages, Nisha and Tulika had returned from school. They rushed to greet her as she entered the house. They were keen to tell her about their day, and even though Alka was in no mood to listen, she feigned interest.

But Nisha immediately caught on. 'Mummy! You aren't listening,' she admonished her.

'Sorry, baby, I'll pay attention now. Mummy was thinking about something else.'

Just then, Alka's phone rang. It was Krish.

'Alka, there's been a complication,' his voice was grave.

Alka sat up straight and then walked away from the girls.

'What happened, Krish? Is he—' she asked, not completing her sentence.

'He seemed to be fine, but the doctors have now spotted an inter-cranial haemorrhage. It's a serious complication and apparently it rarely happens. He needs a second surgery to drain it.'

'Oh good Lord, Krish. I'll start from here immediately,' she said.

When Alka hung up, she found two worried faces staring at her. The girls had followed her out.

'Is Appa dead?' Nisha asked.

'No! No! He's going to be okay,' Alka tried to reassure her. 'He needs another surgery, but he will be fine after that.'

'Mummy is lying so that we don't worry,' Tulika said. Alka was taken aback at her astuteness.

'Listen, you two, Mummy needs to go to the hospital now. Your Appa is a fighter, and he will be fine, all right? I don't know when I'll be back though.'

'Mummy, we will listen to Selvi Akka and do all our homework. Don't worry. I will take care of Tulika too,' Nisha assured her.

'No, I'm a big girl now. I can take care of myself,' Tulika announced.

'You both will take care of each other, okay?' Alka said as she walked briskly to the bedroom and taking out a duffel bag, threw some of her clothes into it.

She called out to Selvi and asked her to inform Shanker that they would be leaving for Bangalore immediately.

Alka was glad Selvi was taking care of everything at home. From supervising the girls' homework, keeping an eye on their playtime and feeding them their meals to even ensuring that they washed themselves and brushed their teeth before bed, Selvi could do it all. She made a mental note to increase Selvi's pay. That girl was worth her weight in gold.

The surgery was already in progress when Alka arrived at the hospital. Krish met her outside the operation theatre. He looked exhausted. He clearly hadn't shaved for days, and Alka had never seen him look this dishevelled. He hugged Alka tight, as though afraid to let go.

'He doesn't deserve this,' Krish said in a small, broken voice.

'No, he doesn't. None of us do,' Alka responded, hugging him back.

When they pulled apart at last, they sat on the metal chairs outside the operating theatre, waiting like they had earlier, both of them too battered to make conversation.

Time ticked by and they lost all track of it. Finally, the doors of the operation theatre opened and the surgeons came out.

'It's all good. The procedure is done and Subbu's fine. You can meet us tomorrow in the consultation room,' Dr Mohan informed them and walked away.

A nurse came up to them and said that they would be shifting Subbu to the ICU in a few hours. She suggested they go home and get some rest.

'You will not be allowed to see him today. Only tomorrow can you visit him,' she stated.

Alka and Krish decided to go to his place.

'Hungry?' Krish asked when they entered his apartment. Alka, however, was in no mood to eat anything and neither was Krish.

'In case you are hungry later, there's some Maggi here.' Krish opened a cupboard in the kitchen and showed it to Alka. She nodded. Then he showed her to the guest room, and gently closed the door on his way out.

'Good night, Alka,' he said as he left.

As soon as the door closed, Alka began sobbing into the pillow. She didn't want Krish to know that she was crying. After a while, when her sobs subsided, she tried to sleep. But she tossed and turned instead, and visions of Subbu lying hooked to the machines kept playing in her mind. How much pain was he going through after this second surgery? She imagined the doctors cutting through his skull to reach his brain, and couldn't bear the thought of it. How much more would Subbu have to endure?

Alka's heart began pounding and her mouth felt dry. Her breath came out in short gasps and she sat up. She didn't know what was happening; all she knew was that she wanted to be held. As though in a trance, she got up and walked to the door of her room. The curtains in the living room were not drawn, and light from the adjoining building dimly illuminated the room. She remembered Krish mentioning that his bedroom was upstairs and found herself walking up the stairs. She identified his room easily—the door had been left slightly ajar, and she could see his form huddled on the bed.

She heaved a sigh of relief.

'Krish?' she called out hesitantly.

'Alka? What's wrong, Alka?' Krish sat up instantly. 'Did the hospital call you?'

'No … no … I … I am terrified, Krish.'

'Come here,' he said.

Alka's knees buckled as she collapsed into his arms, and they embraced desolately, sinking into Krish's bed.

'I am very scared too,' Krish confessed as he held her.

'Can I sleep here? I am unable to sleep, unable to think of anything else but Subbu lying there in the hospital.'

'Of course, Alka.' Krish kissed her on the forehead. 'Do you want me to make you some hot chocolate?'

'No, I just want you to hold me.'

They sat in silence for a while. Alka could hear Krish's heartbeat as she nestled her head on his chest. She felt safe within his arms. Her racing thoughts settled down after a few minutes.

'Is this wrong?' she asked.

'Two people who love each other are comforting each other because they are in pain—how can this be wrong?' Krish countered.

Alka held him tighter. After a while though, Krish felt her breathing relax and her grip loosen a bit. He stayed awake, watching her sleep in his arms. When he couldn't keep his eyes open anymore, he eased her into the bed and went to sleep too. It felt like the most natural thing in the world.

The next morning, Alka was the first to wake up. She went downstairs, made two cups of coffee, and brought them up on a tray to Krish's bedroom. Gently waking him up, she held out the tray towards him. Their eyes met as he took the coffee from her.

'Thanks,' he murmured.

This simple gesture felt too intimate to Alka as it reminded her of the times she would make coffee for him after they'd had sex. Krish felt the same way, his heart swelling with love and concern for her.

'Let's get ready and leave for the hospital,' Alka said. She had no choice but to break the spell.

At the hospital, they had to wait for about forty-five minutes before they could meet both Dr Mohan and Dr Murthy. They sat across them in the consultation room, with Subbu's X-rays pinned on an X-ray view box.

'Mrs Alka, the fresh haemorrhage in Subbu's brain has been removed and fortunately, it had only a mild impact on the brain parenchyma. I would see this as good news. However, the swelling in his brain has to reduce,' Dr Mohan said. He explained the images on the X-ray films like he was giving a lecture. Then he joined them at the table.

'Doctor, what are the chances of recovery? Please be entirely honest so that we can prepare ourselves for the future course of action,' Krish said.

'There's no question of being dishonest here,' Dr Murthy said.

'I am sorry, I did not mean it that way. I mean—'

'Yes, I know. We are asked this question all the time. But we're only doctors. We cannot predict things. In the next ten days, if Subbu opens his eyes, there's a good chance of recovery.'

'And if he doesn't?'

'We'll wait and see, all right? We will keep repeating the evaluations on the Glasgow Coma Scale. While his score had begun improving, because of this new complication, it has gone down again. You'll have to give him time to recover. From a coma, he has to move into a vegetative state (VS), and then to a minimally conscious state or what we call MCS. In MCS, he might be able to correctly answer simple yes-no questions; he might be able to smile. MCS people are generally very confused. He may not respond to things all the time. After VS and MCS, how fast a patient recovers and makes progress varies from person to person. For all you know, Subbu might open his eyes and move straight into the MCS state. After MCS, though, he could end up with a severe cognitive problem, or he might not be able to walk. With the brain, we cannot predict anything at all. But yes, Subbu will need long-term rehabilitation once he recovers,' Dr Murthy explained the situation as best as he could.

But to Krish and Alka, each word from the doctor felt like a blow. It seemed like he was telling them that Subbu was a lost cause, a hopeless case. They thanked the doctors politely and left.

Later at the ICU, Alka found Sister Pushpa on duty. She said they could go in, one at a time. Alka went in first. Subbu looked exactly like he had when he'd been first brought in, vulnerable and helpless. He had now had two surgeries performed on him. Alka's insides twisted into a tight knot and her hands went cold. She couldn't bear the pain. The machines connected to Subbu buzzed and beeped. It was hard being in the ICU.

'They will mostly shift him to the room in two days. He is stable,' Sister Pushpa informed her.

'That's good to know, thanks,' Alka replied.

'Look who has come; it's your wife. Don't you want to wake up?' Sister Pushpa spoke to Subbu as though he could hear her. Alka liked that.

'Once he is shifted to the room, you must keep talking to him. Talking helps. We never know what they might respond to,' she advised.

When Alka stepped outside, she told Krish what the nurse had said.

'Yes, we'll do that. But let's get something to eat now,' Krish said.

They walked to the hospital canteen. Alka sat at an empty table while Krish fetched them hot upma and coffees.

When he sat down with the food, he told Alka, 'Listen, I know you might not be comfortable discussing this. But I think we should let Chanda visit Subbu. She's been asking me about him almost every day. It's really hard for her.'

'I don't think I can meet her, Krish. It's just too raw for me.'

'Hear me out calmly, Alka. I have been giving this a lot of thought. Think about it, you and I also had this thing going on. Didn't we keep it a secret as well?'

'That was before marriage, Krish. It was different.'

'What difference does marriage make, Alka? You know we still have a connection. It's what you feel in your heart. Marriage is just something that's been invented by society. If you think about it, it's just a legal and social formality meant to "legitimize" a relationship. You've been married to Anna for ten whole years, but were we able to get over each other? We weren't. Now, just because we haven't had a physical relationship with each other after we both got married, are we at a morally higher place than Subbu and Chanda? Is it all about sex then?'

Alka didn't know what to say. But she knew Krish was right. She and Krish still had a strong connection, and it was evident from how they had sought each other last night. But she had never thought that Krish would bring up the issue of Chanda visiting Subbu like this.

'I … I don't know, Krish.'

'Think about it, Alka. How are we any better than them when we clearly love each other? Why is Chanda a terrible person because she and Subbu are probably sleeping with each other? They love each other. The only thing that differentiates us from them is—'

'We're nothing like them, Krish. He had a child with her,' Alka cut in a bit too quickly.

'That was *before* he got married to you, and he didn't even know about it till she came back and told him. So how is it any different from our situation?'

'He hid it from me.'

'You too have hidden this thing between us from him, isn't it? It's not like you have been completely honest, Alka. What gives you the right to be angry about Subbu and Chanda then? Aren't these double standards?'

Alka sat still as she thought about what Krish was saying. He definitely had a point. If Subbu was guilty, then she and Krish were guilty too. Krish was holding up a mirror of honesty and she did not like what she was seeing.

'I don't want to discuss this right now,' she said finally.

'I understand. But please give it some thought. That's all I'm asking.'

'I will,' Alka said. 'Now let's change the topic.'

'All right, tell me about the renovations going on in the cottages. I think it's a brilliant idea.'

Relieved to not think about Chanda and Subbu, Alka updated him about what they had decided to do with the cottages.

'I really appreciate how you're managing the whole thing, Alka.'

Alka beamed. Then she told him about her conversation with Gowri and how she had spoken to Mr Chinappa as well.

'I am meeting with the CoRe team soon. I'll keep you posted.'

Alka decide to return to the estate as there was nothing else for her to do at the hospital. Krish walked her out to the hospital porch.

'Bye, Krish,' she said, and as their eyes met, she could see all the pain, the longing and the helplessness within them.

'Take care, Alka. We will get through this, and no matter what, I'm here for you,' he assured her. Then he leaned in, kissed her on the cheek and walked away.

Alka stared after him. She blinked back her tears as she got into the car. As the car made its way back to the estate, she kept thinking about everything Krish had said. She and Krish had presumed that they had buried the love between them. But they were wrong.

That was the thing about love. You could bury it for however long you wanted, but you could never kill it. If it was true, it would always live on. For Alka, love had lain dormant all these years. But it had now emerged without her permission, exactly when it wanted to, at the most inconvenient time. And she didn't have the strength to fight it anymore.

By the time she got back, she decided she would call Krish and tell him he was right. She would tell him to let Chanda visit Subbu. That was the decent thing to do.

20
THE MEETING

2006-2007

Ten days after the second surgery, Subbu was moved out of the ICU into a private room. His condition was stable and the doctors said he was recovering, but he hadn't opened his eyes yet.

Krish told Alka that it was a relief to have Chanda visit Subbu. She came every single day, spoke to the nurses, and even brought home-cooked food for him. Krish didn't have to be at the hospital all the time now as Chanda had readily taken on a huge portion of the hospital duties.

'She's quite a nice person, Alka. Maybe you should meet her,' Krish suggested.

'Not yet, Krish. I am glad she is helping you though,' Alka replied.

'How are the cottage renovations going?'

'Muthu is a wizard! He has managed to hire a local architect whose forte is renovating old heritage properties. He is doing a splendid job of restoring each cottage to its original glory, using local artisans and local material. He's really good.'

Alka had visited Subbu four more times since his second surgery. It became Krish's job to regulate Alka and Chanda's visits so that at no point would they run into each other. Alka said she didn't want to know anything about Chanda's visits.

On one of these visits, Alka had brought Nisha and Tulika along with her. Though she had prepared them, they were completely shocked to see their father's state. They didn't speak a word, neither at the hospital nor on the way back home. When Alka asked if they were okay, Nisha said, 'I am so sad, Mummy. I hate God.'

'Is Appa a bad person?' asked Tulika.

'Of course not, baby,' Alka replied.

'But my teacher said that God punishes bad persons. So is Appa getting punished for something bad that he did?'

'Umm, it's not like that Tulika. God is not like humans who punish people. God is just good thoughts and deeds. He or she is kindness and love, and all things that are good and positive, okay?'

'So, if we hope and pray and think good thoughts, will Appa be okay?' Nisha asked.

'Yes, yes, he will. He will get better, and he'll be back with us soon,' Alka assured them with a confidence she was not feeling.

Between her trips to Bangalore, supervising the renovation work in the cottages, managing her home and worrying about Subbu, Alka was in a constant state of exhaustion. There were dark circles under her eyes—most nights, she couldn't sleep and would lie awake in the dark, wondering what would happen to the estate and whether Subbu would ever make a full recovery.

When Alka wanted to visit him for a fifth time, Krish asked her not to.

'There's no point of your leaving everything there and coming over, Alka. It's such a strain for you to travel up and down on the same day. Not to mention the money spent on fuel. Stay there. I'll let you know if there are any changes here.'

'That doesn't mean I do not even visit him.'

'I know. All I am suggesting is that you visit when there are some developments. Otherwise, all you can do here is simply stand in the room for a few hours and then head back. Let's be practical about these things.'

Alka reluctantly agreed as Krish had made a valid point.

One morning, Alka received a call from Mr Chinappa, asking if she could meet with the members of the CoRe team at the Planter's Club at 11.30 a.m. the next day.

'Yes, of course, I'll be there. I've been waiting for your call,' Alka said.

'Join us for lunch, young lady,' Mr Chinappa said before hanging up.

The next day, Alka met with Mr Chinappa and three other members of the CoRe team at the appointed time. The group, all in their mid-sixties to early seventies, were seasoned planters whose families had been in the business for many generations.

Mr Chinappa, short and stout with a head full of salt and pepper hair that he had combed back neatly, was dressed in a formal white shirt and navy-blue trousers, paired with smartly polished shoes. He introduced the others in his group—Mrs Daisy Bopiah, Mr Umesh Bidappa and Mr Antony Paul. Once

Mr Chinappa had made the introductions, they all insisted that Alka call them by their first names.

'We're young at heart. Only the silver in our hair makes us look old. Except for Antony, who obviously uses hair dye,' Daisy said, her eyes twinkling. She was dressed in a cream saree that she had paired with a sleeveless blouse. She had short, bobbed hair and wore dangly earrings and bright red lipstick. Alka liked her instantly.

'Hey, hey! Don't be jealous of my hair. It's all natural,' Antony quipped, and everyone burst out laughing. He exuded a youthful air and seemed to be lively and witty.

Umesh seemed to be the quietest one in the group. His smart outfit was accentuated by a striking gold watch. Alka realized that this was a well-dressed bunch.

As she took her seat, she could sense the friendship and camaraderie within the group.

'Thank you for meeting me,' she said.

'We're sorry we couldn't meet you earlier, Alka. Two of our members were travelling, and they got back to India only a few days ago,' Mr Chinappa said.

'I've known Subbu since he was this tall,' Antony said, holding out his hand a few inches above the ground. 'Subbu's father and I were very good friends. He was gone too soon, and Anandi was distraught after his death. But Subbu stepped right into his shoes.'

'Yes, we all admired how stoic Subbu was and how he took charge of the estate. It's a shame he has to go through something like this now,' Umesh remarked.

'How is he doing? And how are you holding up?' Daisy asked.

'He had to undergo a second surgery, but the doctors say he is making progress. As for me, I am taking each day as it comes. It is hard, but it's not like I have a choice. My only focus now is the estate,' Alka explained, and the members of the group nodded in understanding.

'How do you all know each other?' Alka asked, desperate to change the topic. It was hard to talk about Subbu and she didn't want them to ask any more questions about his condition.

'Oh, we all go back a long way,' Chinappa said. 'Umesh and I were classmates. We went to the same school. Antony and Daisy were our juniors in college. Antony here is totally in love with Daisy, he has been since our college days.'

'Yes, and I asked her to marry me after she lost her husband. But she turned me down,' Antony complained, making the whole group laugh.

'Men are useless as husbands. Just keep them as your boyfriend or keep them pining for you. Once you get married—that's it. They begin taking you for granted,' Daisy retorted, flicking back her hair in an exaggerated gesture. They all laughed again.

Alka was shocked at their candidness and sense of humour. When she'd first spoken to Mr Chinappa, she hadn't imagined the CoRe members to be like this at all. She felt relaxed around them.

'What would you like to eat?' Antony asked her.

'I'll leave it to you. I don't come here often,' Alka said.

They ordered almost all the delicious starters on the menu—chicken 65, roasted masala peanuts, fish fingers, potato wedges and some whisky. Alka said she would settle for some orange juice; she wasn't used to drinking in the middle of the day.

'Nothing like doing business over a couple of drinks,' Mr Chinappa said.

'Business? I, er, I thought this was just all of you giving me some tips,' Alka said.

'Ha ha ha! My dear girl, we don't do things for free,' Chinappa laughed. 'We do help estates out. But in this case, I am guessing you will need a lot more than just some tips.'

'Of course, if you only want tips about how to run the estate, we are open to that as well. We will share what we know and send you on your way. But if you want to do business, then it's going to be a proper business deal,' Antony announced.

'I would definitely like to hear what the business deal is,' Alka replied.

'Good call,' Daisy nodded. 'Let me explain what we do. See, we have formed a proper company where we're all equal partners. We have invested our own money in it. What we do is take over sick estates and then manage them completely for the owners. We pay off the loans, we handle the administration, we manage the entire running of the estate. In about two years usually, sometimes three, the estate transforms completely. The first year, we invest in shade regulation, pruning and the development of adequate irrigation facilities. We replant, if necessary. Then we desilt the tanks and increase the production capacity,' Daisy explained.

Alka nodded, her brain quickly absorbing all the information. 'What do you get in return?' she asked.

'Until the estate begins to make profit, we get a fixed remuneration. Once the estate has been restored back to health and it starts making money, we switch to a profit-sharing mode. The turnaround usually takes two to three years. Once we take over, we do everything needed. You'll have to give us the autonomy to do so, of course. We open a joint bank account, and all the transactions are transparent. You can carry out checks at any time. We maintain detailed monthly accounts. We deduct the fixed remuneration amount and the estate's expenses, and then the rest is transferred to the owner,' Chinappa answered.

'Hmm, interesting. What will the percentage of profit sharing be?' Alka asked. She was furiously calculating the numbers in her head.

'See, it varies from estate to estate. But we cap it at thirty per cent. That is thirty per cent for us, and seventy for you. In the first year itself, you will see a massive change. We need at least a five-year agreement so that we can completely turn things around,' Daisy replied.

'But what if I want to exit the contract in between?'

'Then there's an exit sum to be paid, and this is applicable to both sides. We sign a memorandum of understanding after doing an estate inspection.'

'What if there are losses?'

'My dear girl, we only take over loss-making estates. So, there's no question of the estate incurring further losses. Once we take over, we shoulder all the responsibilities. You don't have to do anything. We've now revived over twenty-five coffee estates, including your friend Gowri's. When we took over her estate, the yield was hardly two hundred bags of coffee beans. Now it's over a thousand bags. Our aim is to make the estate self-supporting, profitable and sustainable. So far, we have never failed in any of the projects that we have taken over. Our first priority will be to clear the bank loans. Many owners hastily sell off a portion of the estate because they get caught in the debt trap. But we prevent that, and we get all the documents back from the bank. We also focus on the pepper crop, in addition to coffee, because it is a high-paying crop. Everything said and done though, the owner has to be agreeable to all our terms and be a team player, else it will hinder our work,' Chinappa informed her.

'I understand fully now. Let me think this through. I will get back to you soon,' Alka said.

'Yes, please think it through carefully and let us know your decision in a week. We take up only a limited number of projects and our decision is based on many factors, including the circumstances that lead estate owners to us. All of us feel terrible about Subbu, and we want to help. But it is ultimately your call.'

Alka thanked them and expressed her appreciation for their support. As lunch continued, the conversation drifted towards other topics, with all of them sharing bits of gossip and anecdotes, and generally catching up on what was happening in their lives. Alka thought about how fortunate they were to be part of this group where each person genuinely loved and enjoyed the other's company.

On the way back to her own estate, Alka thought about everything the members of the CoRe team had told her. It would be a relief if she could hand over the day-to-day management of the estate to them. That would leave her with ample time to focus on the homestay. The CoRe team seemed fairly certain that they would be able to turn things around. When it came to coffee production, each of them knew ten times more than what she did. But despite knowing that their combined knowledge and experience was formidable, Alka hesitated before taking such a big decision. She would have to consult with Krish on this one. While she understood that handing over the estate to the CoRe team would be the right thing to do, she also realized that Subbu had had this choice too, and yet he had not taken it.

The next morning, Muthu informed Alka that he had a surprise for her. He drove her to Silver Brooks and when they arrived, Alka stood gaping at the transformation. The cottage looked remarkably different from when she had first seen it. Every wooden beam had been polished, the cracks were sealed, the broken windowpanes replaced and the entire cottage had a fresh coat of paint. It looked warm and welcoming. With the right linen and upholstery, and a few additions here and there, Alka could imagine just how pretty and picturesque it would look.

'Madam, even the fireplace is functional now. The chimney has been cleaned as well,' Muthu said. 'The guests can light a fire if they wish. We will have to provide the firewood and also give them safety instructions.'

The transformation exceeded Alka's expectations and she was ecstatic.

'This is beyond fantastic, Muthu! Such a well-done job!' she exclaimed.

Muthu revelled in her praise. He had overseen every detail and worked closely with the local architect.

'Madam, it is not fully ready yet. All the electrical wiring has been done but the fixtures are pending. You'll have to choose the fittings,' Muthu said.

'We'll have to try and get very similar fixtures then. If we get modern ones, they will take away from the charm of this place,' Alka said.

'I already spoke to a person in Hassan who specializes in replicas of antique fittings. He's coming to give us a quote for all of it.'

'That is a good find, Muthu.'

'Madam, we also have to clear all the payments that are due to the renovation architect.'

'Yes, I'll write out the cheques.'

Once she was home, Alka began having her doubts about the economic viability of the project. Even though she had sounded gung-ho earlier, she was not feeling entirely confident. On paper, the numbers and projections she had made looked great. But the reality she faced worried her. She had withdrawn almost all the money that she had saved over the years in order to fund the renovation of the cottages. She hoped she was doing the right thing. It was imperative now to get people to visit the estate and book the homestays. If that did not happen, she would have no money left at all. The thought of being poor reminded her of the time when she had been at the mercy of Mrs Shetty. It made her shudder. If the venture failed, she would have repaired and refurbished all the cottages for nothing. She couldn't afford for it to fail—they would go bankrupt.

She desperately hoped the CoRe team would deliver on what they had promised.

Once Alka had cleared all the bills, her bank balance was less than sixteen thousand rupees. She broke into a cold sweat. At this rate, she wouldn't even have any money to pay her children's school fees.

She knew she could always ask Krish for money, but the very thought of it went against every fibre in her body. She did not want charity. She had to make this work. She spent the whole night thinking about it, and it was only in the wee hours of the morning that she was able to finally fall asleep.

21

YELLAVARIGE NAMASKARA

2006-2007

At 4 a.m. the next morning, Alka sat up with a start; she thought she'd heard a noise. Her room was cloaked in darkness with only the faint glow from the moonlight casting feeble shadows on the walls. Her dishevelled hair clung to her forehead as beads of sweat formed on it. The air hung heavy inside the room with the silence of the sleeping world broken only by the occasional rustling of leaves outside her window. She had barely managed to fall asleep again when she was jolted awake. For a few seconds, she wondered if her disoriented mind was playing tricks on her. Perhaps a branch from a tree had snapped off and fallen down. She shut her eyes again. But when loud, incessant knocks reverberated through the stillness, Alka knew this was no nightmare. Someone was at the door. Her heart raced and adrenaline coursed through her veins, snapping her to full alertness.

In the dim room, she fumbled for a moment, groping for her slippers on the floor. When she found them, she put them on hurriedly and with a deep breath, Alka rushed down the stairs. She was not afraid of intruders as the estate was very secluded. She wondered if Selvi was in some kind of an emergency. When she opened the door, it took her a few seconds to make out the outline of Muthu.

'Madam, very sorry. It's an emergency,' Muthu said. 'The workers are at the line houses. They're threatening to burn them down. They have fire torches. You'll have to hurry, madam. I have left the supervisor Sabanna to handle them, but I don't know how long he can hold them off.'

'Oh my God, Muthu! Give me a second to get dressed,' Alka said. She was wearing only a thin nightgown. She rushed to the bedroom downstairs and slipped on one of Subbu's thick jackets hanging in the closet. She washed her face hurriedly and pulled her hair into a bun.

'Let's go,' she said, and they ran towards the waiting jeep.

'What happened?' she asked as Muthu started driving.

'Madam, Mallama's daughter's body has been found. It's in a decomposed state. The workers are saying that it's two of the migrant labourers who raped and then strangled her. The hate narrative has spread all over. They want the migrant labourers out of the estate. They are furious, madam.'

'Oh good Lord, let's hurry Muthu.'

Muthu drove at breakneck speed and Alka held on for dear life, fearing what lay ahead and how she would handle it.

As they pulled up outside the row of line houses, Alka saw a sea of angry faces all around. A palpable tension crawled through the air. Alka did a quick headcount and noted that around twenty people had gathered. It wasn't as massive a crowd as she had imagined.

'What is happening here? Why are you all here?' Muthu raised his voice and walked towards the group.

A young man, seething with anger, stepped forward. 'They have brought nothing but trouble. First, they beat me up, saying I had eloped with Chandrika. Now she has been found dead. They killed her,' he screamed, his eyes burning with a mix of sorrow, resentment and hate.

'Oye! Keep quiet. How do you know it was them?' Muthu yelled back.

This made the group angrier. Emotions were already frayed, and Muthu's words had only added fuel to the fire.

'Send them back. We won't work with them anymore,' an elderly man said.

Muthu was about to speak when Alka raised her hand and stopped him.

'Okay, okay. You all have valid points. What is your name?' she asked the elderly man.

'Dayanna,' he answered.

'Are you Mallama's brother?'

The man nodded. He seemed surprised that Alka knew who he was.

'I am really, really sorry that this has happened. It is very unfortunate,' Alka said.

'Unfortunate? It is terrible. Even animals will not do something like this. They don't deserve any mercy. Burn their houses down,' a voice cut through the crowd like a sharpened blade.

'Yes, burn them down! Burn them down! We won't tolerate this! They are coming over to our land and committing crimes against our women!' The words echoed like a war drum as the group surged forward.

'Okay, okay. Their houses deserve to be burned down, but to do that you will have to go to Assam and Bihar.'

Alka's words silenced the angry men for a few seconds. She took advantage of the silence and pressed ahead. 'Burning down these cottages won't solve anything. The loss will only be ours. Our estate will suffer. Will you burn down your house if you find a rat inside?' Alka asked. Her heart was pounding and her hands were clammy with sweat.

'Rats! That's what they are. They deserve nothing but to be drowned in the Cauvery,' one of the men thundered.

'This is a heinous crime and the criminals must be punished! We need to feel safe in our own land,' Alka agreed with them. That mollified them a little and they nodded in agreement.

'But we should not punish the innocent. We can't just decide that an entire community is bad. Do you have any proof that it was they who did it?' Alka asked.

'Mahalingappa saw Chandrika talking to them, many times,' Dayanna said.

'When was this?' Alka asked.

'It has been going on for a while, madam. The workers talk. They all know.'

'Then why was Shiva here beaten up? You are Shiva, right?' Alka asked the young man.

'Yes, madam,' Shiva said. 'I told them I had nothing to do with it. But they wouldn't listen.'

'Did the migrant workers beat you up?' Alka asked.

'No, madam. It was the local men, Mallama's men. Apparently, when her mother questioned her after hearing the rumours, Chandrika told her that she had been talking to me. Hence the misunderstanding.'

'See, our own people have created trouble. And how quickly you all blamed the migrant workers. How is this fair?' Alka asked.

The crowd had no answer.

'We have to catch the culprits who did this. We cannot let them get away. Muthu will be going to the police station to personally track the progress of this case. Rest assured, we will catch the culprits. But I request you all to not indulge in criminal acts like burning down these houses. You cannot solve one crime by committing another,' Alka said.

'You have given our houses to them. We don't have a place to stay. You've been unfair,' one of the men yelled.

'There are rumours that Subbu sir is dying and that you are going to sell the estate to some hotel. That's why you are renovating the cottages,' another man called out, emboldened by what the man before him had said.

Alka drew in a sharp breath when she heard that.

'Subbu sir is unwell, yes. But please be assured that the estate is not going to be sold. You all have a right to know what is happening. And I shall address all your concerns. But not like this. I would like to speak to *all* of you. Not just a few. I shall have answers for you this evening at 5 p.m. You have my word on this. Now, please return to your homes and cooperate with the police. They will be making enquiries and you should give them all the information you have so that the criminals can be caught,' Alka said.

Somewhat placated by Alka's words, the men reluctantly began to disperse, their disgruntled murmurs fading into the stillness of the early morning.

After the last of them retreated, Alka let out a breath she hadn't realized she was holding. Her hands trembled.

'Madam, are you okay?' Muthu asked.

Alka nodded in response, although her eyes betrayed her true emotions.

'Let's go back home, Muthu,' Alka said wearily.

'Madam, you handled it very well,' Muthu complimented her as they drove back home.

Alka felt relieved to be within the familiar confines of the vehicle. The interaction with the workers had shaken her. She knew she had diffused the situation, but she still needed to address the labourers. The discontent that had spread could flare up anytime. As Muthu manoeuvred the jeep through the estate's winding roads, Alka stared out of the window, her thoughts racing. Dawn had painted the skies in soft oranges and yellows, a stark contrast to the ugly confrontation that had just unfolded.

When they reached home, Alka knew what to do. She decided not to go on the estate rounds that morning and instructed Muthu to do it by himself. Once he finished, he was to go to the police station, find out all the details about the case, and then report back to her. She had a plan in mind and she needed his help to execute it.

When Nisha and Tulika woke up, oblivious to what Alka had just been through, they chattered away about their school activities.

'Mummy, will you be able to come with me for the competition in Delhi?' Tulika asked.

'How about I send you with Gowri aunty? Do you think you can travel with her?'

'No, Mummy! I want you to come.'

'I will have to be here at the estate, baby. We are doing a lot of work and I cannot leave now,' Alka sighed.

Tulika pulled a long face.

'Can't you see that Appa isn't here? Mummy is now the boss of everybody working here. She is no longer just your mummy. If you are a big girl like you always claim, you should be willing to go without Mummy, no?' Nisha admonished her sister.

'See, we still have some time before the competition. Let's see what happens, okay?' Alka consoled Tulika.

Alka sat in her study after the girls left for school. She thought about the workers being angry over losing their homes. Alka, having craved for a place to call home all her life, knew how deeply hurt they must have been when they were asked to evict the line houses. Their resentment was towards those who were living there now, the migrant labourers. She knew she had to address their insecurities. She thought long and hard about what she could do to alleviate the concerns and solve the problem. Then she took out a piece of paper and began writing.

When Muthu arrived, he informed Alka that the police had already started questioning people and were making good progress.

Alka then asked him to send word out to all the local workers to assemble at the yard in the evening. 'I have a lot of things to tell them, Muthu, but I need your help,' she said, and handed him the paper on which she had written a speech. When he finished reading it, Muthu was full of admiration.

'Madam, you should enter politics. This is great!' he beamed.

'Now help me translate this to Kannada.'

Muthu and Alka spent the next hour translating the speech. Muthu wasn't too sure of some words, so Selvi was called in to help. She was amused and astonished on being asked for assistance. She came up with words which Muthu contested, saying they meant something else.

'Both of you better be sure! I am trusting you to translate this properly,' Alka warned. She had grown up hearing Mrs Shetty speak Kannada, and had picked up the language after she moved to Bangalore. But it was not something that came naturally to her.

Muthu and Selvi, after a few playful arguments, settled on the appropriate words, which Alka promptly wrote down using the Devnagari script.

'Muthu, when the labourers gather, see that they are served tea and biscuits. Selvi, please go to the yard ahead of time and ensure that the tea is made. Take some of our bigger saucepans with you. Muthu, you'll have to go into town and buy paper cups, milk, sugar, tea leaves and biscuits,' Alka instructed.

'But Selvi, be back before the girls come from school,' Alka added.

Once Selvi and Muthu left, Alka memorized what she had written. She rehearsed it over and over again while looking into the mirror. In school, she had always been a good student and on a couple of occasions, she had also won some elocution competitions. So she knew how and when to stress on certain words and lower her pitch for others.

When Selvi got back from the yard, she reported that all the arrangements had been made as per Alka's instructions. 'We got everything, Akka. There was a person making vadas in town. So Muthu sir also placed an order for vadas. He said there was no need to check with you and that you would approve.'

'Vadas are indeed a nice touch,' Alka agreed.

When Nisha and Tulika got back from school, Alka sat with them as they did their schoolwork. While she was with them, she forgot about all the troubles plaguing her and genuinely enjoyed their company—laughing with them, going through their schoolwork and listening to everything they had to say. She was determined to give them a childhood that she herself had been denied.

When it was time for her to go and address the labour, she sent the girls out to play and asked Selvi to keep an eye on them. Then, she got dressed in a very simple handloom saree and drove to the yard.

As Alka's vehicle rolled to a stop, a low undercurrent of whispers rippled through the crowd. All the labourers and their families had assembled in the yard. Alka spotted Muthu overseeing the distribution of the tea and snacks. Never before in the history of the estate had the labourers assembled like this.

Rumours flew thick and fast. Some said that they would all be homeless soon because Alka was selling the estate since she wouldn't be able to manage it without Subbu. Others whispered that this was going to be the last meal they would have at the estate because they would be asked to leave. Although they were all being served tea and refreshments, the faces of the people reflected concern and worry. Alka noticed that Muthu had assembled a makeshift stage using some old wooden crates. She felt like a politician about to address her people as she assumed her position on the stage.

She waited for a few minutes for the people to quieten down, and then spoke loudly and clearly in Kannada. '*Yellavarige namaskara*,' she began with the customary greeting. This took them all by surprise. Since they all knew that she was from Delhi, they had not expected Alka to speak in Kannada. Her words created an instant bond with them, breaking the language barrier and solidifying her connection to the soil.

Alka was nervous. But she hid it well. She had rehearsed the speech many times and she knew her memory was good.

'Ladies and gentlemen, and children of Anandi estate,' Alka spoke flawlessly and without hesitation.

'I stand before you today not merely as an estate owner but as a custodian of dreams, a guardian of our shared destinies.'

The people present looked at each other, astonished by the terms she was using and her command over the language.

'We deeply mourn the loss of Chandrika, and all our hearts are heavy with sorrow. We shall fully cooperate with the official police investigation and see to it that the culprits are booked. Muthu has been to the police station this morning. The police have assured us that they have a solid lead, and that they are closing in on the culprits. We shall not spare them; Chandrika's death should be avenged.'

A murmur of approval went through the crowd. Encouraged, Alka continued.

'As I gaze upon this gathering, I see the faces of very hardworking people, faces weathered by sunshine and the hours of toil that continue through the storms, through the rain, through spring and summer. You all have become an inseparable part of this land. There are rumours going around that Anandi estate will be shut down and that I will sell it. I want to assure you that none of these rumours are true. Nobody will lose their jobs or homes. All your jobs are safe.

'To all of you, my fellow comrades, I extend my deepest gratitude for your hard work, and I promise that I shall never sell the estate to an outsider. Never.'

The people broke into an applause now.

'Subbu, my beloved husband, is fighting for his life in the hospital. I need each one of you to pray for us in these difficult times. He needs your strength. Will you pray for his speedy recovery?' Alka asked. Her voice was now a plea and she was finding it hard to go on.

'Yes! Yes!'

'Anjaneya will protect him.'

'Sir will come back soon. Everything will be okay.' Different voices from the crowd spoke up one after the other.

Alka felt reassured.

'I have something more to share. Our estate has been steadily making losses for the past many years. In times of difficulties, we have to take some tough decisions. The migrant labour will soon go back to their hometowns. This means that the line houses will become empty again. But I cannot allow any rent-free accommodation on the estate.'

Alka could see the anger and disapproval on the faces of those in front of her.

'But I have a solution for you,' she said. 'I present to you, a new venture: Anandi Homestays. This will be a new chapter, a new beginning for us. We will welcome guests and give them an estate experience. I have done the calculations, and the numbers are very lucrative. We will need cooks, cleaners, housekeeping and garden staff for this new venture. I will hire experts from the industry who will train you in all aspects of hospitality. I will not be able to pay you salaries till this project starts generating money. But once it does, I promise you an excellent pay.

'Today, I extend an invitation to each one of you. An invitation to join hands, to become architects of change. If you would like a job in this new venture, please sign up at the office. You will be given accommodation in the line houses. But if you aren't working for the estate or the hospitality venture, I am afraid there's no place for you on our estate. There are other coffee estates that need additional labour, and you are welcome to migrate to those if you don't want to stay here.'

Alka looked at the crowd as it stirred a little restlessly. She could sense not just an excitement and a willingness to join her new venture, but also uncertainty and fear. In the faces of the women present, Alka had seen her mother. These were women who hoped for nothing more than a better future for their children. They reminded Alka of her childhood. All her life, she had hidden her past, her poverty, and the fact that her mother had worked as a domestic help. But today, looking at the anxious faces in front of her, Alka felt that she had to show them she understood their hardships, that she was one of them. She was on their side. But this was that part of the speech which she hadn't rehearsed.

She took a deep breath and then said, 'I have one last thing to tell you all. And this is my story. I grew up in a one-room house in Delhi. My "house" was just a room, smaller than any of your houses here on the estate. My mother worked as a domestic help in a big house. We cleaned vessels, we cooked, we slaved for them the whole day. In exchange, we were given a measly salary and a tiny room to live in. So believe me when I say I know what it feels like. My mother and I were taken advantage of. I do not want that for any of you.'

Alka was speaking from her heart. She was speaking from the years of desperation she had suffered. She was speaking from a place of deep empathy and understanding.

'Once we turn profitable, I will be raising your salaries. If we make more profits, you will earn more. But if we run into losses, let me reassure you that I will be absorbing those losses myself, like we have been doing with the estate. The last few years have been very hard for us. We have been incurring big losses. But we have not let that affect your earnings at all.

'I do not just want your labour. I want your partnership and your belief that our estate will succeed. I have taken the help of the CoRe group and they assure me that the estate will become profitable in three years.

'With the hospitality venture and the estate both making profits, your wages will go up. This is a solemn promise I make. Our destinies are intertwined, so let us script a tale of triumph together.'

The faces of everyone assembled broke into wide smiles. It was almost as if they couldn't believe what Alka was promising. No one had treated them this way. No one had spoken to them like they understood their problems. They saw Alka differently now.

Applause rang through the yard. The excitement and hope in the air was now palpable. It was clear that Alka had won the people over. Already, a long line of people wanting to sign up for employment at the homestay venture was forming. It made Alka happy.

'Madam, that was outstanding. I've never heard anything like this in my life. I … I did not know about your background, madam. Your story is deeply moving,' Muthu told Alka on their way home.

'We cannot let them down, Muthu. They are our people, and we have to take care of them.'

Later that night, Alka sat alone in the living room with a glass of wine. She had given an excellent speech and won the labour over. Now come what may, she had to make the venture successful. She couldn't disappoint these people when they were willing to work for no money and also place their complete trust in her. But she didn't know how she would accomplish this and whether she would succeed at all.

22
EYE OPENER

2006-2007

The next morning, when Alka got back from her estate rounds, Selvi told her that Krish had called and said that it was urgent. Alka rushed to the phone and called him back, fearing the worst.

'Hey, Krish, is everything okay?' she asked.

'Yes, Alka, there has been some new development. Chanda has been visiting Anna every single day, as you know. She speaks to him a lot when she's here. This morning, she was sitting with him and talking to him. Her son was also with her, and when he squeezed Anna's hand, they detected a movement in his legs. He responded to his son's voice and touch! This is good news, Alka. I rushed to the hospital as soon as Chanda called me,' Krish said, his voice carrying a sense of urgency and excitement.

'Oh my God, Krish, this is fantastic! I just can't believe it. What are the doctors saying?'

'They are very optimistic. They see this as a major development. But Anna hasn't opened his eyes yet.'

'Oh, I see. Nevertheless, this is indeed a major piece of news. I'll come there today itself. I can start out once the girls come back from school. Tomorrow is Saturday, so we do not have to rush back too.'

'And it goes without saying that all of you can stay with me. But, Alka, do you think it's a good idea for them to visit him? He still has all those tubes and machines attached to his body. They were very upset when they saw him the last time.'

'True. I'll ask them if they want to come along, and if they do, I will bring them,' Alka said. 'I have to update you about the developments here in the estate. I also want to discuss what the CoRe team has offered. There's so much that has happened here in the estate over the last few days.'

'I can't wait to hear it all. See you this evening, then,' Krish said.

Alka eased into Subbu's favourite chair in the verandah. She called out to Selvi to fetch her a cup of coffee and then sat back thinking about all that had happened over the last couple of days. What a roller coaster it had been. She had never pictured herself running the estate, talking to the labourers and managing every single detail. She had been terrified when confronted with the angry mob, but she had discovered a courage she had not known she possessed.

In the midst of all the chaos, Alka had also had a profound realization: that this unexpected turn of events had, in fact, revealed her life's purpose. She was *meant* to take care of the hardworking labourers and the estate. It felt like a reawakening. With the CoRe team promising that they could help bring the estate back to its feet, and the labour saying they were happy to work at her new venture, she felt a sense of excitement. But the very next moment, it was replaced with a great nervousness. It was like walking a tightrope. One wrong move could make you plummet, but tiny, careful steps fuelled by adrenaline could keep you going. She couldn't afford to fall. Too many people depended on her now.

She wondered what Subbu would say when he got back. While the news of him responding to touch filled her with joy, a part of her was also filled with jealousy. Subbu had responded to Chanda's son's touch and not to her own daughters'. While the boy was Subbu's son too, it was easier for Alka to think of him as 'Chanda's son'. She did not even know the child's name. She still couldn't digest the fact that Subbu had a son with another woman.

She thought about how shocked Subbu must have been to learn of his son's existence. Alka recalled a week-long trip that Subbu had made to Bangalore when Nisha was three. When Alka had asked him about the reason behind his extended absence, Subbu had been vague in his reply, citing meetings with potential business associates as the cause. She remembered how he had returned with a subdued demeanour. It dawned on Alka that it was probably during this time that Chanda must have disclosed the secret.

Even contemplating the term 'his son' felt like a visceral blow, but Alka resigned herself to the reality she now faced. She would have to endure it.

She thought about how she could proceed with the homestay venture. She decided to call Gowri and discuss it with her. But, as it turned out, Gowri was on a trek.

'Alka! I am in the Himalayas! Is everything all right? The network signal is pretty weak here, but I can call you from base camp,' she yelled over the whooshing sound of the wind.

'Gowri, just enjoy your trek. No need to call me back. I only wanted to have a casual chat,' Alka improvised. She did not want Gowri to rush down to the base camp to discuss the homestay venture.

After hanging up, Alka remembered that Manasi had told her to reach out if she needed anything. She could discuss things with her.

Manasi answered the phone almost immediately.

'Hey, Alka. What's up?' she asked.

'Is this a good time to speak? Are you busy?'

'No! In fact, today is one of those days when I am completely free. I was idly flipping through my movie collection and trying to decide what to watch. Rajat has taken Sanal out. That is a first! He has never been anywhere without me, except of course while he's at school. And him trusting Rajat enough to go out with him—I can't tell you what a big achievement it is! But that's enough about me. You tell me, what's up?'

The easy manner in which Manasi spoke, her joie de vivre and, most importantly, the warmth and the love in her voice were like a comforting hug. Overwhelmed by emotions, Alka couldn't speak for a few seconds.

'Hello? You there?' Manasi asked.

'Yes, my friend. I'm just thinking that I hit the jackpot when I found you as a friend. Remember when we both first met during our MBA course, how you were lugging your suitcase up the stairs?'

'Haha! Yes, I do remember that. But I don't know why you think you hit the jackpot. I didn't even stay in touch with you for many years,' Manasi admitted with a self-deprecating laugh.

'You were not in a mental space to do so, Manasi. You've been through a lot,' Alka said gently.

'I know. Life hasn't exactly been a cakewalk for either of us,' Manasi said.

Alka found herself opening up to Manasi about everything—how there was trouble at the estate, how she had given a speech, how she wanted to make the homestay succeed and, finally, how she had learned about Subbu's secret son.

'Wow, woman! This is a lot to handle. How are you even managing?' Manasi exclaimed.

'Why do you think I am calling you? Help! I am drowning.'

'No way will you drown when I am around. I'm your lifeboat!'

Both of them giggled, feeling like they were back in college—they had always been there for each other.

'First things first, do you want to get a divorce from Subbu?' Manasi asked.

'The man is still in the hospital, Manasi. What kind of a heartless bitch would I be to abandon him in this condition?'

'The best kind. He has his Chanda and his son. Walk out,' Manasi said.

'We have time to decide on that. Let it be for now. Tell me, how I can make the homestay succeed. Honestly, more than my marriage or what Subbu did, making this new venture succeed is my priority. There are so many people who have signed up for jobs there already; I cannot let them down.'

'Hmm. We're putting our MBA degrees to good use at last. Let's brainstorm over the next few weeks and come up with a solid business plan.'

'Yes, we need one. I need to spread the word about the homestay once my staff is trained. The cottages are looking incredible, Manasi. You should come and stay. Bring Rajat and Sanal too.'

'I don't know if Sanal is ready for such a big trip yet. We are taking small steps. Once he becomes comfortable with Rajat, I can leave him and visit too.'

'That would be fabulous. Can't wait to see you here,' Alka said.

'All in good time, my friend. But coming back to your homestay venture, we need all the publicity we can get, Alka.'

'What do you think about getting travel magazines to write about us?'

'That's a good idea. I'll reach out to my contacts and see if I can get any leads. You could even invite travel bloggers. Blogging is a big thing now.'

'All good suggestions, Manasi. If enough people come to stay, I can recover my costs.'

'They will come once they get to know about your charming homestay. If they like the food and the hospitality, they will tell their families and friends about it, and before you know it, you will have a waiting list of people wanting to book a stay. I could do the publicity for you. Most Mumbaikars crave experiences like an authentic estate stay. Warn them about the leeches though,' Manasi laughed.

'Oh my God! Do you remember how they clung to my leg?'

'How can I forget? Both the brothers rushed to take care of you,' Manasi said.

'And you asked if the leeches would "spread",' Alka laughed. She was surprised at how there was not the slightest hint of resentment in Manasi's voice when she spoke about Krish.

'Most people sound bitter when a marriage ends. But you sound so much at peace,' Alka remarked.

'I think we're all at peace when we finally unite with our soulmates. Rajat is a darling, and I feel fortunate to have found him. I never thought anyone could bond with Sanal. But Rajat has, and he treats me like I am precious. We all deserve that kind of love, Alka. Most of us settle for the security that marriages offer. But it is only when we seek the things that make our souls happy that we lead authentic lives.'

Manasi's words left Alka with a lump in her throat.

When the girls got back from school, Alka asked them if they would like to visit their father at the hospital.

Tulika was very clear that she did not want to.

'Appa can't hear us or see us. He won't know that I have come,' she reasoned.

'It is not to make him see us that we should go with Mummy. We should go because we love him,' Nisha replied, sounding like a sixty-year-old.

'You don't always have to show your love. It is okay to keep it inside you,' Tulika retorted.

Alka listened keenly to the conversation her daughters were having. She wondered if children had a certain inherent wisdom which surfaced when they were subjected to traumatic experiences.

Alka asked Nisha, 'Are you sure you want to come? Aren't you tired after a full day of school?'

'No, Mummy. I want to see Appa,' Nisha said.

'All right, get ready then. And tell Selvi to help you pack for a day. We will stay in Chikkappa's house and return tomorrow.'

When Tulika heard that they would be staying at Krish's place, she was tempted to join them. But then she thought about her father lying on the hospital bed and the smell in his room which she hated. She couldn't bear the thought of seeing him with all the tubes sticking out of his body. She wanted him to be okay and moving around, like he used to. So, she decided to stay back.

Alka was brushing her hair when the phone rang. It was Krish.

'Have you left yet?' he asked.

'No. We'll leave in the next twenty minutes. It'll be me and Nisha. Tulika isn't coming. Why do you ask?'

'There has been some further development, Alka. Anna has opened his eyes.'

'Krish! That is wonderful news! Our prayers are being heard!' Alka almost shrieked.

'Indeed. But just to prepare you, he's not responding to things yet and he isn't focusing on anything either. So don't expect more right now.'

'All right. But it's still exciting! It's still progress!'

'It is huge progress. The doctors are delighted. Chanda hasn't left his side since the time they first detected movement in his feet. And he opened his eyes while she was speaking to him. Chanda is convinced that he can hear her. But Alka, at this point, I don't think it's right on my part to tell her to leave just because you don't want to see her. I wanted to warn you about this before you started from the estate. She will be here when you arrive.'

'I see,' Alka said. 'Have you told her that I didn't want to see her? And that I told you to regulate my visits so I wouldn't run into her?'

'Of course not. Why will I do that?'

'Then what have you been telling her so far? How did you manage to keep our visits separate?'

'She's an extremely understanding person, Alka. She herself asked me to let her know about the days you would be here so she could stay away. She has been here day and night since Anna was shifted to the room. She goes home only to shower and comes right back. She says she can't leave him alone, and she hasn't let me stay overnight with him, not even once. She said she could manage things at work as she is her own boss whereas I have to report to work. I didn't want to tell you any of this earlier since I felt you might not want to hear about it, but I am telling you now because you asked. I can't tell her to leave, Alka.'

'Yes, of course. I get it, Krish, and it's okay. I'm coming over. It doesn't matter if she is there or not,' Alka said with a false sense of bravado. She was bristling inside—whether it was anger, jealousy, hurt, resentment or relief, she couldn't tell. At this point, her emotions were a jumble. On one hand, she was happy that Subbu seemed to be recovering, but on the other, the last person she wanted to deal with was Chanda.

Nisha slept for most part of the journey to Bangalore and Alka was glad she got to rest. When they pulled up at the hospital, Nisha woke up, fresh as a daisy. Alka had packed sandwiches, which Nisha wolfed down before stepping out of the car.

'Are you ready to meet Appa?' Alka asked.

'Yes, Mummy,' Nisha nodded solemnly.

'His eyes are open, Nisha, but he may not recognize us. We have to be prepared for that. It will take him some more time to get better.'

'Okay,' Nisha replied.

That was it—a calm acceptance of whatever the present situation brought, no questions asked. Alka wished she could be as calm as Nisha. She held Nisha's hand and walked into the hospital, with feelings of dread and anticipation clouding her heart.

When they reached Subbu's room, she gently knocked on the door. A couple of moments later, the door was opened by a boy who looked a little older than Nisha. He was tall for his age. He greeted them with a big smile and said, 'Hello, I'm Gaurav. You must be Nisha, and you must be Alka aunty.'

Nisha smiled back and shook his hand shyly.

Alka, however, couldn't say a word in response. She stood gaping at him, unable to believe her eyes.

The boy was a spitting image of Subbu.

23

CHANDA'S STORY

2006-2007

'Mummy! Where are your manners? Say hello to Gaurav,' Nisha nudged Alka.

Alka's composure wavered as she managed to murmur a hesitant 'Hello, Gaurav.' She had been so busy mentally preparing herself to meet Chanda that she had momentarily forgotten about the child. Upon seeing him now and noticing the unmistakable resemblance between him and Subbu, Alka found herself completely thrown off balance. In that moment, she wished she could simply vanish. Meanwhile, Krish stood by the window, looking awkward and unsure of how to deal with the situation.

In the next second, Alka's eyes fell on the woman seated next to Subbu.

Chanda.

The one she dreaded meeting.

Subbu's secret.

Alka looked at her, hoping she wouldn't get caught staring. Chanda seemed comfortable and at ease in the hospital room. She was much shorter than Alka—just about four eleven. She was dressed in a black saree and maroon blouse, and wore a bindi, a pair of jhumkas and a light pink lipstick. Her thick hair fell in waves around her heart-shaped face and her eyes were large and kohl lined. She looked graceful—like a dancer.

'Hi, Alka, I'm Chanda. It's nice to meet you,' she said as she slid off the stool next to the bed and walked up to her. Smiling genuinely, she then held out her hand towards Alka.

'Hello, Chanda, thank you for being there for Subbu,' Alka said. She had to force each word out of her mouth and do her best to not grit her teeth.

'How could I not? This is horrible for all of us,' Chanda said.

If she was aware of the effect she was having on Alka, she definitely did not show it.

'We'll give you some time alone with Subbu,' Chanda said as she led Gaurav outside.

Krish was about to follow Chanda out of the room but Alka mouthed, 'Stay here, please.'

He nodded.

Alka walked up to Subbu and looked down at him. His eyes were open but unfocused.

'Hello, Subbu. I am here and so is Nisha,' she said.

Nisha stood next to Subbu's bed. She held his hand and said, 'Appa, your eyes are open. Can you see me?' She waved her hand in front of Subbu's eyes but they did not follow her hands at all, nor did he turn his face towards her. He seemed like a wax statue, lying still and silent.

'Appa, I know you can hear me. You are going to get better soon, okay?' Nisha said.

Alka couldn't bring herself to talk to Subbu or even touch him. She stood mutely by the side of his bed, staring at him.

Krish tried to ease the situation a little. 'Anna, look who is here. It's Alka. She's managing the estate all on her own. Don't you want to help her? You have to try harder to get better soon, okay?' he said.

'Subbu, there is a lot going on at the estate,' Alka managed to say finally.

But Subbu lay staring vacantly at the space in front of him.

'I don't know what else to say,' Alka told Krish as she walked out of the room with Nisha in tow. Krish followed her out. Chanda and Gaurav were waiting outside.

'Are you done?' Chanda asked Alka in surprise.

Alka nodded.

'I'll see you later. I need some coffee,' she told Chanda and walked away with Nisha. She couldn't bear to meet Chanda's eyes.

'I'll come along too. It's time for Subbu's cleaning anyway. The nurses will be here soon and they don't allow the patient's attendants to stay inside the room during the cleaning. The whole thing will take at least thirty minutes,' Chanda said and, much to Alka's discomfort and horror, followed her and Krish to the cafeteria. Gaurav seemed to know the way as he half-skated and half-walked across the smooth hospital corridors.

'Want to come with me? I know a shortcut,' he told Nisha. Nisha looked at her mother for permission and when Alka nodded, she smiled and followed Gaurav.

Great. Alka couldn't help her thoughts. *I seem to be the only one having a problem with Chanda. Even my daughter seems to have taken a liking to her son.*

Both Gaurav and Nisha were already seated when Alka, Chanda and Krish entered the cafeteria.

'Shall I place the order?' Gaurav asked enthusiastically. Chanda smiled at him and handed him the menu card.

'Sure, ask everyone what they want,' Chanda told him.

'Let me pay for this please,' Alka said, reaching into her bag for her purse.

'It's already paid for, Alka. The hospital has a cafeteria card system for the attendants and caregivers of long-term patients. Gaurav loves to do this. Simply tell him what you want. He will place our orders and also bring the food for us. Just sit back.'

Alka nodded and sat down. As Gaurav politely asked each one of them what they would have and then walked up to the cafeteria counter to place their orders, she couldn't help thinking how well-mannered and gentlemanly he seemed to be.

'Alka, I would have really liked to meet you under different circumstances,' Chanda said.

'I'm sorry, Chanda, but I wish I could say the same,' Alka replied. The second the words were out of her mouth, she was mortified. Chanda had been nothing but sweet and polite. And here she was, taking out her anger and frustration on her. But her reply did not seem to faze Chanda.

'I know, and I would've felt the same way had the roles been reversed. You see, while Subbu has spoken so much about you and the girls to me, he did not mention me to you at all. I knew about you all along. But my existence itself has come as a shock to you. So I completely understand how you might be feeling right now.'

Alka looked at Chanda with utter disbelief. How could she be so calm and kind? She was right though. She had known about Alka all along, but for Alka, it had indeed come as a shock.

'Alka, I want to talk to you at length. But not in this hospital cafe. I'd like it if you could spare me about an hour or so.'

'Today?'

'Yes, today, if that's possible. It's important. Please,' Chanda looked at Alka, her eyes pleading, begging her to agree. There was something so honest in her expression that it made Alka uncomfortable.

Gaurav returned just then with a plate of idli for Chanda. Nisha had wanted only a milkshake while Alka and Krish had both ordered khara bath. Krish got up to help him carry the rest of the food to the table.

'I'll do it, Krish uncle. I'll get them one by one,' Gaurav said.

'You do it every day. Let me help you this one time. There are more people today,' Krish replied as he walked to the counter to collect the food. They were both clearly comfortable with each other. Alka could see how well Krish bonded with Gaurav. *After all, they share the same genes*, Alka thought, bitterness creeping in again.

'I know you probably hate me, but I really do want to speak to you, if you are willing to listen,' Chanda told Alka.

'Fine,' Alka conceded with a sigh. 'Go ahead and tell me whatever it is that you need to say. I'm all ears,' she added, cringing inwardly at the unfriendliness in her tone. Her resentment, though unintentional, was difficult to conceal.

'Let's go to my place then. It's close by, and we can talk more comfortably there. We can take the children along. Gaurav is very good with younger kids; he can look after Nisha while we talk. And thank you for agreeing to come to my place. I can't tell you how much this means to me,' Chanda said.

Alka could only nod, hoping that her face did not reflect her squeamishness.

Krish and Gaurav came back with the piping hot food, and they all dug in, the chatter of both the children making up for any awkwardness the adults were feeling.

'That was delicious,' Alka said. She hadn't realized how hungry she was.

'Krish, will you be with Subbu for a couple of hours? I am taking Alka and Nisha home,' Chanda asked.

'Of course. I can be with him the whole day today. I've taken the day off from work. Please, take your time.'

Chanda owned a Hyundai Santro. Gaurav and Nisha climbed into the backseat while Alka got into the passenger seat. Chanda then drove them to her home.

'It's a good thing it's barely a five-minute drive away,' she said.

Alka found herself smiling as she listened to both the children chattering away nineteen to the dozen. Gaurav was telling Nisha about the different types of Pokemon cards that he had collected and Nisha sat wide-eyed, absorbing everything he said.

Chanda's apartment was situated in a lane adorned with towering pink trumpet trees that created lush canopies on either side. The residential complex she lived in boasted of a charming children's park with an array of vibrant climbing structures, swings, slides, tunnels and bridges. The park floor was covered with thick rubber mats, and a covered area housed a ball pool. The delightful park immediately captured Nisha's attention, prompting her to sprint towards it the minute the car stopped, all before Alka could even utter a single word.

Gaurav ran after her.

'I'll look after her, Alka aunty. Don't worry about her,' he said

'Thank you, Gaurav,' Alka said. It was hard not to like this well-mannered teen.

'Gaurav, will you bring her home when she is done playing?' Chanda called out to him.

'Yes, Ma, don't worry. I will take care of her.'

'Has he always been like this? He is so well brought up,' Alka remarked as they walked towards the elevators.

'Thank you. He's been through a lot, but I've tried hard to instil good manners and kindness in him,' Chanda said. They got into the elevator and she pressed the button for the ninth floor. When they reached her apartment, instead of reaching for her keys, Chanda rang the bell. The door was opened by a young girl, dressed in a salwar kameez. She seemed to be in her early twenties.

'Hello, madam,' she smiled cheerfully.

'Hello, Kusuma. Alka, meet Kusuma. She lives with me and helps me so much,' Chanda said.

'Hello,' Alka greeted the girl as she entered the apartment.

She noticed immediately how bright and spacious it was. The living room was adorned with Indian artefacts, intricately carved wooden pillars, tasteful décor pieces and brass lamps. Suspended from the ceiling was a large six-foot wooden swing, complete with a comfortable mattress and an array of vibrant cushions. Opening up from the living room was a spacious balcony that offered a breathtaking view of a picturesque lake. Outside, the bright blue sky played host to lazy white clouds, and the shimmering water in the lake reflected the warmth of the sun. A flock of white cranes gracefully soared overhead. The balcony itself was a lush oasis, filled with various plants. Placed opposite each other were a pair of cozy woven cane chairs with deep cushions. Under them was a beautiful bohemian rug.

'This is a beautiful place,' Alka couldn't help saying.

'Thanks, it's my shelter, my refuge, and it has taken me years to shape it exactly the way I want. What will you have to drink?' Chanda asked as she walked towards the cane chairs.

'Nothing.' Alka followed her.

'But you did not have anything to drink at the hospital either. How about some filter coffee?'

'It's fine, really. You can just tell me whatever you wanted to say,' Alka said as she continued to stand.

'I know this must be uncomfortable for you. But it will take a while, Alka. Could I please request you to sit down?'

Alka did not know how to refuse such a polite request, and so she sat down.

'Coffee then?' Chanda insisted.

'All right,' Alka agreed.

'Kusuma, two coffees please,' Chanda called out as she sat opposite Alka.

Alka was surprised at how *normal* all of this seemed on the outside. They probably looked like two friends meeting up over coffee. Nobody would have guessed the real relationship between them, she thought.

'Alka, even though I am repeating myself, I want to tell you how much this means to me. I never thought our children would even meet. After all, they're half-siblings.'

Alka nodded. Up until now, she had been thinking of Gaurav as 'Chanda's son', but she could see now just how much of Subbu and Krish was there in him.

'I am glad they are getting along well, too. Er, does he know?'

'Sorry, who are you referring to?'

'Gaurav.'

'Know what?'

'That Subbu is his father.'

'You know, I've debated whether to tell him or not. It's something I struggle with every single day. I haven't told him yet. I feel it is too big a burden to place on a child. In the eyes of society, he'll be an illegitimate child.'

When Alka heard that and thought about Gaurav, she realized how cruel society was to label an innocent child.

'He just knows Subbu as Subbu uncle. He thinks my ex-husband is his father. But he doesn't ask about him much,' Chanda explained.

Alka was silent, thinking about how hard it must be for Chanda to hide such a big truth from her son.

Kusuma arrived with their filter coffees then. She had also brought a plate of banana chips.

'Oh, but we just ate!' Alka protested.

'Try these. They are not your usual banana chips. They've been made specially by Kusuma's mother who gets the plantains from her village.'

Alka bit into one, and the crispy, crunchy flavours exploded in her mouth.

'This is good!' she exclaimed.

'It is, isn't it? For me, filter coffee is never complete without these.'

Alka found herself relaxing and unwinding in Chanda's presence. She had a calming quality about her.

The two women sat on the balcony, enjoying the coffee and snacks.

They were halfway through their coffee when Chanda looked at Alka and said, 'Alka, I want to tell you my story. Between me and Subbu, it's not at all what you think. It's not like we're having a torrid, illicit affair. I know that people might see it that way. I was young and naïve, and I paid the price for it. Let me explain.'

Alka nodded, sipping her coffee.

'I have to tell you the whole story, and it's a total Bollywood drama. Except that it actually happened to us. As you know, I grew up in Sakleshpur. It is a small town, and everyone knows each other. I had met Subbu at various social functions, and over a period of time, we both fell crazily in love. Everyone commented that we were made for each other, and they assumed that we would get married. But then my father got wind of it. When he asked me, I admitted that it was all true. He then made some enquiries and found that Subbu hadn't graduated. I, on the other hand, was doing my post-graduation in Travel and Tourism. For my father, education was very important. My older sister who is in Australia now, had done her PhD and married a doctor. My father was very proud of that. He felt that my marrying Subbu would make him lose face in society. My mother was a mental health patient, and she would have psychiatric episodes every now and then. My sister and I had been taking care of her since childhood; we were used to it. She was totally under my father's influence. She believed everything he said and thought that he could do no wrong.

'My father was a very powerful man. He told me he wanted to meet Subbu, and pretended that he had no issues with our relationship. When Subbu came over for the first time, my father said he would be happy to get me married to him, provided Subbu did his graduation. Subbu and I were ecstatic. Subbu entrusted the running of the estate to the manager and immediately enrolled himself in a college in Bangalore. But the moment Subbu was out of Sakleshpur, my father's friend's family came over to my house to "see me". I couldn't speak up in front of them. But when they left, I made it clear to my father that I was not interested in getting married to his friend's son. I called up Subbu, and he immediately rushed to Sakleshpur. My father insulted him badly. The kind of things my father said, I wished I could die. Subbu returned to Bangalore, totally dejected. He called me up and said that he wanted to drop out of college because he didn't see any point of continuing now. He was in a bad state of mind. Two days later, the police arrested Subbu. It was my father who was behind it. He implicated Subbu in a false case of sandalwood smuggling. Back then, abundant sandalwood grew in the estates. Cutting down the sandalwood trees and trading in them was a huge crime. To transport the sandalwood to buyers in Kerala, the smugglers would steal cars from Bangalore, pack the sandalwood in the cars, drive them to Kerala and then abandon the cars there. One such gang was nabbed by the police and when questioned, they said Subbu was the one who master-minded their operation. Subbu spent three nights in jail. I was young and frightened. I didn't want anything to happen to Subbu. It was only when I agreed to marry the man my father had chosen that he bailed Subbu out.'

'Oh my God,' Alka exclaimed. 'Does Krish know about all this?'

'No. No one knows he was in jail. Subbu didn't want his mother or Krish to know. He didn't want to give them any grief or stress. Especially since his mother wouldn't have been able to take it. So, he told them that we had broken up. They couldn't understand why though. I got married within a month and moved to the US. My ex-husband's mother lived with him, while his father lived with his other brother. They were not on good terms. We never knew any of this till I got married. By this time, however, I discovered that I was pregnant. I suspected that the child was Subbu's. But I wasn't sure, and of course, there was no way I was telling my ex-husband about it. He was an extremely controlling, jealous man. Initially, he and his mother abused me verbally. Then the physical abuse started. By the time Gaurav was a year and a half old, I was being regularly beaten up, starved and kept away from him on the silliest of pretexts. I still can't believe how I bore it all. When Gaurav was three, my mother killed herself. I came back to India for her last rites and then simply never went back. My father didn't believe me when I told him about my ex-husband's abusive behaviour. He said that it must have been "my fault". I cut off all ties with him then. My sister helped me get a job, and for a few years I worked with one of the biggest international travel agencies here. Later, I started my own business.'

A mix of shock, empathy and sadness played across Alka's face as she listened to Chanda's tragic tale of deception and abuse. Alka couldn't fathom the emotional toll everything must have had on Chanda.

'This is all so shocking, Chanda. And forgive me if I sound intrusive, but why did you decide to get the paternity test done and when did you tell Subbu about Gaurav?'

'Again, I must apologize to you for this, Alka. I got the paternity test done because my ex-husband was harassing me for child custody. Once I proved that the child wasn't his, he raved and ranted. But he was in the US and I was in India, there wasn't much that he could. So he left me alone and agreed to the divorce. Meanwhile, I knew Subbu had gotten married to you. I had never kept in touch with him after my own marriage. But a mutual friend who is a bit of a prankster, a slightly insensitive guy if you ask me, thought it would be great fun for me and Subbu to meet. He invited me over to meet the old gang at a catch-up he had organized. He didn't tell me that Subbu would be there. Subbu didn't know either. When I saw Subbu, I started crying and fled the scene. Needless to say, everyone was shocked, and the get-together didn't go quite the way they had planned.

'Subbu called me up later to make sure I was okay. I couldn't keep it in me then. I had to tell Subbu that Gaurav was his son. Subbu went through a million emotions that day. He said he wanted to tell you everything, that he couldn't cheat you. I told him that I didn't want to be the reason his marriage broke up. Subbu's whole life is in that estate while my life is here. There's no way we could be together. I convinced him that the best way forward was for us to live apart and not tell anyone about this.

'Subbu began visiting us regularly after that. But Alka, not once has he stayed the night here. He always goes back to Bangalore Club and stays there, no matter how late it is. We have also never met without Gaurav. And in case you are wondering, we have never slept together either. I know it sounds hard to believe, but this is the truth. Subbu is so joyous around Gaurav. You have to see them together, Alka. You will know what I mean.'

Chanda paused to take a sip of her coffee. Her eyes filled with tears as she continued, 'He always said my home was his secret refuge. Whenever he was too stressed about things at the estate, he would come here. He has never told me about any fights that he's had with you, even though there have been times when I've guessed it. He spoke highly of you, Alka. He said you deserved someone better. He praised how you had bonded with his mother. He adores Nisha and Tulika, and he feels guilty about keeping this huge secret from you. He was sure that if he told you, you would leave him, and he didn't want to have to choose between his daughters and his son.

'I had never expected to see him again after I got back from the US. So I was content with whatever little time he was spending with us. His presence in our lives was a blessing. Gaurav and I eagerly looked forward to his visits.

'I am extremely sorry, Alka. Subbu and I couldn't tell you about Gaurav without the risk of Subbu losing his daughters. I love him fiercely, with all my heart, and I will do anything for him. I put him before me, and it was for his happiness and maybe my own too that I hid everything from you. I hope you understand, Alka, please pardon me.' Chanda started crying softly. She looked into Alka's eyes, hoping desperately that Alka would understand.

In a strange way, Alka did understand. After all, she and Krish had carried their feelings for each other in their hearts for years. She knew how Chanda felt. She loved Krish the same way Chanda loved Subbu.

'Anyway, now that you know my story, I really hope you have it in your heart to forgive me,' Chanda said as she wiped away her tears.

Alka remained silent for a while. The weight of Chanda's revelation hung in the air as they sat sipping their coffees. Breaking the silence at long last, Alka spoke gently, 'I do understand, Chanda. Life throws unexpected challenges at us, and we navigate through them in ways we believe are the best. I understand fully. Thank you for sharing your story with me.' She reached out and held Chanda's hand, offering a gesture of understanding and a sense of acceptance.

24

TRUST AND BELIEF

2006-2007

Later that night, Alka and Nisha went back to Krish's home. Nisha was very excited about having met Gaurav. As far as she was concerned, he was a new friend she had made.

'He's really nice, Mummy! And Chanda aunty's house is so pretty. Do you think Chikkappa's house is better than Chanda aunty's house?' she asked Alka.

'They're both different, baby,' Alka said, still feeling overwhelmed by Chanda and Subbu's story.

'You have to pick one!'

Nisha's current favourite game was that of giving two choices to either Tulika or Alka and getting them to pick one. Most of the time, Alka would indulge her. But today she said, 'We will be reaching Chikkappa's house soon. Why don't you see for yourself and then we will decide together, okay?'

'Okay, Mummy.'

Nisha's curious eyes widened as she stepped into Krish's apartment a little later. She had never seen such a luxurious house before. Her fingers traced the textured fabric of the sofa, and she couldn't resist sinking into its plushness.

'Wow, Mummy! Chikkappa's place is so fancy!' she exclaimed, a sparkle of excitement in her eyes.

Alka smiled. 'It is, isn't it? Your Chikkappa has always had a taste for elegance,' she said, catching Krish's eye. Krish smiled back at her.

Nisha glanced around, her gaze zeroing in on the white hand-tufted rug that adorned the floor. 'This rug is so soft! It feels like a hundred teddy bears lying together on the floor.'

Krish laughed at Nisha's imagination.

'Are you hungry?' he asked.

'Yes, a little bit.'

Krish carried his niece to the kitchen. 'Ask your mummy if junk food is okay just this once,' he said, taking out a bag of potato chips.

'Yes, I suppose so. It's been a long day,' Alka replied.

Krish then led them to the private pool on the terrace of his penthouse. He told Nisha that it was too cold now, but she could swim the next morning if she wanted to. Nisha's jaw dropped open. 'Wow, Chikkappa! All of this is just for you?'

'Yes, but tell you what, I'll share it with you and Tulika too!' Krish winked at her.

'This place is a palace. I wish I could live here forever!' Nisha exclaimed.

Alka ruffled Nisha's hair affectionately. 'Well, whose house is better? Chanda aunty's or Chikkappa's?'

Nisha rolled her eyes in mock annoyance. 'Of course, Chikkappa's. Do you even have to ask?'

It took Alka some time to settle Nisha down, and by the time she drifted off to sleep, it was long past her usual bedtime.

Krish handed Alka a mug of hot chocolate as they sat facing each other in the living room. They had finally found the time to talk to each other in private.

'Chanda shared a lot with me, Krish. I don't know if I should be telling you this, but Subbu is your brother, and you have a right to know. Besides, it all happened a long time back, so I don't think I should hide it,' Alka said.

'Hide what? What did she tell you? Is it such a big secret that you can't share it with me?'

'A big secret, yes. Sharing it with you, well, I am about to, if you let me speak!'

'Yes, yes, sorry. Please continue. It's just that I am so relieved to see Anna open his eyes.'

'Oh, yes, me too.'

'Sorry, I interrupted you again. What is this big secret that you were about to reveal?'

'Krish, Subbu went to jail a long time back.'

'What?! Jail and Anna? I can't believe it.'

'It came as a shock for me too. That's actually the real reason why he and Chanda split up. Apparently, he spent three nights in jail. Chanda's father framed him in a sandalwood smuggling case and refused to bail him out unless Chanda got married to the person he had chosen for her.'

'Oh my God, and how is it that we had no clue about any of this?'

'He didn't want you to stress about him and he didn't want Amma to worry.'

'Oh God, that's just horrible. And that is so like my brother. To become a martyr in order to protect his family from any pain.'

'It is. All this while, we thought that whatever we had between us was a secret. But looks like Subbu's secret was even bigger.'

Alka then narrated everything that Chanda had told her.

'Alka, I can't imagine what he must have gone through. He suffered silently all those years ago. And then he had to hide Gaurav's existence as well.'

'I know, I was thinking the same thing. And Gaurav is such a sweet kid. I can't help feeling affectionate towards him. He looks exactly like Subbu, doesn't he?'

'Oh, yes, a carbon copy. He is like a mini Anna walking around!'

'You know what, Krish? After listening to Chanda, I am not the least bit angry or resentful anymore. Earlier, before I knew her whole story, I was angry. But given her situation, what else could she do? We do whatever we can according to our circumstances and the best choices available to us; that's what Chanda did too.'

'See, I told you she isn't at all what you imagined her to be.'

'Yes, that's true. We're too quick to judge people and slot them into boxes. But the thing is, we slot them into boxes which we have made up on the basis of our perceptions. And our perceptions can be so wrong,' Alka reflected as she wrapped her hands around the mug of hot chocolate and drained it down in one go.

'Yes, I couldn't agree more.'

The next morning, Alka and Nisha left for Bangalore. Alka was so lost in her thoughts that Nisha had to repeat herself twice to get her mother's attention.

'Mummy, you aren't answering me. You are just muttering hmm hmm,' Nisha complained, her eyebrows knitting up and the corners of her lips turning down into a pout.

'Sorry, baby, I didn't hear you.'

'I know. I asked you who you like more, Chanda aunty or Gaurav?'

'I don't know, baby. This one is hard.'

'You have to pick one! I like Gaurav because he played with me even though he is older than me, and I also like Chanda aunty because she gave me storybooks when we left. She didn't forget Tulika either. And, she told us to come visit her again. She is very nice, Mummy.'

'Yes, that was indeed nice of her. I like both of them, equally. I can't pick one,' Alka said.

After a while, lulled by the motion of the car, Nisha fell asleep and Alka sighed with relief.

She was exhausted by the constant up and down between the estate and the hospital. These trips were taking a toll on her. She would have to visit Subbu again soon, even though she knew Krish and Chanda were taking care of him. The stress of executing the homestay project weighed heavily on her mind too. Though Manasi had offered to help, Alka was worried about actually getting people to stay at the cottages. She leaned back into her seat and closed her eyes. By the time she opened them again, they were already pulling up at the estate. Alka had been sleeping for hours, but it just felt like a few minutes to her. Nisha, having slept in the car, was very chirpy and she eagerly recounted the whole trip in minute detail to Tulika, who listened wide-eyed. In Nisha's narration, Gaurav came across as a superhero.

'He is very nice. He carried me in the ball pool, piggyback style, and he pushed my swing really high up,' Nisha said, stretching her arms up in the air. She described Chanda and Krish's homes too, going on and on about the latter's private pool. She mentioned that Krish had said he would be happy to share his home with both Tulika and her. After listening to everything, Tulika turned to Alka and said, 'Mummy, why didn't you take me along? You always leave me behind.'

'Baby, you didn't want to come. I had asked you.'

'No, you didn't take me.'

It took another hour to comfort her. Alka had to play a board game with both the girls to pacify Tulika who felt that she had missed out on too much of the excitement.

Over the next few days, Alka became so busy with the affairs of the estate that she didn't know when one day ended and the other began. The hours went by in a blur. She also realized how different her life was without Subbu. When he was at the estate, her life had revolved around him and the girls. She adjusted everything in her schedule according to them. But now it seemed like she was the centre and the world revolved around her.

The CoRe team arrived during this time, and they took three days to do a thorough recce of the estate. Alka and Muthu accompanied them everywhere. The team got in experts who studied the soil, assessed what had been planted and where it had all gone wrong. They dipped into their funds, cleared the estate's bank loans and took back the property papers. Alka heaved a sigh of relief when they handed the papers to her triumphantly.

'This is just the beginning, wait and see what we do,' Daisy said. The team also appointed Daisy's nephew, Tarun, as the project head. The young man held a post-graduate diploma from the Indian Institute of Plantation Management, Bangalore. Alka introduced Muthu to Tarun. She told him that he would be reporting directly to Tarun, and that executing whatever plans the CoRe team made would be his job. Muthu was more than happy to assist Tarun. Daisy said that they would have to do an audit of the processes. Tarun swung into action and executed the audit under the team's guidance. The irrigation systems were not up to the mark and could be hugely improved. Alka was also shocked to discover that there was at least twenty-five per cent pilferage happening on the estate.

'Though it's unpleasant, we have to police and plug the leaks,' Tarun said. He then put watertight systems in place, where every single sack of coffee beans was accounted for. He appointed more supervisors to monitor the labour. The CoRe team identified fifty acres where they would have to completely change the crop and replant it. 'We will do it in phases so that we still have some income coming in from the rest of the estate, don't worry about this,' Chinappa assured Alka over the phone. At every step of the way, Alka was kept apprised of what the team was doing and why they had decided on a particular course of action. Tarun or one of the other members would brief her regularly. Alka noted that all of them were equally involved with the project and knew what was happening at any given moment. She felt grateful for their presence on the estate.

At the end of two weeks, Alka could tell that the estate was beginning to slowly change for the better. There was a sense of urgency and purpose in the air that hadn't been there earlier. The sleepy, placid estate was now the hub of activities and it buzzed with energy.

Alka accompanied Muthu on the estate rounds every single day to ensure that the instructions of the CoRe team were being carried out. Even though Tarun had assured her that she could sit back and relax, she discovered that she simply couldn't. It was her land and she wanted to be on top of things. So, she went out at the break of dawn daily and came back exhausted. When she couldn't manage going in the morning, she would ensure that she went in the evenings. At times, she reached home only after Nisha and Tulika had already slept off. She was happy though that Selvi was there, taking good care of them.

On the days when Alka did not go on the estate rounds, she spent her time discussing the plan of action for the homestay venture with Manasi. Between them, they drew up a decent business plan.

'Do you know anyone who can come and train the staff? We need a trainer for soft skills, and that is the first hiring you have to do,' Manasi advised.

Muthu identified about four people who could do the job, and after interviewing all of them, Alka chose a lady named Gayathri who had set up her own training institute after a decade-long career in the hospitality industry. She had worked with many five-star hotels, and her aim now was to provide employment opportunities to girls belonging to economically weak families from Hassan and Sakleshpur districts.

'Don't worry about them. By the time their training is done, they will be ready for employment at fancy hotels like the Taj,' Gayathri assured Alka.

Muthu and Alka quickly interviewed the applicants from within the estate and identified the people who would be sent for training to Gayathri's institute. The training itself would take about three weeks, and since Gayathri's institute was an NGO funded by many corporates, the cost was nominal—something that Alka was happy about.

'You know, Manasi, I am terrified I will go bankrupt,' Alka confessed to her during one of their chats.

'You worry for nothing. You'll have income from the estate too, won't you?'

'That's only after two years, when the estate starts becoming profitable,' Alka clarified, but Manasi told her she was being paranoid.

Manasi could not understand her fears because Alka had not told her about the circumstances she had grown up under. Manasi had never experienced poverty, and being an only child, she was well supported by her wealthy family.

But Krish, having known Alka's background, understood her fears perfectly. It had become a routine for Krish and Alka to call each other after dinner. Initially, he used to call to keep Alka updated about Subbu's progress. Soon, however, the phone calls between them grew longer and longer. Alka found herself sharing details about the day's activities at the estate. They chatted about life, about the choices they had made, their intertwined fates, everything that happened at

Krish's workplace and many other things. For both of them, these conversations became the highlight of their day, a special 'treat' which they both looked forward to. When they finished talking, which was often well past midnight, Alka would fall asleep as soon as she hung up the phone and her head hit the pillow.

During one such conversation, Krish told Alka about how he felt that Manasi was so much happier now.

'I know, Krish. She sounds like the old Manasi now.'

'I feel no resentment towards Rajat,' Krish said. 'In fact, I am happy that Sanal is bonding with him. But I also feel like a failure as a father. I couldn't connect with him the way Rajat has. Can you believe Sanal went out with Rajat? That is like a HUGE deal, Alka. I have struggled so much with him. Even a simple task like making him a sandwich the way he wants was so hard. Sanal has extremely specific requirements. Even if a small thing is not done the way he wants, he throws the whole thing on the floor.'

'I know, Krish. Amma used to tell me a lot of things when she would return from visiting you all. She told me how difficult it was and how much you tried to bond with Sanal. Also, she was glad that you had your work to escape into. Those were her exact words. She was very proud of all that you have accomplished at work. Don't beat yourself up, Krish, you did your best.'

'Yes, I did. The distancing from Manasi wasn't deliberate, you know.'

'I know. The important thing is that Sanal is becoming more sociable, from what Manasi tells me. By the way, she has some great suggestions for the homestay, but I am extremely worried, Krish. This venture has to succeed at all costs.'

'It's okay even if it fails, Alka. At least you would have tried something new.'

'Krish, it cannot fail. It simply *must not*,' Alka said.

Her pride didn't allow her to tell him that she barely had any money left. She would need a cash inflow soon, and if the cottages didn't generate an income, she would actually have to borrow money from Krish. She hated the very thought of it. It took her back to the life of poverty she had escaped from, and she shuddered imagining it.

Manasi helped Alka come up with uniforms for the newly appointed staff. For the women, they got jade green sarees and deep green blouses. For the men, they got half-sleeved shirts in the same jade green and deep green lungis. The staff was very excited about the uniforms. They smiled widely for the professional photographer Alka had hired to take their pictures for the brochures she had decided to print. The photographer also clicked photographs of the cottages. Manasi had designed the brochures and written a beautiful description of the cottages and the facilities on offer. Once printed, the brochures looked stunning and extremely inviting. Alka mailed two hundred of them to Manasi, who said she would spread the word in Mumbai. She also sent a few to Krish who was full of admiration for her efforts.

'The cottages look so splendid, Alka. You've done a magnificent job! I feel like staying in those cottages myself.' Alka revelled in his praise.

After meeting all these expenses, however, Alka's bank balance had dwindled to a mere four thousand rupees. This caused her immense anxiety. She knew she desperately needed a few bookings to come through immediately.

Manasi and Alka waited and waited, hoping they would get some enquiries regarding the cottages, if not actual bookings. But there were none.

'I don't get it. Why don't people want to go on a vacation to this beautiful place? Each person I have reached out to said it looks promising and they will consider it. But why aren't they making a reservation?' Manasi pondered.

Alka had no clue.

As the days passed without any bookings, Alka's anxiety turned into a gnawing fear that threatened to consume her. The looming possibility of the venture being a colossal failure clawed at her heart. Manasi, however, was still optimistic.

'Maybe it's because the schools are not closed yet. Or maybe people have already booked their vacations, and they will book our homestay as their next vacation spot. Perhaps they are waiting for reviews?' Manasi tried to rationalize it.

But for Alka, the desperation and the uncertainty weighed heavy. Every rejection from potential guests felt like a stab, a confirmation of her deepest fears and insecurities. Perhaps she wasn't good enough. She was cut out only to be in Subbu's shadow forever. She did not have a business sense. She was a fool to have ventured into this. How would she face all the people whom she had assured a promising future and a generous compensation? They had placed their trust in her and believed in her vision. She had let them down. Very badly so. The crisp uniforms and the empty cottages now seemed to be mocking her.

The all-consuming anxiety showed on Alka's appearance and health. She pushed food around her plate at mealtimes, unable to eat much. At night, she dreaded going to bed, for she knew it would be yet another long night of tossing and turning and being eaten up by worry. Sleep would evade her as her mind played out various scenarios of failure and humiliation. The stress-induced sleepless nights and the erratic eating pattern manifested themselves as dark circles under her eyes and visible weight loss. Alka felt constantly exhausted and on the edge.

Selvi worried about her. 'Akka, please eat properly. Don't worry, Subbu Anna will be back soon,' she would say, presuming that Alka was haunted by Subbu's absence. Alka would simply nod, unwilling to voice her fears.

Krish noticed the change in Alka's voice and manner as well. Initially, he attributed it to a physical tiredness that arose from her looking after the estate and all the travelling she had been doing. But soon he realized that it was something deeper.

'What is worrying you, Alka? I know there's something eating you up. I thought you would actually be happy and relieved now. The CoRe team has taken over and Anna's health is improving day by day. The doctors say he is getting better. You're definitely hiding something from me. You have to trust me here, Alka. Tell me, what is it?' he cajoled her gently.

It was the kindness and the concern in Krish's voice that broke Alka. She cried, unable to form the words to express what was in her heart.

'Hey, hey, it's okay. Whatever it is, I am here for you. We will sort it out together. You aren't alone, Alka,' Krish said.

When Alka composed herself enough to speak, she said, 'Thanks, Krish. The thing is, my bank balance will soon hit negative if things continue at this rate. I am so worried I won't have anything left to pay for the household expenses and Nisha and Tulika's school fees. I am afraid of losing face with the staff I have hired. I promised them a bright future but now everything is falling apart.'

'Alka! How can you even worry about this? You know I'll be more than happy to help you out monetarily, right? Come on! My money is sitting idle in some investments. I can straightaway transfer five lakhs to you. That would be more than sufficient for now, isn't it?'

'Krish, I appreciate your offer. I really do. But borrowing money, it just takes me back to when my mother and I were at Mrs Shetty's mercy for every single penny. I can't stand it. I hate the thought of owing anything to anyone. Even if it's you, Krish. I simply do not want to borrow. The reason I didn't tell you about all this till now is that I knew you would immediately offer money. I hate to be a charity case, Krish. I detest it.'

'Alka, you being a charity case is a thing of the past. It happened in another lifetime. That part of your life is over. Every successful entrepreneur borrows funds. Do you really think they all invest their own money? Bank loans exist for a reason, Alka. You have started a big venture and it's going to take you some time to break even.'

Alka nodded, appreciating Krish's support. What he said made sense. But she found it hard to shake off her deep-rooted belief that come what may, she could neither owe any money to anyone again or be at the receiving end of anyone's charity. Krish understood her hesitation perfectly.

'Okay, how about this? I will invest in your venture and you can give me a share of the profits? You run the daily operations, you handle it all, but give me a percentage of your profits. That way, you don't have to feel obligated about having borrowed from me.'

Alka thought about it.

'But tell me, Krish, aren't you doing this only because you want to help me out? Would you still invest in this venture if we didn't know each other?'

'I would do so without a doubt, Alka. If we were strangers and you made a business pitch to me, I would invest in your homestay venture. But we're not strangers. I know you. And I trust you. I believe in you.'

As Krish's words slowly sunk in, Alka felt something deep shift inside her. Trust and belief—that was what he was offering her. At that moment, it felt more powerful than love.

25

THE ROLES WE PLAY

2007

The next evening, Chanda called Alka. She was bubbling with excitement as she spoke.

'Alka, Subbu has started visual tracking! His eyes are moving. He's able to follow a finger or an object as it moves. The doctors say this is an excellent sign!' Chanda was almost screaming as she apprised Alka. She couldn't contain her joy.

'Oh wow! That is fabulous, Chanda. How long have we waited for this!'

'It is fabulous. It is! The return to consciousness is a slow process. Very slow, especially since he's had two surgeries. I can't tell you how happy I am, Alka. It might seem like a small thing because he cannot do anything else, but it's a massive achievement. Sister Pushpa says it's excellent news and she thinks he'll be out of the hospital soon.'

'Really? How soon?'

'The doctors say it's not possible to give a definitive date because it all depends on the progress he makes. But you know how Sister Pushpa is. She predicts he'll be out of the hospital in less than a month.'

'Chanda, that is amazing!'

'He will still need a lot of assistance, but his being out of the hospital will be a relief.'

'I feel wretchedly guilty about not being there enough. I haven't been able to visit Subbu in a while now. The estate has been undergoing major transformations and I am immersed in things from morning to night. On top of that, the homestay hasn't taken off at all. We haven't had a single booking so far.'

'Oh, don't feel guilty at all. Sadly, Subbu still doesn't recognize anyone, so it doesn't make any difference to him whether you are there or not. But wait, you have a homestay?'

'I call it a homestay, but it's much more than that. There are these heritage cottages here in the estate—gorgeous ones from the British era. I have sunk in a lot of money and refurbished them beautifully, staying true to their original style. I also got the staff for this venture trained by one of the best people in the industry. We've all been waiting for guests to book a stay with us, but there've been no takers so far and it's disappointing, to say the least.'

'My dear woman, you do know that I run a travel agency, right? Why didn't you tell me earlier about this venture of yours?'

'Umm, I guess we were busy catching up on our life stories and I was trying not to hate you?'

'Touché! Well, why don't you send me all the details about the cottages now? I'll see what I can do about it. From what you tell me, they sound fabulous. I remember looking at the cottages many years back and telling Subbu that it was a pity they were locked up.'

'Oh yes! I told him the same thing. But you know how adamant he has always been about things at the estate. It's something I never understood about him. But you should see the cottages now, Chanda. They are picture-perfect!'

'Do you have any promotional materials? Anything I can use?'

'Yes. I have tons of brochures that provide all the details about the homestay.'

'Could you please send them over to me?'

'Of course! I'll do it today itself. By the way, I meant to ask you, how do you manage things at your travel agency while being in the hospital at the same time?'

'My manager, Seby, is very efficient. He has worked with me for over a decade now. He handles all my major clients. Seby's been a rock, really. Also Alka, along with the brochures, send me some additional information about the place—more photos, plans, anything that you have. I've been in the travel business for so many years now that I know what unique angles will appeal to what sort of clientele. I shall pitch your property to magazines and newspapers with a strong presence in the travel and tourism sector. Let's see who bites the bait. Rest assured, I will definitely be sending some clients or at least some travel journalists your way.'

'Chanda, that would be wonderful. I can't thank you enough for all that you are doing.'

'Don't thank me just yet, Alka. When something solid materializes out of my efforts, then you can. Now, will you tell Krish the good news about Subbu or should I?'

'What? You mean you haven't called him yet?'

'No. I wanted you to be the first to know.'

'That is so very thoughtful and kind of you, Chanda, really. How can you have this big a heart and be this selfless?'

'I don't know! I guess it's because I have learnt to value love now. I would've probably not appreciated the presence of loved ones so much had I not gone through the awful situations that I did in the past. Subbu has been nothing but kind and generous towards me. Now it is time for me to give back.'

Chanda kept her word. Just like she'd promised, Alka's phone started buzzing non-stop about a week later. There were at least eight to nine enquiries about the homestay every day. She'd come home for lunch when the first call came in. She was so excited after that, that she cancelled her plans for the rest of the day and stayed at home because she didn't want to miss a single call.

Alka managed to confirm at least fourteen bookings. She had categorized Gurgling Waters as the premium cottage and charged a hefty amount for it. The least expensive of the cottages was Silver Brooks, but the amount she had charged for it was substantial nevertheless. She maintained a meticulous record of the bookings and wrote down the dates when the clients would be checking in and out, the cottages that they wanted, the number of guests, their dietary restrictions, if any, and the activities they were likely to enjoy. She offered them a choice between a tour of the estate, a trek to the waterfall, walks to picturesque viewing points at sunrise and sunset and campfire evenings. If the guests were staying for more than three nights, they could choose any two activities free of cost. The rest would be chargeable. If they were staying for two nights, Alka offered them one complimentary activity. All these were Manasi's ideas. A majority of the bookings were for the following month. Alka informed the guests that a fifty per cent advance payment would have to be made upfront. This amount would be non-refundable. Most clients were okay with this arrangement, but a few backed out when they heard that. When Alka told Manasi about the bookings, she was delighted.

'It's really nice of Chanda,' she commented. When Alka told her about the clients who had backed out because of the advance payment, Manasi told her not to bother about them.

Among all the calls Alka received, none sparked as much excitement as did the calls from two journalists, one representing a famous international travel publication called *Magnificent Earth*, and the other from a well-known Indian travel magazine called *Wanderlust*. Both the journalists expressed their interest in visiting the cottages. The prospect of *Magnificent Earth*, known for its comprehensive travel guidebooks covering every facet of travelling to and exploring different destinations, considering Alka's property for a feature was a huge milestone.

Magnificent Earth's publications were, in truth, more than just simple travel guides; they were carefully curated compendiums that included information about where to go, where to stay, what to expect, the costs involved and every other conceivable detail about a place. Alka was aware that their endorsement was not easily earned. A property had to meet stringent criteria and pass rigorous parameter checks before it got listed in *Magnificent Earth*. But being featured by them would open the doors to a global audience throughout the year. The homestay could very well start attracting visitors from all corners of the world.

'This is terrific! I am happy to hear this. Just make sure that you stock an ample amount of toilet paper and ensure that everything is spotlessly clean,' Chanda said when Alka rang her up to give her the news. 'Also, see to it that there are no rats or cockroaches around. Once, they refused to list a really good place because the journalist who'd gone to review it spotted a tiny cockroach somewhere in the room.'

'Yikes! No, absolutely no cockroaches or rats, but there are leeches here. I'll print instructions on how to handle the leeches, just in case the guests encounter them. I'll also provide protective galoshes. I'm glad you warned me,' Alka said.

Chanda had a few more tips for Alka. 'Train your staff about the personal space aspect. Tell them there should be a distance of at least ten feet at all times between them and the guest. A client of mine, a young woman travelling solo from Brazil, felt intimidated once when the porter who had brought her luggage into the hotel room stood very close to her. These foreigners are not used to the staff doing everything for them. They are extra sensitive. Anyway, *Magnificent Earth* is likely to send someone from their London office,' Chanda said.

Alka thanked Chanda profusely for her tips and for the lead.

'I am really happy this is happening. But I think the credit for this one should go to Seby. He cracked a deal with a major tour operator abroad. This tour operator, in turn, tipped off the right travel magazines about an exciting new, unexplored destination in India. Plus, I did call up everyone I know, and the response has been good. You will definitely get more calls, Alka. Be prepared to get busy.'

'Please thank Seby for me!' Alka replied.

Alka invited both the journalists from *Wanderlust* and *Magnificent Earth* to visit at the same time. She allotted the two best cottages, Gurgling Waters and Misty Blue, to them.

She instructed the homestay staff and made them understand just how important the two visitors were. She told them that one of them would be coming from London, and that she might have light eyes, blonde hair and very fair skin. She gave instructions that at no cost were they to ever stare at her. Alka knew that the staff had spent all their life at the estate and they would've never seen a foreigner before this.

'What if we do not understand what she says?' one of the girls asked.

'Don't worry, just give her a big smile and say, "I will call madam." I'll take care of it,' Alka replied.

She told the cooks to prepare a feast fit for royalty. When the visitors finally arrived at the estate, Alka was personally there along with her staff to welcome them with garlands and betel leaf wine. She told them how the cottages had lain neglected for years, how they had been recently restored using local resources, and how she was hoping to give everyone a taste of the 'authentic coffee estate life', which they might never get a chance to experience otherwise. After the journalists were properly fed and rested, Alka took them on an estate tour, just like Subbu and Krish had taken her in the past. She organized campfires for them in the evenings, and took them on her favourite trails around the estate. She showed them the waterfall where she and Krish had sat and spoken their hearts out. She took care of every single detail to ensure that the two guests had a vacation they would never forget.

The staff was nervous about catering to the two journalists, but Alka was around all the time and she reassured them, telling them that they were doing a great job. She also explained the staff's background to the journalists.

'For all of them, this is an incredible opportunity to learn and grow, to step away from the labour-intensive tasks they do at the estate. This is their first foray into the hospitality industry. They might not always understand what you say, but I assure you they are trying hard to. They are the first in their families to get an education. Their parents, grandparents, all of them have been illiterate,' Alka told the journalists.

This deeply moved the journalist from *Magnificent Earth*, who told Alka that her friend at BBC World might be interested in this story about how a woman entrepreneur was changing the lives of many families in a coffee estate deep in southern India. She asked if it would be okay to connect her friend to Alka. Alka was obviously over the moon, but she hid her excitement and said that she would be fine with it.

The visit went smoothly as Alka micromanaged every detail. She guided her staff and encouraged them to always have a smile on their face. The visitors didn't miss this. They loved every moment they spent at the estate. They were full of praise for the genuine smiles and the warm hospitality of the staff. They felt completely relaxed and rejuvenated and promised to write great reviews. While Alka had been slightly nervous in the beginning, she felt at ease when she saw how friendly both the journalists were. She had thoroughly enjoyed taking them around and showing off the estate. She never saw it as an encroachment on her privacy the way Subbu did.

After they left, she shared her experience with Manasi, Chanda, Gowri and Krish. All of them were very pleased for Alka.

Six weeks went by. Alka's cottages managed to make it to the listing in *Magnificent Earth*. *Wanderlust* too, featured the homestay prominently. Both the journalists, full of praise for this new venture, had written great articles about the cottages. Combined with the ethereal photographs they had clicked at the estate, the reviews were fantastic pieces of publicity, and Alka's homestay gathered unprecedented attention. Many newspapers called her up, wanting to send their reporters over, and now Alka had to carefully schedule the stays. She decided to keep only one cottage for the press and allot it by turns. Visitors to the cottages had begun to pour in, and Alka couldn't afford to lose any revenue. Upon Chanda's suggestion, she also decided to keep the cottages free of any guests for four days in a month and dedicate those days for maintenance activities.

'When you have a steady influx of visitors, wear and tear of the property is natural. But you have to keep everything in mint condition because you are now on the international circuit, and you are charging a premium amount as tariff. Take a break from continuously renting out the cottages. Use this time to get all the fixtures, plumbing, drainage and electrical points inspected and fixed. See if any of the linen are looking a bit frayed. If so, replace them. Do not try to cut costs here. There shouldn't be even the slightest of stains on your linen. This attention to detail will pay off well in the long run,' Chanda advised.

When Alka discussed all of this with Manasi, she agreed that they were excellent suggestions. 'Also, it will give you a much-needed break from the constant running around.'

A break was what Alka really needed. She had forgotten what leisure felt like. She was constantly on her feet, supervising things, instructing the staff and being around guests. A break of four days would give her the time to recharge too.

Work at the estate was going on in full-swing and Tarun was there every day before sunrise. Alka loved how much better the estate looked now. Even Muthu agreed that never had it looked so pruned and tiptop the way it did now.

In addition to their daily calls at night, Alka and Krish had also begun speaking every morning after she returned from the estate rounds. If she didn't call, Krish would. Krish had started going to the hospital at the crack of dawn. Chanda would then go back home, send Gaurav to school, grab a shower and some breakfast and be back at the hospital to take over. Once she returned, Krish would go back home and call Alka just before he changed and left for work. It was a balancing act that they had fine-tuned.

Krish broke the routine that morning when he called Alka at 6.30 a.m. from the hospital.

'There's big news, Alka! Chanda just told me that Anna answered a simple yes-no question!'

Alka was overjoyed to hear this. Krish also told her that Subbu seemed happier around Chanda and that he responded more to Chanda than to him.

'I know it's not a figment of my imagination. I can feel the change in him when she's around. She just left now,' Krish said.

'I feel I should be there, helping you guys out. Guilt is eating me up, Krish.' Alka said.

'How can you be here, Alka? You haven't had even a moment to yourself. You've been managing the estate, the girls and now the homestay, all by yourself. It would be impossible for you to visit Anna regularly. We've already discussed this. You deserve some rest.'

'I am finally putting my feet up today as we have no guests for the next four days. You know, Krish, many of the publications send their own photographers to the estate. You should see the pictures they click. They make the estate look like heaven, Krish!'

'Our estate *is* a piece of heaven, Alka. Sometimes, heaven is right in front of us, but we don't see it that way. It's only when we look at it through the eyes of another that we see its real worth.'

'I truly wish you could come and see the cottages, Krish. I can't tell you how gorgeous they are!'

'Your wish is my command, madam,' Krish replied and Alka laughed.

It was just when Alka was about to sit down for lunch that she heard a vehicle pull up outside.

'Akka! Krish Anna is here,' Selvi announced.

'What!' Alka gasped in astonishment as she rushed to the verandah. Her heart skipped a beat as she saw Krish emerging from his car, taking two steps at a time towards the house. He looked stunning in a crisp white full-sleeved shirt that complemented his light blue jeans and a pair of semi-formal suede shoes. The aviator sunglasses he was wearing added just the right amount of oomph.

'Krish!' she exclaimed, grinning from ear to ear. Her heart, unable to contain the surge of happiness, pounded in her ear. 'How on earth are you here?'

'I told you. Your wish is my command. I wasn't kidding,' Krish said, removing his sunglasses and gazing into Alka's eyes. For a moment, Alka forgot the world around.

Krish drew in a sharp breath. The feeling was mutual. When he was around Alka, nothing else mattered. Alka's freshly scrubbed face, her loosely knotted hair held in place with a sparkly clip, her loose pink T-shirt and the white baggy pants made her look sweet and vulnerable. He could sense her exhaustion even though her eyes were sparkling with joy on seeing him. Each time he saw Alka, all he wanted to do was draw her into his arms, hold her tightly and never let her go. It was only Selvi's figure looming in the background that prevented him from giving her a hug now.

Over the past few weeks, with their daily phone calls, they had grown even closer to each other than before. Subbu's unfortunate accident, their concern and sorrow over his situation, the time spent together during the hospital visits, the interactions with the doctors, the presence of Chanda and Gaurav—all these collective experiences had bound them so tightly together that there was no longer any hesitation in either of their minds about crossing a boundary. They needed each other to get through life. And that was just how it was.

'Anna, did you eat? Lunch is ready,' Selvi said.

It was only then that Krish broke his gaze away from Alka.

With Selvi around serving them lunch, they made mundane conversation as they ate.

'The chicken curry is nice, Selvi.'

'Thank you, Anna. Akka taught me this. Please, have some more.'

'Try the jackfruit pappad, Krish. They are delicious.'

'Where did you get these from? Amma used to make them.'

'My mother made them at home! Anandi madam had taught her how to make these,' Selvi told him.

When they were done with lunch, Alka told Selvi that she was going to show Krish the cottages.

'Let's go in my car,' Krish said. He was driving a third generation Honda CR-V that had just been launched.

'New car?' Alka asked.

'Yes, ma'am. It has the comfort of a sedan with the sporty sturdiness of an SUV. But that's not why I want to take my car,' he said as he held the door open for Alka.

'Oh! I thought you wanted to show off your new car,' she teased as she got in. She felt light and carefree as he slipped into the driver's seat beside her. It was a feeling she had forgotten. She got a whiff of Krish's familiar perfume, and pleasure shot through her.

'No, I wanted to give you these,' Krish said, leaning over to the rear seat and picking up a massive hand-tied bouquet of Oriental pink lilies and peonies, their stems wrapped beautifully in a delicate white lace fabric. 'I didn't want to turn up at your doorstep with a big bunch of flowers. I don't know whether my gifting you flowers is appropriate or not, but I just had to get them for you,' he said, his voice low.

Alka took the flowers and brushed them against her cheeks. She held out her hand then and Krish intertwined his fingers through hers.

'Which cottage do you want me to see first?' Krish asked.

'Gurgling Waters.' It took Alka a few seconds to reply, and when she spoke, her voice was a hoarse whisper.

They drove to the cottage in silence, not daring to look at each other. When they reached, Krish parked his car and took a few seconds to look at the cottage.

'This is magnificent, Alka. But you already knew that,' he said. He still hadn't let go of her hand.

Later, Alka would be unable to recall how they made it from Krish's car to the bed. She remembered Krish leaning against the doorframe while she fumbled with the key to open the cottage. As soon as they were inside, they were in each other's arms. Neither of them uttered a word. She clung to him, burying her head in his chest and inhaling deeply. All their self-control had finally blown away. Krish kissed her forehead and her eyes. He unpinned her hair, and it cascaded to her shoulders.

'Oh, Alka, you're beautiful,' he whispered as he ran his hands through her hair. She fumbled with the buttons on his shirt until he pushed her back frantically towards the bed and then stripped off his own clothes in a hurry. He lay down beside her, slipping his hands under her T-shirt, kissing her gently on her lips, his fingers lightly exploring her waist, her stomach until she couldn't stand it anymore. She removed her T-shirt with one hand and then quickly unhooked her bra, throwing it on the floor as she guided his hand to where she wanted it the most. She hooked a leg around his waist, arching towards him, aching to have him inside her. But Krish would not be hurried. He teased her till she moaned and begged him to take her. Their bodies had changed over time, and there was both familiarity and wonder as they gently made love to each other.

Later, their bodies spent and limbs heavy, they lay in silence for a while, Krish spooning against Alka's back, both dizzy with happiness. The room was warm and sunlight filtered in through the net curtains, illuminating Alka's face.

'We must be the worst people on this planet. Me, cheating on my husband, and you, sleeping with your brother's wife,' Alka said.

But Krish silenced her. 'Shh. We don't get to choose who we fall in love with.'

They lay in silence, aware of each painful minute that ticked by, reminding them that they would soon have to return to the real world where they both had their roles to play—brother, father, wife, mother—and where they could no longer be just Alka and Krish, two people deeply in love with one another.

26
FAMILY

2007

In the weeks that followed, Alka and Krish found it hard to be away from each other. Alka messaged him at every opportunity she got, and whenever Krish could manage to get away from work, even if it was for ten minutes, he would call her.

'I've never used the mobile phone so much! And it's hard to type out these long messages and then find a spot where I can get some network signal,' Alka complained.

'It's easier to type on a Blackberry than on a Nokia. I'll get you one,' Krish offered.

'No, Krish. The signal at the estate is erratic. Here, even mobile phones are a luxury. And in case you've forgotten, we do not have internet. Imagine me roaming around with a fancy Blackberry. The only berries here are coffee berries, not blackberries,' Alka laughed.

With money pouring in from her homestay venture, and the estate being in the CoRe team's safe hands, Alka was no longer as stressed as before. Her sleep improved and the dark circles under her eyes vanished. She regained some of the weight she had lost. Her skin radiated happiness each time she spoke to Krish. Even her daughters noticed these changes.

'Mummy, your face is glowing,' Nisha said one day.

'It's because Mummy is now a boss lady,' Tulika replied. She wasn't wrong, Alka thought. It felt wonderful to be in charge of a successful business.

The BBC correspondent had reached out to Alka and fixed a date for an interview and a shoot. Alka asked the team to come on one of the days when the homestay was closed. The interview and the shoot lasted for an entire day. The journalist who came to interview Alka, also interviewed the staff, and all of them raved about their 'Alka madam'. Once the homestay had started making money, Alka had fixed a generous remuneration for them. Most guests who booked the cottages were very affluent people, and they also tipped well, which added to their income.

'Never before have I made so much money. With my own earnings, I purchased a TV, a washing machine and a fridge for my family. This is the first time we are using all these appliances in our home. I have only seen them in the movies,' one of the girls, Srilakshmi, announced with pride. Later, this quote would appear prominently in the article which would talk at length about Alka's journey from being a domestic help's daughter to a successful entrepreneur employing over sixty women. There would be no mention of Subbu at all. Alka had once felt ashamed of her past, but now she wore it proudly like a badge. However, when she thought of all that she had accomplished, it was always a bittersweet moment, for she missed her mother intensely.

Alka called up Renuka Mavshi to share the news of her success, and she was delighted to hear about it.

'While I am sad about Subbu's accident, none of this would have happened if he was hale and hearty. He would have never allowed you to run the homestay. So, there is a reason for every mishap that happens,' Renuka Mavshi wisely pointed out.

Tulika's art competition was just around the corner. Even though Alka trusted Gowri to take good care of Tulika, this was the first time she was entrusting her child to somebody else's care. When the day of their departure came, she grew worried as she saw Tulika leaving with Gowri.

'Listen, Alka, at some point we have to let our children go. But trust me, she will be okay,' Gowri assured her.

'Renuka Mavshi, my mother's close friend, lives in Delhi. Do you think you can take Tulika to visit her after the competition is over? It's a huge favour to ask for, I know. But if you can manage it, that would be great.'

'Consider it done! And it's not a huge favour at all. Delhi is like my second home,' Gowri said.

While Tulika had initially been disappointed about Alka not accompanying her, she had ultimately understood that it would be hard for her mother to leave the estate since she had to supervise everything at the homestay. When Tulika returned from her trip a couple of days later, she was full of excitement. She described everything in detail—the flight from Bangalore to Delhi and back, the extra chocolates which 'Airhostess aunty' had given her, all the big stores in Connaught Place where Gowri took her shopping, the gol-gappas she ate, and everything else that had caught her fancy. She described Renuka Mavshi's house and Manish and

Kavita's hotel as well. She told them that Renuka Mavshi had said that she was her 'junior grandma'. She had pampered Tulika and sent a salwar kameez set for both Nisha and Tulika. Alka was touched and overjoyed when she heard that. Nisha, meanwhile, listened to Tulika's stories with a growing envy.

'Don't worry. We'll go again, and this time we'll tell Gowri aunty to take us both. She's very sweet and she won't say no,' Tulika declared confidently, making Alka smile. She felt lucky to have a friend like Gowri.

A week later, Chanda called Alka and said that there was a new development with Subbu. She wanted Alka to come down to Bangalore as soon as she could.

'Is it bad news, Chanda?' Alka asked nervously.

'No! Not at all. It is exciting actually, but I want you to see it for yourself,' Chanda assured her.

Alka heaved a sigh of relief.

'We are running at full capacity for the next three days. Since we're still new, I want to be around for these bookings as the staff might not be able to manage without me. But after that, we have only one booking which they can manage. Is it okay if I come then?'

'Yes, of course. And I've told Krish not to tell you as well. We want it to be a surprise,' Chanda said.

Alka was so busy over the next three days that she did not have the time to think about what the surprise could be. When she spoke to Krish, he said that Chanda had specifically instructed him not to tell her anything. 'But it's good news. In fact, it's excellent news, so don't worry,' he said.

'All right.'

'Will you be bringing the girls when you come over?' Krish asked.

'They have school, Krish. I can't.'

'Will you stay over?'

'Yes, I will leave the next morning,' Alka said softly.

They both knew what it meant.

Alka left for Bangalore early the following morning. She had given detailed instructions to her staff even though they all knew what to do by now. She put Srilakshmi in charge of the overall arrangements. 'At any point, if you have any questions, please call me. My phone will always be with me,' Alka told her as she left. And as far as the girls were concerned, Selvi had looked after them so many times that she needed no instructions.

Shanker drove Alka straight to the hospital where Krish and Chanda were both waiting for her at the entrance. Alka was happy to see Chanda and gave her a tight hug that lasted quite a few seconds.

'I really owe you, Chanda. If not for your help, this venture wouldn't have taken off,' she said.

'You've put in the work too,' Chanda said, hugging her back.

'Hi,' Krish said quietly, hoping it wouldn't be obvious to Chanda that he was smitten by Alka.

'Hi, Krish,' Alka replied, trying not to smile too much.

'So, what is this good news that both of you are keeping from me?' Alka asked as she followed them to Subbu's room.

'Come, see for yourself,' Chanda smiled as she held the door open.

Alka walked in and stood there in stunned silence. Subbu

was sitting up in bed and there was barely any medical paraphernalia in the room. He wasn't staring blankly into space anymore either. As soon as she entered the room, Subbu turned and looked at her. The scars on his face had faded quite a bit. He had clearly been given a shave and a haircut as well, and he was looking somewhat like his old self.

A mixture of astonishment and relief swept through Alka when Subbu's eyes met hers.

'Subbu! How are you?' she asked tenderly, stepping towards him. Her eyes brimmed with tears. She couldn't believe the fact that he was sitting up and looking into her eyes, actually *looking* at her.

Subbu hesitated for a moment and then said, 'I am fine, doctor. Thank you.'

Alka looked at Chanda, shock and confusion writ large and clear on her face.

Chanda touched her arm gently and nodded, gesturing to Alka that it was okay. Then she turned to Subbu and said softly, as though she were speaking to a child, 'Subbu, this is not the doctor. This is Alka.'

But Subbu frowned in confusion. He looked blank as he shook his head. There were no signs of recognition on his face.

'Your wife, Subbu. This is Alka, your wife,' Chanda said.

Subbu looked at Krish and said, 'Krish?'

'Yes, Anna?' Krish was immediately by Subbu's bedside.

'I don't know who she is, Krish. I've never seen her before. Tell her to go away,' Subbu told him, turning his face away, indicating very clearly that he did not want to talk anymore.

Alka's heart sank as the sharp sting of Subbu's rejection hit her. She hurried out of the room, her head low, her shoulders drooping. Subbu had recognized Chanda and Krish. But he had not recognized her. Was it because he was still angry with her? She couldn't believe it.

Distraught over what had happened, Chanda followed Alka outside.

'I am so sorry, Alka ... I told him this morning that you are coming, and he said he was waiting to see you. But now he seems to have forgotten everything. I ... I didn't expect this to backfire,' Chanda said.

'Does this mean that he has completely forgotten who I am? Does he remember the girls at least? How is it even possible that he is calling out to Krish and you but not recognizing me and asking me to go away instead?'

'Alka, just give him time. We have to be patient with him. He is slowly adjusting to regaining his consciousness. It will all come back to him.'

'But he isn't even recognizing me, Chanda.'

'He will. Until recently, he was only following instructions. But now he is speaking on his own. He is able to identify Krish and me, and Gaurav too. Soon, he will remember you also,' Chanda said.

'I told you springing this surprise was not a good idea, but you insisted on going ahead with it,' Krish said. He had followed them out after seeing how upset Alka was.

'Krish, he did remember Alka this morning. He even seemed excited about her visit. I am certain it's only a matter of time before he recognizes her,' Chanda replied.

Krish pursed his lips and said nothing. He was trying to hide his annoyance with Chanda. While she had obviously meant no harm, Krish did not like seeing Alka so dejected.

'Look, Alka, you know that Krish and I have been meeting him every day. Perhaps that is why he recognizes us easily now.' Chanda consoled her. Alka hoped she was right.

'Anyway, we have to meet the doctors today. That was the other reason we wanted you to come over. The doctors wanted to have an assessment meeting to discuss when he can be discharged,' Krish told Alka.

'I am sorry about this whole thing,' Chanda said.

'It's okay, Chanda. It's not your fault,' Alka replied.

Alka and Krish met with Dr Mohan and Dr Murthy at the consultation room.

'He has made excellent progress. Congratulations,' Dr Mohan said.

'He doesn't seem to remember me, doctor. Will this be permanent? Is his memory affected?' Alka blurted out. She couldn't keep the apprehension out of her voice.

'See, he is recovering from the minimally conscious state, the MCS,' Dr Murthy replied. 'He might act lost or confused. He may not be able to keep track of where he is or what time it is. He might even see things that are not there. However, this is all good news as it means he is reacting to his environment, engaging with it.'

'Doctor, what can we expect going forward?' Krish asked.

'Well, you will have to handle him with a lot of patience, love and care. Object recognition, communication, command following, all of it might be inconsistent at this stage. Treat him like he is a small child who has to learn everything anew. Some children learn fast, some learn slowly. But at some point, they will all level up,' Dr Mohan explained.

'What specific things would we have to do to help him?' Alka asked.

'We will be prescribing quite a few medicines which have to be given to him regularly. These will help with his recovery. He will also need to work with a speech therapist and a physiotherapist every day. But he doesn't have to be in the hospital for that. He doesn't need professional nursing anymore. We can simply treat him as an outpatient. In fact, we recommend moving him home since it will aid in his recovery,' Dr Mohan said.

'Every week or so he can come for a check-up and we can closely monitor his progress,' Dr Murthy added.

Alka and Krish looked at each other as they took in all the information.

'But I live in Sakleshpur, doctor. If the check-ups have to happen weekly, I'll have to bring him from there.'

'Sakleshpur? How far is that?' Dr Murthy asked.

'It about 220 kilometres from here,' Alka answered.

'Oh! He cannot travel that far. It would be a strain on him and it's not advisable. Short distances are okay. You'll have to take that call—whether to keep him at home or in the hospital,' Dr Murthy said.

'His brain is showing remarkable improvements and he is regaining movement too. With regular physiotherapy, he'll be able to walk soon. That's indeed excellent progress, considering the state he was in. He can be discharged in about three days. But if you decide to keep him here, we will shift him to a different wing.'

'All right, doctors, thank you so much. We will discuss everything and let you know of our decision,' Alka said.

Alka and Krish walked back to Subbu's room and found Chanda sitting next to him, stroking his hand. Alka stood outside the door, not want to risk upsetting Subbu again.

Krish walked in and said, 'Anna, is it okay if Chanda comes out for a cup of coffee? She'll be back soon.'

'Yes, go, Chanda. Eat something too,' Subbu replied.

'I won't be long, all right? The nurses are outside. If you need anything, just press this button, okay?' Chanda told Subbu. She kissed him on the cheek, and Subbu looked at her with so much love in his eyes that Alka had to look away. There was no mistaking that look. It was the exact way that Krish looked at her.

'Will Subbu be okay on his own?' Alka asked.

'Yes, we've been leaving him alone for a couple of hours every day. The doctors said it is important to do so as it gives him time to think and recoup his mental energies. They said he might become too dependent on us if we don't do this,' Chanda replied. 'What did the doctors say about him being discharged?'

'We will tell you everything in detail. We want to discuss all the options. I think it's best if we go to my place. The hospital cafeteria is too noisy,' Krish said.

'Yes, let's do that. I'll get Shanker to follow us,' Alka said.

'Are you guys sure that you want me to be a part of this discussion? After all, you are his family and I—'

'Come on, Chanda, you are family too,' Alka interrupted. 'Have you forgotten that our children are half-siblings?'

That made Chanda smile, and without a word, she followed Alka and Krish to the parking lot and got into the car with them.

27
SELFLESS LOVE

2007

Alka and Chanda sat in Krish's living room while Krish made elaichi tea for all of them.

'Quite the place you have, Krish. So well-coordinated too,' Chanda commented as she looked around and admired the opulent but tasteful furnishings.

'Thank you. This tea, I can assure you, is better than the one served at the hospital canteen,' Krish said as he joined them. He placed the woven cane tray with the teacups on the centre table and sat down next to Alka.

On the way to Krish's place, Alka and Krish had told Chanda about everything that the doctors had mentioned.

Now, as they sat sipping the tea, Alka thought about how strange this gathering was. She was with her husband's brother, the man she deeply loved and the one she could've had a future with, and a woman who was her husband's true love and now her good friend too. Capricious were the ways of fate, forcing their paths to intersect because of the choices each of them had made.

'I am really happy that Subbu can be discharged in three days,' Chanda said, resuming the discussion.

'But taking Subbu to Sakleshpur is out of the question because the doctors have explicitly forbidden it,' Alka said.

'I suggest we bring him here to my place. I'll hire a fulltime caregiver. Anna will be comfortable here. You both have seen how comfortable this place is,' Krish said, leaning back into the sofa.

'That's generous of you, Krish, but you know how much he has benefitted from my being around,' Chanda replied.

'Hmm, I'll give you a key to my place then. You can let yourself in whenever you want,' Krish shrugged.

'Listen, Krish, I don't think that's a good idea. I know you want to look after your brother. But the fact is, he is responding well to me and to Gaurav. You've been a witness to that. Think about how inconvenient this arrangement would be for me. I'd have to commute between my place and yours multiple times a day because I would want to be at home when Gaurav gets back from school. Not to mention, I would have to commute to work too. I can't be here all the time.'

'Do you think keeping him at the hospital is an option then? Are you suggesting that?' Alka asked.

Chanda looked at Alka indignantly. 'Of course not! I can't imagine leaving him at the hospital. Even though he will receive great nursing care there, it's impersonal. He needs the comfort of a home,' she said.

'Well, how do we manage this then?' Krish asked.

'If both of you are okay with it, I would like to move him to my place. That way, Gaurav and I can both interact with him. He'll be right there when Gaurav gets back from school. Krish, you're most welcome to visit whenever you like. Same goes for you, Alka. You are welcome to my place, along with Nisha and Tulika, anytime you want. I do have three bedrooms, and the spare bedroom can be set up to accommodate Subbu,' Chanda said.

Both Krish and Alka were absolutely stumped. The possibility of Subbu moving to Chanda's place hadn't occurred to them at all.

Chanda spoke again, clearly explaining her rationale.

'Alka, right now Subbu needs a lot of attention and care. Your homestay has just taken off. You also have the responsibility of looking after the girls and the estate. Subbu being shifted to Sakleshpur is out of the question. And Krish, you have an extremely demanding job. It *is* going to keep you occupied. We know how late your meetings run. If Subbu is at my place, it becomes so much easier for me to look after him as it saves me the commute to your place. That's why I think my place is the best option for his homecoming,' she finished.

Alka sank back into the sofa as she mulled over what Chanda had said. She was right. Subbu being with Chanda was indeed the best option available. Yet a small part of her couldn't accept it. Even though she had told Chanda that she was now 'family', Alka found pangs of jealousy shooting through her. Subbu was *her* husband. How could she 'allow' him to be with someone else? She felt irrationally possessive about Subbu.

Krish, meanwhile, looked thoughtful.

'What do you think? Alka? Krish?' Chanda asked again, her eyes reflecting her earnestness.

'I think what you are saying makes a lot of sense, Chanda. But it's a massive responsibility. It's not going to be easy to execute it. I mean you are not ...' Krish trailed off.

'Not what, Krish?'

'Nothing …'

'Not his wife? Not obligated to take care of him? Of course I know that. More than anyone else, Krish. I've been taking care of him for so many weeks now. Do you think I don't know how big and daunting a task it is? And if you're worried about what society will say, I think it's time we stop bothering about that. I want what is best for Subbu. And I am determined to help him get back to his normal self,' Chanda declared. She crossed her arms and sat stiffly.

'The doctors said that there is a possibility that his progress might be very slow. What happens if he … if he just stops making progress and God forbid, remains this way forever?' Alka asked in a small voice.

'Then I will think of him as a child and continue caring for him. I love him, Alka. I'll do anything for him. Anything really,' Chanda declared.

Alka knew Chanda's words came from a place of selfless love. Her voice rang with the certainty of what she wanted. She wanted to care for Subbu, and she wasn't backing down.

'This is not something that can be decided over a cup of tea. I know your feelings are genuine, Chanda. But please, could you give me some time to think about it?' Alka asked.

'Yes, I understand how you must be feeling. But let go of the guilt, Alka. He may not be married to me, but he is the father of my son too. Take your time and think about it, both of you. Talk about it too. I do think this is the best option. But I don't have any authority or any right to take the final call. That's on both of you,' Chanda said. 'I am leaving for the hospital now. When you've decided what to do, let me know.'

Krish sat silently with his head in his hands as Chanda got up to leave.

'Wait, how will you go? You don't have your car,' Krish said as she reached the door.

'Let me get Shanker to drop you. I'll accompany you to the basement,' Alka said, getting up.

In the elevator, Chanda turned to Alka and said, 'I don't mean to be pushy, Alka. Not the least bit. I only want what is best for Subbu's quick recovery.'

'I know, and that is what I want too,' Alka replied. But she was still feeling uneasy and unsettled about accepting Chanda's proposal.

As soon as she came back to Krish's apartment, Alka sat down next to him and automatically reached for his hand. He held her hand and kissed it.

'What do you think?' she asked.

'She loves him deeply.'

'That she does. And he loves her too, very much so. All of us have married the wrong people.'

'We were young, and the young are foolish,' Krish said.

'Me, a bigger fool than you for having walked away from you like that. I thought I was being a great friend, making the ultimate sacrifice for Manasi. How naive I was. We cannot force ourselves to be happy if there's no love in the relationship. It has to come from the heart. It has taken me years to realize that.'

'I think there was some pressure from my mother as well. She was very keen for you to get married to Anna. Anyway, it's all in the past now. There's no point lamenting about it. Let's come back to the present.'

'True. Logically, Chanda makes sense, Krish. Subbu will be better off at her place. But his home is in the estate.'

'Yes, the coffee estate is Anna's life. But right now, he needs to heal. Once he recovers fully, he can go back to the estate.'

'Oh, this is such a hard decision, Krish!' Alka rested her head on his shoulders.

'I know. It's hard for me too. He's my brother; I should be the one taking care of him.' Krish squeezed her hand.

'I am jealous too. I will never admit it to anyone but you, especially since I am painfully aware of what a big hypocrite I am, considering I am in love with you. I am also a little angry that Chanda is so generous and so genuine. I ... I really don't know why I am angry about her love for him being so true. Is it because I am upset that Subbu did not recognize me? I am worried that he may never recognize me,' Alka said, her voice quivering as she spoke.

Krish looked at her in surprise. He hadn't expected that outburst. But he understood what Alka was going through. He knew she was hurting.

He kissed her gently on the head.

'Hey, it's okay. I am angry too even though I know what she said is infuriatingly right—that she can care for him better than I can. But we will get through this together, okay?' Krish said as he turned towards her and hugged her tightly.

They sat embracing each other for a long time. As Alka thought about everything she had faced in the last few months, she started tearing up. Until then, she had been strong. But in Krish's arms, she felt safe enough to surrender to her emotions. The daily estate rounds with Muthu and Tarun, handling the bookings at the homestay, being warm and hospitable to the reporters and guests even on the days when she didn't feel like it, taking care of Nisha and Tulika, rushing to the hospital whenever she could to see Subbu—all of it had taken a massive toll on her. She also felt a deep regret for not marrying Krish when she had the chance to. She thought about how unfair it was that Subbu was suffering so much. She wondered if he felt helpless, trapped as he was within his own mind. She thought about Chanda's fierce love for Subbu and the way Subbu had looked at Chanda. All the emotions that she had suppressed—sorrow, jealousy, helplessness—everything converged inside her, drowning her. Alka let the tears flow freely now.

Krish held her till her sniffles subsided. Her nose was running too. When she finally pulled away from him, she said, 'My face must be a mess. Do I look like a racoon? My eyeliner wasn't waterproof.'

That made Krish laugh.

'What? It's true. Look at these black streaks,' she said as she touched her cheeks and held up her finger.

'Alka, whether your eyeliner runs or not, you're still gorgeous and brave and fabulous. I am very proud of you,' Krish said as he held her face in his hands and kissed her lightly on the lips.

Alka kissed him back, and then walked to the bathroom to wash her face.

She wiped off all the makeup and didn't bother to re-apply it. She simply brushed her hair and came out.

'Let us look at it this way. If what has happened to Anna had happened to you, I would never hesitate for even a second to bring you to my place and take care of you. For life,' Krish said. 'That is what Chanda is doing too. She *wants* to do this, Alka. I don't think it would be right on our part to not allow her to do that.'

'She said she wants what is best for Subbu. And at this point, Subbu is happiest when he is with her. So, let's go tell Chanda that we will move Subbu to her place,' Alka said.

But deep down, she still felt profoundly sad about it.

28

MEDIUM-ROAST ARABICA

2007

It had been nine weeks since Subbu had been shifted to Chanda's home. While he was at the hospital, Alka had not felt the need to visit him every week and was satisfied with the updates she received from Krish and Chanda. She had also been extremely caught up with establishing the homestay venture. But now that Subbu was living in Chanda's house, Alka felt an urge to visit him at least once a week. Sometimes, she even visited him twice a week. She would wake up at 3 a.m. and leave Sakleshpur by 4 a.m. so that she could spend the day with Subbu and then be back the same day to attend to the guests who had booked the cottages. The travel was exhausting, but she felt a pressing need to continue doing this. On some of her visits, she ran into Krish, but mostly, she would reach only after he had already left. Amidst it all, she and Krish continued their morning and evening phone calls, discussing their days in detail. They never ran out of things to talk about.

'I don't understand my need to visit Subbu so often,' Alka confessed. 'I know Chanda is caring beautifully for him, and he is extremely well looked after. And even though he still doesn't recognize me or the girls, I want to be there. At least he is not asking me to leave the room now like he first did.'

'I know what you mean. Even I feel a compelling need to see him twice every day, once in the morning and once in the evening. I think it's because, subconsciously, we want to convince ourselves that we haven't abandoned him,' Krish said.

'Maybe you're right. It's good we decided not to allow any visitors, even though the doctors said it was okay to,' Alka replied.

'Yes, I would hate for them to see him the way he is now. I don't think anyone will truly understand. Also, we can't possibly know who wants to visit Anna out of genuine concern and who wants to come out of idle curiosity so that they can gossip about him later.'

'Not to mention that it would be an additional strain on Chanda to receive visitors. She has been so hospitable and welcoming to both of us, even though we are constantly going in and out of her house.'

'She is the sweetest, Alka. So selfless. And Gaurav too, he's such a sweetheart. I love how he chatters away around Anna, and how Anna listens patiently to everything he says.'

'I also think we got lucky with Rashmi. She's a good physiotherapist.'

'Yes, she is. She's doing a splendid job. She talks to him, encourages him and then dutifully reports everything back to Chanda. Not that Chanda needs her updates. She's there all the time, with her ears literally glued to that room.'

'I know! I noticed that too. Her devotion to Subbu is beyond remarkable, although she insists that it's what anyone who loves another person deeply would do.'

While Alka, Chanda and Krish took Subbu every week for his check-ups, it was only Krish and Alka who met with the doctors.

'You can brief me later about what they said,' Chanda told them. She felt it was better if Krish and Alka met the doctors and she did not want to encroach.

The doctors were pleased with Subbu's progress as well as the physiotherapy reports. They assumed that Subbu was staying with Krish, so they instructed them to continue giving him the same care. When Alka asked them why Subbu did not recognize her or the girls, the doctors had no answer for her.

'We do not know exactly what goes on in the minds of patients like Subbu. Perhaps his mind is still struggling to access memories of his immediate past. But since he is beginning to remember other things about his coffee estate and that part of his life, let's hope he will recognize you and your daughters soon,' the doctors said.

On one occasion, when Rashmi was working with Subbu, Krish was at Chanda's home and he couldn't help overhearing their conversation.

'I have to go now and supervise the workers. If we don't do the off-shooting today, the crop will fail. And we can't incur any more losses, don't you get it?' Subbu demanded from his chair.

'What crop? Can you explain?' Rashmi asked as she gently moved Subbu's legs to get the blood circulation going.

'The crops, the plants,' Subbu frowned, trying hard to remember what he was saying. He was unable to recall that the right word to use would be coffee bushes.

'Do you know who I am?' Rashmi asked.

'Rashmi. You are helping me walk.'

'That's very good!' Rashmi smiled. 'Now, can you put a little weight on your feet and try to stand up?'

'Why do you have to help me? Why can't I walk on my own?'

'Because you had an accident, Subbu. Do you remember the elephant?'

Subbu frowned again. 'Everyone tells me about this elephant. But I don't remember anything. Are you all trying to fool me?'

'No, Subbu. But don't worry about it. All of it will come back to you. You are making good progress. Now try and stand up.'

Subbu grasped the support bars kept in front of his chair and pushed himself up with great effort, but a second later, he collapsed back onto the chair.

'Very good! Let's try once more, please,' Rashmi encouraged Subbu. And Subbu tried again. This time, he managed to stand up for a little longer than before, but he wasn't able to make his legs move even though he wanted to. His brain was not able to command his legs to move. It was almost as if his legs weren't attached to his body anymore.

'Very good. That's enough for today. I will see you again tomorrow, okay?' Rashmi said as she got up to leave.

'How was he today?' Krish asked Rashmi when she came out into the living room.

'He remembered my name today. So I would say that's a good thing. Keep talking to him. Keep reminding him of things.'

'I will do that,' Chanda said.

She entered Subbu's room and smiled at him.

'I want bisi bele bath,' Subbu said, giving her a wide smile.

'Of course,' Chanda said. 'Shall I make your favourite coconut chutney with it?'

'What?'

'With bisi bele bath? Do you want some coconut chutney?'

'What is bisi bele bath?'

'You said you wanted it, no?'

'No, I didn't.'

'It's okay, Subbu. You just did and you don't always remember what you are saying. That is okay. Do you want to do some colouring now? Gaurav will do it with you.'

'Is he here?'

'Yes, he's back from school.'

'Gaurav is my son.'

'Yes, my darling. Gaurav is your son.'

'But who are you?'

'I am Chanda. I am Gaurav's mother.'

'No, you are not. You are *my* Chanda.'

'Yes, I am your Chanda.' Chanda squeezed Subbu's hand and he squeezed it back.

Krish watched the tender scene unfolding before him and tried to keep his eyes from welling up. In that moment, he realized there was no force more powerful than love.

'You have to fight this, okay? You will start walking soon,' Chanda said as she stroked Subbu's hair, pushing the strands away from his face.

'I will start walking soon,' Subbu repeated, not taking his eyes off Chanda.

'Do you know who is coming to see you this weekend?' Chanda asked.

'Nisha.'

'And?'

'Tulika'

'Very good. And who is coming along with them?'

'I don't know.'

'Try, Subbu, try to remember. I told you this morning, no?'

'Leave me alone, Chanda. You ask me too many questions and I don't like it. I want to sleep now.' Subbu sulked and covered himself with a blanket. Within minutes, he was asleep. Chanda sighed.

When she came out of the room, she told Krish, 'On some days, he is like a three-year-old child. And then on some days, he talks in detail about the places we went to when we were dating, the things we did. I am astonished, really.'

'I am too. I never knew his recovery would take this route. Even though the doctors have assured us that confusion about people and places is common at this stage, it is still hard to watch Anna like this.'

'He will be completely okay, Krish. He only needs time. See, barely a month ago, he wasn't even able to stand up. Today, he stood for a few seconds.'

'I know. The way you are encouraging him is incredible.'

'I do feel he is fighting to find his way back to us. We have to be patient, that's all,' Chanda said.

But it was harder still for Alka. Her visits to Subbu were a painful reminder of the reality of their situation. She also had to explain to Nisha and Tulika why their Appa had to stay at Chanda aunty's house.

'He needs his weekly check-ups and he cannot travel up and down from Sakleshpur every week,' she told them.

'Why can't Chikkappa keep him?' Tulika asked.

'Because Chikkappa has to go to office, silly,' Nisha replied.

The girls had unquestionably accepted that Chanda aunty was a very good friend of their mother. They had also quickly accepted that their father would take time to recover and return home, and that they had to continue talking to him even if he didn't seem to be listening to them. Nisha was better at it than Tulika. She would bring her school textbooks and show Subbu the assignments she had scored good marks in. Subbu would sometimes say things like 'well done' and sometimes he would just nod and then turn away, as though trying to find the right words to say. Tulika, however, was unable to speak to Subbu. She found it too difficult. So she would stand silently beside Nisha and let her do all the talking.

Both Tulika and Nisha were happy each time they visited their father because it meant that they could also spend time with Gaurav. The girls adored Gaurav. He, in turn, waited for them to visit. The trio got along like a house on fire. Gaurav would think of games to play, and the three of them would spend hours together, pretending to be superheroes, or policemen or secret agents. Gaurav orchestrated the game plans and Nisha and Tulika followed him around like little puppies, hanging on to every word he said. Looking at the three of them playing, chattering away and bonding, Alka's heart filled with joy, as did Chanda's.

'I never thought, not even in my wildest dreams, that they would meet, let alone have this kind of a connection. I used to feel bad about him being an only child. But he isn't one now. He has two sisters,' Chanda said.

'Do you think we should tell them that they are half-siblings, at some point in time? It seems cruel to keep it from them,' Alka said.

Alka and Chanda were standing in Chanda's balcony, sipping lemonade and watching their children play in the park.

'Yes, we should definitely tell them. But not now. Let's wait till they are a bit older and can understand these complexities,' Chanda replied.

Each time Alka went back to the estate after visiting Subbu, Muthu would enquire about him. Alka had told Muthu that Subbu was recuperating in Chanda's house. Muthu had met Chanda a few times at the estate many years ago. He had always assumed that she and Subbu would get married. He had also seen how heartbroken Subbu was when Chanda had been married off. Although he was surprised to hear that Subbu was now living in Chanda's house, he didn't ask any questions. Years of working under Subbu meant that he was discreet and tactful about everything involving Subbu or the estate.

Muthu's worry and concern touched Alka. One morning, Muthu expressed his desire to visit Subbu.

'Do you think it's a good idea to let Muthu visit him?' Alka later asked Chanda.

'Subbu spent all his growing-up years with Muthu, accompanying him on his estate rounds. Maybe it will help?

But let's check with Krish, too. I don't want to spring any more surprises,' Chanda said.

When Alka asked Krish about it, he agreed that it might be a good idea. On Alka's next visit, therefore, she brought Muthu along with her.

'Thank you for bringing me, madam,' Muthu said just before entering Subbu's room.

'Hello, Subbu sir, how are you?' Muthu asked.

Instead of answering him, Subbu looked at Muthu for a few seconds. Then, his face broke into a wide grin. 'Muthu! Where have you been all these days?'

With a warm smile, Muthu approached him.

'Sir, I've been here only. You should see the estate; it's flourishing very well. I brought you something special. Your favourite coffee beans. I got these roasted specially for you. I thought you might enjoy a taste of home,' Muthu said as he opened his bag and took out a packet of freshly roasted coffee powder.

As the rich aroma of coffee filled the room, Subbu closed his eyes.

'Medium-roast Arabica, the organic batch that we planted near the waterfall,' Subbu said, inhaling deeply and identifying the coffee the way only a true connoisseur could.

'Wow, sir! Ten out of ten!' Muthu exclaimed in delight.

'This will make a smooth, perfect blend. Call Alka madam,' he said.

Alka had been sitting outside the room, listening in on the conversation. She could not believe her ears now! Subbu had called out for her! She rushed inside.

'Yes, Subbu?' she asked eagerly.

'Brew this please, Alka, and let us all enjoy this premium coffee. Do you know how hard Muthu and I worked to get this?' Subbu asked.

Alka couldn't contain her excitement.

'Oh Subbu, I've missed you so much!' she exclaimed softly.

'But why? I was always here,' Subbu said.

'Yes, you were. Anyway, let me make the coffee right away,' Alka said as she hurried out. She did not want to start crying in front of Muthu and Subbu.

Chanda too had heard the whole interaction.

'Wow!' she mouthed as Alka rushed to the kitchen to make coffee for all of them. She couldn't wait to tell Krish about the development.

After Muthu's visit, Subbu started talking about the coffee estate a lot. He told Rashmi that he had to quickly learn to walk again so he could go on the estate rounds.

'All in good time, Subbu. You must learn to walk without any support first, no?' Rashmi told him. The thought of going for the estate rounds filled Subbu with a renewed determination. He was more than willing to push himself as he struggled to do all the exercises that Rashmi assigned him. Chanda told him she was proud of him, but in private, she cried because it was hard for her to witness the physical pain he was going through. Subbu now had to go for a check-up every fortnight. After a few such check-ups, however, the doctors said that it would suffice if he came in once a month. He was making wonderful progress, and they were more than satisfied.

'Why can't I hear the birds chirping? Why are there buildings in the estate?' Subbu asked Alka on one of her visits.

'Subbu, we are not at the estate. We are in Chanda's house, remember?' Alka said.

Subbu looked at her in shock. 'How do you know Chanda? Who told you?' he demanded.

'It is okay, Subbu. Chanda and I are friends now,' Alka said gently.

Subbu looked confused. 'You and Chanda are friends?'

Alka nodded.

Subbu didn't say anything for a few seconds. Then his face broke into a grin. 'Alka and Chanda—friends. It's good,' he said.

On the next visit to the doctor, Subbu managed to walk into the hospital with a stick. He no longer needed the support frame that he had used in the initial days. After his check-up, he waited outside with Chanda while Alka and Krish spoke to the doctors.

'While he has made remarkable progress on the physical front, he is still confused about many things,' Alka told Dr Mohan.

'Yes, that is common at this stage. But you can clearly see the progress he has made, mentally too. He is able to recognize people and describe events from his past. From time to time, he might still have serious cognitive problems such as slowed thinking and memory lapses. Continue with the same care routine and talk to him like you are doing now. Over time, the confusion will decrease and you will see significant improvements.'

Later, when they were back at Chanda's place and Subbu was fast asleep, Alka, Krish and Chanda sat in the living room and talked.

'It's so emotionally draining when he goes into a confused state. How do you manage to be so patient?' Krish asked Chanda.

'When you love someone, it is never a chore to take care of them. Yes, it's disappointing when he gets confused about things. But if I give up on him, how will he have the strength to fight back? We have to be there for him,' Chanda said.

'You are great, Chanda. You are really great,' Alka said.

'Oh please, you don't have to put me on a pedestal. If you had been in Bangalore instead of me, you would've cared for him the same way.'

But Alka wasn't sure if she would ever have been able to care for Subbu as lovingly as Chanda had been doing.

29

THE HOMECOMING

2007

The more progress Subbu made physically and mentally, the more frustrated he began feeling in Chanda's house.

'I like being out in the estate, Krish. I don't like these buildings or these city noises. How much longer will I have to stay here?' Subbu asked.

'I understand your frustration, Anna. Let us speak to the doctors and see what can be done.'

Subbu frowned. 'Why do the doctors get to decide? I am okay, am I not?'

'Yes, you are. But let's just check with them once. You will have to travel from Sakleshpur to Bangalore for your check-ups. Maybe you can stay with me then and go back the next day. You haven't seen my house yet, Anna. I am dying to show it to you.'

'Where will Chanda stay?' Subbu asked.

'Chanda will stay here. This is her house, remember?'

'And Gaurav?'

'He will stay with her.'

'But I want them to stay with me. Not here, but at the estate. Please Krish, don't take me away from them.' Subbu looked so forlorn and anxious that Krish had to turn away. He couldn't bear to see his brother like this.

Over the next twelve weeks, Subbu's recovery progressed tremendously. He managed to take his first faltering steps without the support of a walking stick. He stretched both his hands out in front of him and took tiny steps, his gait a little funny, much like that of a penguin. Then he looked proudly at Chanda who clapped and said, 'Well done, my love! Well done!' She had to wipe away her tears and Subbu could not understand why she was even crying.

'Are you sad that I am walking?' he asked, confused.

'No! No! I am happy that you are walking. These are tears of joy,' Chanda said.

'Tears of joy. They're good for coffee. Coffee needs tears. Not tears, but rain …' Subbu trailed off, knowing that something he said was not right. He still had trouble saying the right things, but he knew what he wanted very clearly. He wanted to be back at the estate.

On the next visit to the hospital, when Subbu proudly walked in without a stick and expressed his desire to be back at his beloved coffee estate, the doctors said that he could return to Sakleshpur. He was fit enough to travel and could come for a check-up once every two months. They also told Alka and Krish to continue with the care and the therapy that he had been receiving. 'Now that he has started clearly communicating what he needs, he might sometimes experience expressive aphasia. This means that the patient knows what they want to say, but they are unable to get it out. Don't get frightened if that happens, it's a part of the healing process. The key thing is to maintain an atmosphere of love and kindness,' they said.

Alka was both happy and nervous at the prospect of taking Subbu home.

'We'll have to make a ramp that he can easily climb to get to the house. Those steps leading up to the house might be a challenge,' she told Muthu. He promptly got in touch with the contractor who had refurbished the cottages. In no time, they had fabricated a metal ramp that was sleek and sturdy with a non-slip surface and a gradual incline.

Tulika had mixed feelings about having Subbu back home. 'It means we will no longer be able to play with Gaurav,' she said.

'Gaurav can visit us,' Alka replied.

'Appa cannot stay there forever. Appa's home is here at the estate, not at Chanda aunty's house,' Nisha said.

That night, when Alka spoke to Krish, she said, 'I am happy about Subbu coming home, Krish. I truly am. But I am also terrified about what he will say once he comes to know that I have handed over the management of his beloved estate to the CoRe team. Right now, we have a routine in place. Tarun, Muthu and I go on the rounds and tackle things together. What if Subbu tries to disrupt what Tarun has put in place? Also, what about the cottages, Krish? When Subbu sees that I have refurbished them and that there are guests occupying them, he's going to be furious.'

'You're thinking too far ahead, Alka. Anna is still healing, and I don't think he can process all of that yet. Anyway, you aren't alone in this. I will come over frequently and we will gently make him understand the situation. You did what you did because of the estate's dismal financials. He should be proud of you for saving the estate and turning it all around. At some point, I think he will be able to understand how deep in debt the estate was.'

When Alka told Selvi that Subbu would finally be coming home, she was overjoyed. So was Gowramma, having returned from the village by this time. The mother-daughter duo got busy cleaning Subbu's room thoroughly. They put the mattress out in the sun, changed the bedsheets and the pillow covers, and dusted the entire room twice so that it was spotlessly clean. On the day of Subbu's arrival, they decorated the entrance to the house with garlands made of yellow marigold flowers and mango leaves. They made a large, colourful rangoli at the entrance and lit a lamp. They also made akki payasam with coconut and jaggery, one of Subbu's favourite dishes.

'You've made this look like a house where a wedding is about to take place!' Alka said when she saw all the effort they had put in.

'Yes, madam. This was the same rangoli I had made when you had come as a bride. How can we not celebrate sir's homecoming?' Gowramma asked.

❧

Alka left with the girls to bring Subbu back home. It had been agreed that Krish would come back with them as well. He would drive his car as the ride back would be more comfortable with two cars, rather than one.

'I bagsy riding in Chikkappa's car,' Tulika said while they were on the way to Chanda's house.

'There's enough space in his car for both of you. Now don't start fighting over that,' Alka said sharply. That made both the girls keep quiet for a while. Their mother did not normally use that tone with them.

Krish was already at Chanda's place when Alka and the girls arrived. When Alka entered the house, she saw that Chanda had packed all of Subbu's clothes in a large suitcase and placed it in the living room. It had been over eleven months since Subbu's accident, and his collection of clothes and personal belongings had grown. Chanda, Subbu and Krish were seated at the dining table, and Kusuma was serving them hot vadas.

'Come, Alka, join us,' Chanda said. Alka could see that while she was trying to be cheerful and pretend that everything was fine, there was a sense of sadness and finality in the air around Chanda.

'I've packed everything,' Chanda said when she saw Alka's gaze lingering over the suitcase.

'Where is your suitcase?' Subbu asked Chanda.

'You are going with Alka and Krish. We talked about it, remember?' Chanda told him. Alka could see the pain in her eyes.

'Yes, but I want you and Gaurav to come along with me.'

'Anna, if you want to be at the coffee estate, you will have to stay with Alka, Nisha and Tulika,' Krish said gently.

'Appa, there is a new ramp for you. You can run down its length and go flying,' Tulika said.

'Is it?' Subbu asked, struggling to remember what the house looked like.

After the children had some snacks, they went out to the park to play with Gaurav.

'Where are they going?' Subbu asked.

'To the park.'

'Tell them to be careful. That swing can cause accidents. Krish had fallen down from a swing and got hurt badly once,' Subbu said. Krish was surprised to hear Subbu talk about a childhood incident that he himself had almost forgotten.

When it was time to leave, Subbu insisted once again that he wanted Chanda to come along.

'I can't go with you this time. But I will come and visit you soon,' she assured him.

'When will you come?' he asked. He reached out and held her hands tightly.

'Soon, my love,' Chanda whispered softly, but both Alka and Krish heard it.

Chanda went to the balcony and called out to the children.

'Gaurav, the girls need to leave now. All of you come upstairs please!' she said.

The children came upstairs grudgingly. Tulika was not happy about her playtime being shortened.

'Mummy, we just got here and we are leaving again already. We both want to spend more time with Gaurav.' She looked at Nisha for support and Nisha said hesitantly, 'Can we take Gaurav back to the estate with us? Please, Mummy?'

Subbu's eyes lit up at the suggestion. 'Yes, Gaurav can play with Nisha and Tulika at the estate and spend time with us,' he said with a big smile. It had been a long time since Alka had seen him smile like that.

'He is more than welcome to come back with us, provided he wants to come and Chanda aunty has no problem with the plan.'

'I would like that very much, Alka aunty. Thank you,' Gaurav said. Then he turned to his mother and asked, 'But how will you manage alone, Ma?'

'I have Kusuma with me. I am not alone! Go on if you want to. You have a weekend coming up. Are you sure you'll be okay?'

'Of course, Ma. I am old enough now,' he said.

'Yes, I keep forgetting that,' Chanda said as she kissed him on the forehead. 'Go, pack a few clothes then. And don't forget your toothbrush. The three of you can have fun over the weekend.'

'Yay!' both girls screamed.

'Double yay!' Subbu said. That surprised everyone and they all laughed together. Subbu joined in the laughter as well, but he looked a little unsure about why they were all laughing.

When it was time for them to finally leave, Alka hugged Chanda tightly. Her heart was full of gratitude. The three kids were excited to travel in Krish's car. Alka and Chanda looked fondly at how happy the children seemed in each other's company without having any idea that they were half-siblings. Alka and Subbu were to travel with Shanker. Krish walked to Alka and Subbu's car, folded the front passenger seat, and told Subbu that he could rest his feet on it if he felt tired during the journey. Chanda had come downstairs with them to see Subbu off, and she placed a soft pillow behind his back once he was seated in the car.

'Are you comfortable?' she asked, her voice quivering slightly.

'Yes, when will you come to the estate?'

'In a few days, I promise. Gaurav is going along with you, so have fun with everybody, okay?'

'Okay.'

Both the car engines roared to life, and Alka, Subbu, Krish and the kids embarked on the journey to the coffee estate. The kids were chattering excitedly in the back seat. Nisha and Tulika were describing the coffee estate to Gaurav. He had never been to a coffee estate before and he listened to them with rapt attention.

Chanda stood alone outside her apartment complex, a gentle breeze playing with her hair as she waved goodbye. Her eyes were a mixture of emotions—pride, love and a deep sadness that only those left behind would truly understand. She watched the cars disappear round the corner, her hand still raised in a farewell gesture.

Subbu kept looking at Chanda's figure in the rearview mirror and watched it grow smaller and smaller till it finally disappeared from view.

Krish adjusted his rearview mirror as he drove. When both vehicles halted at a signal, they were so close that Krish could see the other car clearly. Alka, seated next to Subbu, was gazing out. Then she looked directly at him and their eyes met in the car's mirror.

The road stretched ahead, winding through the hills as both cars made their way towards the coffee estate. As they climbed higher into the mountains, the joy on Subbu's face was evident. With each mile the car gained, the air became cooler and Subbu's happiness surged. He rolled down the window and put his head out, inhaling the fresh mountain air and chuckling in delight. Alka couldn't help laughing along with him. His unbridled joy was infectious.

When they reached home, Muthu was waiting there along with Gowramma, Selvi, Srilakshmi and the entire estate's labour force as well as the staff that worked at the homestay. They had brought hibiscus garlands and carried trays filled with flowers, lamps and the auspicious vermillion powder to welcome them, just like Alka had taught them to do when receiving visitors to the homestay.

Alka was astounded at the little celebratory party that had turned up to welcome them. Krish and the children were taken by surprise too.

'Wow! This feels like a royal celebration when kings come home from the battlefield,' Gaurav exclaimed.

'What is this, Muthu?' Alka asked as she stepped out of the car.

'Madam, word spread that Subbu sir was coming home today, and they all wanted to be here to do this. I could not refuse them.'

The entire gathering cheered and clapped when Subbu got out of the car. He looked at them and waved, looking a little hesitant.

Alka and Krish were right by his side as he walked towards the ramp leading to the house.

'Do you need help, Anna? Krish asked, gently holding him by the elbow.

'No, I got this,' Subbu replied as he carefully walked up the ramp, taking slow, careful steps.

It was the perfect homecoming.

ACKNOWLEDGEMENTS

To my father, K.V.J. Kamath, whose love for the coffee estates of Chikkamagalur and other parts of Karnataka introduced me to the beauty of these landscapes in my childhood. This book carries a piece of him—he would have loved it.

To Purvi, my tireless first editor and beta reader—thank you for your keen eyes and thoughtful feedback. You helped me shape this book. And to Atul, for his honest, astute feedback.

To Satish, for being my rock, always. Your steady support and unwavering belief in me have been my strength.

To my mother, whose pride in my achievements is a constant source of joy. Her strength, sense of humour and resilience inspire me every day.

To Gayatri Goswami, for her meticulous editing, and to Rashmi Menon, who loved my work. Both my brilliant editors polished this work to make it shine. Your insights were invaluable.

To Saurav Das, for the cover that captures hearts. The moment I saw it, I knew it was perfect. You have an incredible talent for making art speak.

To Pranav Shah, my lightning-fast technical guru. No glitch stands a chance with you around—thank you for always saving the day!

To Sathish of Sakleshpur and Sahishnu Bagmane, for generously sharing your knowledge about the life and lore of coffee estates. Your detailed explanations have added richness to this narrative. Any mistakes are mine alone.

To my closest friends—you know who you are. Your presence in my life, even in the quiet moments, keeps me grounded.

To Fareeda, my wonderful house help, who ensures that everything is spotless, allowing me the freedom and peace to focus on my writing.

To my cats, Kasper, Bella and Harvey, and the numerous other feline visitors who make my days lighter. And to Lostris, whose loyal spirit and love remains forever in my heart.

Finally, to my readers—your enthusiasm and support mean the world to me. You are the heartbeat of every story I write. Thank you for always waiting eagerly for my next book. I am filled with gratitude to have connected with you through my books.

ABOUT THE AUTHOR

Preeti Shenoy, one of India's most popular authors, has written sixteen bestselling titles and her books have sold over a million copies. Known for her accessible writing style, she tackles complex themes like mental health, gender inequality and socio-economic divides. Preeti has been featured on *Forbes*'s list of influential Indian celebrities, and has represented India at international literature festivals in Birmingham, Sharjah and Abu Dhabi.

Her work has earned praise from major media outlets such as BBC World, *Cosmopolitan, The Hindu* and *The Times of India.* Preeti's accolades include the Popular Choice Fiction Award (2021), presented by the *Times of India*'s AutHER Awards, and Amazon India's Most Popular Self-Help Book of 2021. She was also named 'Indian of the Year' and received the Business Excellence Award from the New Delhi Institute of Management.

In addition to being a writer, Preeti is also a sought-after motivational speaker, having delivered talks at organizations like Walmart, Infosys, ISRO, KPMG and Accenture. A fitness enthusiast, an artist and a traveller, her short stories and poems have been featured in *Condé Nast* and *Verve*. She also writes a weekly advice column and a monthly opinion column for *The Indian Express*, and has previously contributed to the *Financial Chronicle*.

Connect with Preeti:
Website: www.preetishenoy.com
Email: ps@preetishenoy.com
Twitter/X: @Preetishenoy
Blog: Blog.preetishenoy.com
Instagram: Instagram.com/Preeti.Shenoy and Preetishenoyart
Facebook: http://preeti.io/fb
Snap: Preeti.Shenoy
LinkedIn: https://www.linkedin.com/in/preetishenoyauthor/

HarperCollins *Publishers* India

At HarperCollins India, we believe in telling the best stories and finding the widest readership for our books in every format possible. We started publishing in 1992; a great deal has changed since then, but what has remained constant is the passion with which our authors write their books, the love with which readers receive them, and the sheer joy and excitement that we as publishers feel in being a part of the publishing process.

Over the years, we've had the pleasure of publishing some of the finest writing from the subcontinent and around the world, including several award-winning titles and some of the biggest bestsellers in India's publishing history. But nothing has meant more to us than the fact that millions of people have read the books we published, and that somewhere, a book of ours might have made a difference.

As we look to the future, we go back to that one word—a word which has been a driving force for us all these years.

Read.